QUEEN TAKES QUEEN

THEIR VAMPIRE QUEEN, BOOK 3

JOELY SUE BURKHART

QUEEN TAKES QUEEN
THEIR VAMPIRE QUEEN, book 3

Published by
Joely Sue Burkhart

A Reverse Harem Vampire Romance

The Triune's attention is a deadly thing to attract. The world's oldest and most powerful vampire queens devise a plan to ensure the fledgling Isador queen is eliminated before she can call enough Blood to protect her.

But Shara has already drawn formidable and famously powerful Blood to her side: Leviathan, king of the depths. Guillaume de Payne, the headless Templar knight. Wu Tien Xin, the silent invisible assassin. Nevarre, the Morrigan's own Shadow. And of course, her first two Blood, Alrik and Daire, inexperienced—but extremely powerful in their own right.

Though well fed on queen's blood and well loved, six Blood are not enough to stand against the mighty Triune. Shara needs more.

She needs more Blood. She needs allies.

What she really needs is a queen of her own.

For my Beloved Sis.

Thank you to my beta readers, Sherri Meyer, Laura Walker, Melissa Joy Vailes, Alexx Ragan, Rachel Mowry, Jenn VonBerg, Lydia Simone, Francesca Vance, Mads Schofield, Shelbi Gehring, Alyssa Muller, Meagan Cannon West, Amber Lynn Hamblin, Lachaundra LaRue, and Ella Cross

Special thanks to Stephanie Cunningham for naming Eztli.

Amber, Ezra thanks you personally.

1

SHARA

L ounging in bed was a luxury I'd been denied most of my adult life. When you were on the run, afraid for your life, the last thing you wanted to do was close your eyes. Let alone drop your guard enough to actually sleep soundly. Sleeping made me vulnerable, and alone, I couldn't afford to be vulnerable. I couldn't relax one second without worrying I'd end up dead.

That fear was long gone now. I could lie in bed all hours of the day or night and sleep without a single worry. I didn't have to keep one eye on the door, or strain my ears to hear a whisper in the hallway. Because I would never be alone again, not with my Blood by my side.

Before I opened my eyes, I liked to touch each of my six Blood bonds one by one, locating their position. Partly to know who was in bed with me, but also so they would each feel me touch their bond. They'd know I was awake and well, and I'd know *they* were well.

Of course as my alpha and my biggest, baddest Blood, Rik probably knew I was awake before I realized it, but I always felt for him first, even though I knew he'd be right there beside me.

Until he wasn't.

He isn't here.

I jerked upright, my heart pounding. "Rik?"

He hollered from the bathroom. "In here, my queen. Sorry, I didn't mean to worry you."

"Even alphas need to take a leak now and then," Xin said beside me.

Whew. My heart still pounded, but I lay back down beside him and curled into his side. Even in his human form, Xin smelled like a wolf. Well, that didn't come anywhere close to a good description. He smelled like a wolf, paused in a clearing in the middle of an ancient forest, beneath a full moon on a cold winter's night, with frost and snow crystallized on his fur.

Touching him felt so strange with that image in my head, because his skin was so hot and smooth. I ran my palms over his chest and shoulders, enjoying the play of muscle and sinew beneath his skin. He was one of my leaner Blood, but no less powerful or strong than the others. As my second-oldest Blood —born in 712 AD—he had endured centuries upon centuries in a cold, untouchable service to his queen. To say he was starved for touch was the understatement of the year. All my Blood were starved to a point, but he and Mehen, my oldest Blood, who'd been imprisoned as the mighty dragon, Leviathan, definitely felt the need most severely.

I pressed closer to Xin, tangling my legs with his and sliding one hand around to his back. My eyes drifted shut and I relaxed into his embrace, just enjoying the feeling of companionship.

Okay, I was starved for touch too.

"Tell me something about you," Xin whispered against my forehead, stroking my back. "Something no one else knows. Something good."

It would be impossible for me to tell him a secret when my Blood bonds tied our hearts and minds together. They usually knew what I was thinking before I realized myself. But he would at least be the first to hear the words.

Silent a few moments, I tried to think of something not just good, but special. "It's funny, but when you're a kid, you think that your life is normal and everyone else is weird, you know? So I thought everybody had terrible nightmares and saw red glaring eyes outside their windows. I thought everyone was scared of the dark because of the monsters. So when I talked about it at school, I got labeled 'special' pretty quickly. After a few years, Mom took me out of public school and I stayed home with her. Dad was gone by then, but she really tried hard to make things normal and safe for me. Fun, even. But I didn't have any friends, and as much as I loved her, I was still lonely, even before she died."

He made a low sound against my skin. "I said something good, my queen."

"I'm getting there, I promise! I didn't have a lot of friends, and I hung out mostly with Mom. But all through my life, little things happened that made me feel like I wasn't alone. That I was watched over. Like I had a guardian angel. Maybe I'd find a flower on the porch, something tropical and hot pink, when we didn't have anything like it growing on our street. Or a really pretty red leaf in the middle of winter, pressed to the windshield of the car. Or I'd smell something sweet and soothing at night when I was scared, and I'd close my eyes, and it'd feel like someone was there, watching over me. I didn't know then who it was, but now... I think it was my real mother. Even though she was dead and I had no idea of her existence, she was always with me."

I didn't bother saying her name. Thanks to a geas Esetta Isador had placed upon all Aima, no one living could say or remember her name. I didn't have that problem, since I'd technically died the first time I came into my power when Rik and Daire found me just a few miles from here.

My throat ached and my eyes burned, but with happy tears. "Even though she knew I had no idea that she even existed, she still made sure I felt her presence. That's pretty special."

Mom would always be Mom, the woman who raised me, who died to keep me safe, even though she was technically my aunt. But now I had Esetta, too. I had her words she'd written to me. Even if no one else could remember her name, I would always remember.

Thank you, Esetta.

Something soft brushed my cheek like a feather—though I didn't see or sense anything.

"Thank you, my queen," Xin whispered.

He didn't tighten his grip or press against me, but something tugged on my sixth sense in the bond. I sank deeper into his bond, now used to the gray fog that seemed to surround him. Each of my Blood's bonds felt different in my head, and Xin had always been distant. Not that he tried to deliberately hide from me, not at all. His gift of invisibility wrapped his bond and made him harder for me to sense. His former queen hadn't wanted any of her Bloods' emotions to leak into her head, and so he'd learned a long time ago to keep his emotions tightly under wrap. When I first met him, I'd had to jump off a metaphorical skyscraper to find his true self. It was easier now, but I still had to reach to feel him.

Raw need raged through him so fiercely it made my breath catch on a soft gasp. I already knew he was starved for affection, but this... A gnawing black hole ate through his bond. He needed my blood. He needed to fuck. Preferably at the same time. More, though, he burned to be alone with me. To have me to himself. Like this. Just me and him in bed together. Even if only for a few minutes.

He'd never had that. None of my Blood had me alone, except maybe Rik. And even then... How often was I completely alone with even him? With six men all dedicated to protecting me and seeing to my every want and need, it was usually crowded around me.

Especially in my bed.

"Xin. Why didn't you tell me?"

The corner of his eyes crinkled slightly but otherwise his face remained smooth. "Tell you what, my queen?"

Again, he wasn't trying to hide or obscure anything. He honestly didn't know. He was so far removed from his own emotions that he had no idea what I sensed. It was his nature to remain controlled, hidden in plain sight, without complaint, request, or reaction. He was a blade. A weapon I sent to kill my enemies. My food when I wanted it. He had no expectations other than I use his particularly deadly talents.

And that damned near broke my heart. Because he was so much more to me than that. They all were.

I cupped his nape and rolled over onto my back, drawing him toward me. On his elbow, he looked down at me, more curious than anything. Still waiting for my command. He wouldn't act. Not of his own volition.

So be it.

I threaded my fingers in his hair and gave a little teasing tug. "Rik's going to take a walk while you fuck me."

XIN

HER WORDS DID NOT MAKE sense. I stared at her, afraid to breathe or move a single muscle until I understood. A queen never sent her alpha away. An alpha never left his queen's side. That Rik trusted me to guard her long enough to hit the bathroom was already a boon.

A Blood was lucky to have even three minutes alone with his queen in a lifetime.

To have her alone…

Her blood *and* her body…

It was unheard of.

My last queen had never allowed me to touch even her hand. Her Blood did not feed from her directly. Even among her

5

full court, my physical interactions had been limited to feeding from my sibs. Sexual need was a weakness.

Something I'd cut out of myself a very long time ago.

At least so I'd thought.

"You cannot," I finally said, each word cutting my throat like broken glass. "Rik would not allow it."

Eyes smoldering, she smiled slowly, each incremental curve of her lips an invitation to insanity. Soft, full lips. The delicate tip of her tongue. The flash of white fang descending. "Oh really? I'm your queen. I decide who's in my bed. And this queen hungers."

"Take every drop of blood in my body, my queen."

Her lashes fluttered down over her gleaming eyes. "I want more than your blood."

I swallowed hard. "I will give you anything. Anything you ask. Anything at all."

She didn't elaborate, which made my nerves tighten like a drum. She had a need. I must meet it. Whatever it was. That's what Blood did. My alpha would expect no less than I give her exactly what she needed. Even better if I could offer it before she must ask.

But a Blood did not initiate sex with his queen, especially *without* her alpha.

Her hand stroked down my chest, her fingers trailing over each ridge and hollow. My abdominal muscles quivered with her advance. A tiny crack in my control.

The chilled silence of my gift filled my head like impenetrable fog. Still. Calm. Silent. If Rik happened to look at the bed, he wouldn't be able to see me here with our queen, unless he used her bond to locate me. An unfortunate side effect. I didn't want to hide—but I had to maintain my ability to serve. I could do nothing about the erection, but I wouldn't make a sound or demand or request. Never.

"No," she whispered against my lips as her hand closed around my cock. "Look at me."

I hadn't realized I'd closed my eyes. Stupid. Another weakness I couldn't afford. I couldn't shut my eyes when my queen's life was in my hands. When I focused on her face, she tugged me firmly by my cock, pulling me on top of her, her thighs opening to cradle me against her.

Shit. Fuck. Another quiver slipped through the stillness, a twitch that slithered down my spine and made my hips move, dragging my dick through her grip. Wholly involuntary. Wholly unacceptable.

I pierced my bottom lip with my fangs, letting blood fill my mouth. The small pain distracted me enough so that I didn't move again. Even when she wiggled beneath me, sliding into position to take me inside her.

Her thighs came up around my waist and I was almost lost. Almost undone. A crumbled wreck.

In my mind, I fled to an abandoned temple at the top of the mountain near my birthplace, wrapped in fog and lost in time. I went there as a child, my safe and secret place that no one knew of but me. I ran up the treacherous slopes, my lungs burning, thighs aching, and pushed open the tattered woven mat that served as a door.

And found Shara lying on silken cushions, pulling me to her like a ceaseless tide.

"I want your emotion," she whispered against my mouth. Licking my lips. Demanding I give her the blood she must have smelled, even though I carefully kept any from dripping on her. "I want you open to me. Not locked away, lost in silent fog. I want you here, eye to eye, even if it's raw and ugly. Share your mind and heart with me."

"I cannot," I whispered, my voice breaking with the overwhelming failure. I would give her anything. My life. My blood. But I couldn't give her my emotions. I didn't know how. And even if I did figure out how to unlock that door after centuries…

I feared it would leave me broken. Unusable. Could her best blade serve as a killer if I became crippled with emotion?

7

I couldn't think. Not with her muscles tightening on my dick. Her mouth on mine, teasing my lips apart so she could taste my blood.

"Show me," she whispered, her words a caress that my starved body soaked up like a sponge. "Show me everything. I want it. I need it. I want to know you, Xin. I want to *see* you. All of you."

See me.

See me huddled in the corner of my hiding place, hugging my knees to my chest with arms too scrawny, legs like sticks, my back a mass of welts. I learned early not to cry or protest or react in any way. A Blood never asked for mercy or complained at cruelty, and I was born to be Blood. While human children would have been learning to read and write, I killed my first thrall. When other human boys my age would have been thinking about girls, I was tested by the best and most powerful alphas within a week's ride of my home court.

They'd sniffed me. Bit me. Tasted my blood. Watched me fight against the other potential Blood candidates.

But Wu Tien's alpha woke me in the dead of night and took me through the court to stand outside a dark house.

"A threat to my queen sleeps within. She wants this threat dead but no one must see or hear you. If you're successful, she'll call you as Blood."

Most people probably would have asked how many were inside and which one was the target. Which one I should kill.

But not me.

The alpha had chosen his words carefully. If no one must see or hear me...

They would not live to tell the tale.

I had done my duty. Beautifully quick, silent and deadly. Though I had cried without sound when I killed the youngest. A girl, younger than me. Her eyes had opened a moment before my steel bit into her throat, pupils flaring with terror though she

8

didn't cry out. I had felt something in her. Something that called to what I was becoming.

A fledgling queen. Calling a fledgling Blood. Calling me.

I had always wondered what would have become of me if I'd refused Wu Tien's order that night. If I had answered the still, quiet call I felt in that child. Before I slit her throat as my new queen ordered. Though I killed many queens through the centuries, I never felt that call again.

Until Shara Isador pulled me to her side in Kansas City, Missouri only days ago. Would I have killed her on Wu Tien's command? Would I have been able to look down at her sleeping beside Rik and slit her throat?

My gift would have made it possible. Rik would never have seen me. While his queen died in his arms. *Our* queen. Mine.

Her eyes swam with tears. "How many did you kill that night?"

Ice spread through my veins, freezing my marrow, slowing my heartbeat to a ponderous, uneven gait. I couldn't have moved a finger to defend her or myself. "Five. The target was Wu Tien's eight-year-old niece who would be queen one day."

"How old were you?"

"Twelve."

Her eyes flared, her emotions slicing me like the knight's deadly blades. Surprise. Horror. Shock. "You killed at twelve years old?"

"No. I killed much earlier. But I was Blooded that very night. All the Wu queens took Blood early in life. It made us easier to train how best to serve."

"My father was killed when I was six years old. If I had the knowledge of how to kill the monsters, I would have slaughtered them all that night. Without hesitation."

Ice spread through my body, brutal cold that cut through my lungs and encased my heart. It didn't matter. I didn't need to breathe. "If I had known of your need, I would have killed them for you. Your parents would still be here with you today."

9

"I have a need now," she whispered against my lips.

So cold. I couldn't understand why her lips didn't freeze to mine. Why she still found my blood to taste, rather than a frozen river in my veins. "Yes, my queen. Whatever it is. Yes."

She tightened her grip on me. Her fingers squeezed my neck, holding me close. One hand slid down my back, gripping my ass, pulling me into the searing heat of her body. Her thighs hugged me. Her mouth on mine. Heaven. The most exquisite torture.

Her hips undulated in a slow roll against me, her fingers digging into me. Pulling me. Demanding. Something. Her lips were hard on mine. Her tongue slid into my mouth, risking my fangs. I couldn't make them retract and I didn't know why. I'd never bitten my queen until Shara. My fangs throbbed, extending even longer, vicious icicles that would tear her tongue and shred her lips. I would hurt her. Wound her. And not even mean it.

Rik would have my head on a plate if I hurt one hair on her head. I would serve it to him myself.

She groaned, a soft aching sound that cracked something inside me. She needed. My queen. Mine. I fisted my hands in the bedding and ground harder against her. If I could not give her everything she desired, I would at least give her pleasure. She drank blood from my lips, but I drank her cries and sighs and moans, muffled only by my own mouth. More beautiful music I had never heard in my life. I wanted more of it. More cries. Louder.

The crack widened inside me, slicing me to ribbons.

"Yes," she groaned against my lips.

Blood. Her blood. I didn't know if she punctured her lip, or if I did, but I could taste her on my tongue.

Ice shattered. Splintered. Jagged and sharp. I heard a guttural cry, a raw, ragged growl.

That rattled *my* chest.

I had made that sound. Me. The silent, invisible killer.

"I want to hear you, Xin." She arched beneath me, her head rolling back, her throat bared. "Please. Show me. Tell me without words how much you love me. I want to hear it."

My name on her lips. Her throat offered to me. With a plea.

I thrust deep, every muscle straining on a groan that hurt my vocal chords. Again. The headboard thudded against the wall with the force of my thrusts. I tried to draw back, spare her, but she'd have none of that. She kept saying my name. Aloud. Her eyes locked on me.

Seeing me.

Calling me.

My wolf snarled, my spine bulging with the effort of keeping him contained. Claws burst from my hands and I shredded the sheets. Better to destroy the bed than damage my queen. Though her nails raked down my spine and dug into my buttocks, urging me deeper, harder. Her words a whip.

"Yes, yes, Xin, please. Show me everything. Let me in."

I was afraid I would hurt her—but I was the one who cracked open, broken in a million pieces.

All the kills I'd made over centuries in Wu Tien's name. Enough blood to fill an ocean. Wasted. Lives destroyed. Entire bloodlines lost forever.

So much regret.

When I had become a killer who lived only for the hunt?

Emptiness. A million lifetimes lived alone—while surrounded by people. Unseen, unheard, untouched, unneeded. Until my queen pointed at me, and her alpha whispered a name in my head. A target. My prey to hunt.

Never my queen herself though. She'd never touched my bond, my mind, my body. Let alone my heart.

No wonder I lived for the kill. It was all I'd ever had.

I tried to find the boy I'd been. The boy who'd fled to the forgotten temple on the mountain. But that child had died long ago. I'd never known my mother or father. As customary in those times, I'd been taken from my home at age three and raised among the other candidates. I'd shown early promise. They'd seen the wolf in me. The predator who would kill and kill and kill.

Shara tightened around me, her pleasure rising in our bond. Shining like beacon in the dead of night, a star bright enough to dim the noonday sun. I didn't want her to see the centuries stretched out like a graveyard with all the tombstones I'd wrought with my own hands.

How could she love a killer like me? She would turn away. Exile me. I deserved it.

She sank her fangs into my chest and I roared with release. I jammed my dick deep into her. So deep. I wanted to disappear. Into her. Forever. Grunting with effort, I rutted on her like a mad beast, unable to stop coming. I sank my fangs into her throat and drank her pleasure directly from her vein.

In a vast, ancient forest, her scent floated through hoary, twisted trees heavy with vines and moss. A hint of laughter on the breeze. A challenge. My wolf darted after her into the shadows. Silent. Deadly. Hungry.

But cold no more.

RIK

Evidently not even alphas were above jealousy.

Forehead braced against the bathroom door, I fought my need to be with my queen. She needed this time alone with Xin. With each of us.

She needed. I provided.

Even if that meant I was not the one holding her now.

I'd never seen a queen like Shara before. She loved each of us. Really and truly loved us. She wanted to touch us. All of us. She wanted to sleep with us, make love, sleep again, feed, dance, party, eat, laugh, everything. I loved it. I loved her. I loved them.

All of them. I wanted their happiness as much as I wanted hers. But I'd sworn my life to fulfilling *her* every need. Not theirs.

It would be easier if she didn't love us each so much. Easier for me. Not easier for her.

Xin was right. The more I loved her, and the more she loved me, the more I wanted to be alone with her, too. A selfish need, and something I must guard against to ensure my queen received everything she wanted and more. My jealousy would only hurt her, and it would be too easy as alpha to drive them away from her.

I'd seen it happen many times before. Alphas had to be close to their queen at all times, yes. Alphas gained the most power from their queen; they fed her the most, and fed *from* her the most. They needed to be the strongest because they were the last line in her defense.

But that power easily went to an alpha's head. Power to choose who to send on guard duty. Who to allow into her bed. Who would be allowed to feed her first. Ultimately the queen had final say, absolutely. But it was an alpha's job to keep her Blood in line and deal with any discipline and hierarchy issues without drawing it to her attention.

The larger her court, the easier it would be for these kinds of abuses. And it was abuse in my mind, a huge abuse of power. My queen would be stronger because all of her Blood were strong. Because we all fed from her nearly daily. We all shared in her pleasure and her magic openly. She was well-fed and terrifyingly strong.

Which made us all a nightmare for anyone who even thought to harm her.

I would ensure each of her Blood had time with her alone, as Xin did now. They needed it. She needed it.

I lifted my head, sensing the change in her bond. The subtle tug on me that signaled she wanted me with her. I opened the door and paused at the side of the bed.

Xin lay sprawled on top of her, still panting, unable to move.

She'd used him well and hard, breaking through the reserve that had been ingrained in him from his former queen at such an early age. Not an easy feat.

But my queen was up for any challenge.

I hid nothing from her. She felt how hard it had been for me to stay in the bathroom while she fucked another man. Even a man I'd shared her bed with several times before. It was different when it was just him. When I had to stand there and feel her pleasure in our bond and know I had no part in giving it to her.

She met my gaze and held out her hand. *:Thank you,:* she said softly, touching only my bond. *:You're an incredible alpha, and I love you more every day.:*

I settled into bed beside her and lifted her hand to my mouth, pressing a kiss to her palm. *:You're an incredible queen, and I love you more than life itself.:*

"Sorry." Xin lifted his head a little, sweat dripping down his forehead, but quickly dropped his face back against Shara's throat. "Alpha."

I draped an arm over his back and pulled them both into my embrace. "No need for apologies, Xin. You gave our queen exactly what she asked for. You'll never hear me discipline you for that."

"You may change your mind," he panted. "If I'm no use to you now."

"What are you talking about?" Shara's voice sharpened. "Why would you no longer be of use to us?"

Xin shifted off to her other side, but didn't withdraw completely. "No offense, my queen, but you broke me."

He didn't mean to upset or hurt her, but I felt the surge of heartache in her bond and I very nearly thumped him on the head for it. "I give you a boon and you're a dickhead about it."

He blinked, which in Daire or Mehen would have been a very vocal, very loud retort. "I am?"

"You are," I said agreeably.

14

"I've only ever been a killer. A silent, deadly, and most importantly, emotionless, blade." He ducked his head. "I don't know that I can assassinate your targets now, my queen, if I can't find that stillness again."

She cupped his chin and tugged his face back up to hers. Leaning in close, she glared at him, her bond a fierce, white-hot blade of ice. "I would rather have you here, looking at me, talking to me, letting me see into your heart, than ever have an assassin. Even if you never kill again."

"What if your goddess meant for you to send me after Marne Ceresa or Keisha Skye?" Xin asked softly, regret clogging his words. "And now, I'm unable to kill them? What then, my queen?"

She sat up, tossing her hair back off her shoulders. Her face hard as marble, her neck long and graceful, breasts jutting proudly, blood trickling down her throat.

My queen. My goddess. "Then I'll fucking kill them myself."

2

SHARA

I was starting to realize why vampires were always portrayed as nocturnal. I was too busy feeding and fucking all night to see the sun before noon. Okay, two in the afternoon. As we walked up to the main house, I could only hope Gina and Winston didn't tease me about the lateness of the hour. If he'd made breakfast early this morning, he'd definitely be wondering where the hell we were.

Which made me wonder how we were going to handle the workers who'd be wanting to enter my nest. If they were going to be dependent on me to wake up and let people in…

"Anyone carrying your blood can make the decision." Guillaume, my Templar knight, walked on my left. "One of us on guard will always be near the gate during the daylight hours so we can examine anyone wanting entry. Frank can allow people through too, but he may not carry enough of your blood to sense anything amiss. He's an excellent security guard for a human, though, and he does have good instincts."

"But how do you actually allow them to pass?"

"The easiest way is to touch them." Guillaume dropped his

hand on Nevarre's shoulder beside him. "A handshake, a friendly touch. We'll open our senses up, using our power that you've magnified, and if they're fine, we let them pass while touching them. Once they're through, they can come and go at will, and we'll all feel it as they pass the circle. Though if you're sleeping soundly, you shouldn't be bothered. Over time, you can tone down that sense too because security of the nest lies with us."

Rik walked on my right, closely enough I could feel the heat that radiated off his big body. "If you look at the tapestry in your mind, you'll see the nest's boundaries and exactly who is within. You'll know their purpose because they've touched your blood circle."

We stepped onto the back patio, covered with a trellis of old, dead vines. A slider door would let us directly into the kitchen, assuming the door wasn't locked.

Rik made a low rumbly sound that made my spine strum with pleasure. "The doors to your house will never be locked to you, my queen."

I was so used to lining the walls with salt, making sure my room had no windows or easy access points, and all my doors were always locked by dusk. Unlocked doors and huge windows were completely foreign concepts to me. "But we'll have people in and out all the time. Do you really think it's safe to leave all the doors unlocked?"

Guillaume snorted. "Do you really think anyone would dare break in or steal something when a rock troll, warcat, wolf, hell horse, winged snake, and giant bird are guarding your property?"

"That would be raven, Sir Guillaume," Nevarre said. "And the first person who makes an Edgar Allen Poe joke will have the great pleasure of competing against me in a caber toss."

"Good thing Daire isn't here to hear this challenge." Rik laughed. "I can hear his crow jokes already."

At the mention of Daire's name, I automatically felt for his location. He and Mehen were on guard duty together. An odd pairing, but Rik must have had his reasons. Probably a deliberate attempt to torture Mehen a bit more with Daire's antics. Of all my blood, he was the most likely to play a prank or make an inappropriate comment that would probably set the oldest, and yeah, most touchy, Blood's teeth on edge. Xin was further away, alone. I had a moment to worry about him, especially after his comments about being broken. But I felt his wolf slipping through the trees and his bond was full of a wolf's joy as he tracked his prey through the trees. He didn't smell an intruder, but his wolf knew his nature. I wasn't worried in the slightest that he wouldn't be able to kill if he needed to protect me. As for assassinating anyone…

That wasn't really my style anyway.

My Blood stood on either side of the door, watching me. Waiting for me to test the door and verify it really was unlocked. That it would always be unlocked for me. Even this obscure side door that wasn't visible from the main drive.

I laid my fingers on the slider's pull and gave it a tug. Yeah, it opened, though I will admit to holding my breath. I pushed the door open wider for the guys and stepped inside the kitchen. "Hello?"

Smiling, Winston hopped up from the round table in the corner where he'd been sitting with Gina. "Your Majesty, good day. What may I get you?"

Gina stood too. "I've got some interesting television footage to show you."

I groaned. "We made the news again? I'll have whatever you're having, and please, call me Shara."

There were only four chairs at the small table, but the guys were too busy hitting the food laid out on the counter like a buffet to care where they sat. Rik sat me down by Gina and kissed the top of my head. "Trust me to pick something for you?"

I rolled my eyes. "Duh."

Gina turned her laptop toward me and hit the play button. The headline read *"Christmas Miracle—or Apocalypse?"* The video itself was shaky enough to tell me it was recorded by an amateur. A man spoke in Spanish, too rapidly for me to make out any of the words, but a translation ran along the bottom of the screen.

"Do you see where it went? A black shape. Huge. It didn't look like an airplane. I think it was alive."

Breathing hard, he stopped, the camera panning the night sky. Light blazed to the right, and the camera jerked in that direction. A huge pillar of silvery bright light drove down toward the ground like a sci-fi movie tractor beam. Too bright to make out much, but there was definitely something inside the light.

Something that moved.

"That's what we looked like?"

"No," Rik said in his low rumble. "That's what *you* looked like."

The person filming was far enough away that it was hard to see details. Shapes definitely moved on the ground. Large shapes. A horse leaped up like it was soaring over a brutally high fence, the only clear image on the screen.

Guillaume's hell horse. Fuck, he was massive. Neck thick, shoulders broad, huge, powerful haunches. Definitely a warhorse built to carry a knight and all his armor into battle. All four hooves left the ground, his head straining high into the air, well back-lit by the brutal blaze. He'd tried to catch me before I could hit the ground, moments before I was able to shift and stop our fall.

Gina paused the video. "There aren't a lot of horse shifters."

I knew where this was going. I sighed. "So every other queen knows that Guillaume de Payne was protecting a queen. Someone called him to be Blood, and it wasn't Marne Ceresa."

"A fucking powerful queen," he said over his shoulder as he

19

stacked bacon on top of pancakes. "That kind of glow isn't something that every queen can do. They'll know you were feeding on something big, powerful, and winged, in the middle of Venezuela."

"And though Mayte Zaniyah has purposely kept herself off the Triune's radar, it wouldn't surprise me if consiliari were calling her first thing this morning to find out if she knew who had been so near her territory. I'm glad we placed the call to her first, but I wish we could have taken her up on her offer before the news ran."

"So she might be pissed at me, too. If she wanted to stay off their radar, the last thing she'd want is a bunch of people calling her for information."

Nevarre swung one of the bar stools out from the peninsula and sat facing me, his plate in his lap. At least his kilt was long enough to cover his knees, or I might have had to explore despite so many witnesses. "Or, she's gladder than ever that she got to you first."

"How's that?"

"I don't know Mayte Zaniyah, but she's got to be pretty fucking smart if she wants to stay out of the Triune game, and doubly smart if she reached out to you already, but I don't know what she offered."

I forgot that he wasn't with us in Venezuela. "She offered her nest to me."

His eyes widened. "Fuck. Yeah. She's patting herself on the back right now. Don't worry about her reneging on her offer. She wants you badly and if the other consiliari are calling her for information, your stock just went up exponentially."

"I want the Triune afraid of me. Enough to leave me alone. But not afraid enough to come at us full strength. At least not yet."

"Oh I'm sure they're afraid all right." Gina hit the button on the video and let it play out. Something flew up out of the brilliant shaft of light. Something huge. With wings.

Staring at the grainy image of my shifted shape, chills raced down my spine. And yeah, my fangs ached. I remembered how I'd fed so deeply off Mehen that I'd basically sucked his dragon into myself. He'd changed my cobra queen into a half snake, half dragon beast that flew. Granted, it'd saved us both. But it was still pretty freaky to see my monstrous shape captured on television for the world to see.

Rik sat down beside me with two plates. "Not monstrous. Beautiful. I've never seen a wyvern before."

His plate was loaded with normal breakfast food: scrambled eggs, sausage, biscuits, and gravy over everything. My plate: lovely fruit salad and a warm croissant with a bit of chocolate sticking out one end. Staring at the difference, tears burned my eyes. Because he'd been paying attention all along.

"Of course I have, silly." He threw his left arm over my shoulders and pulled me against him. "That's my job."

"All our jobs," Guillaume added as he set a cup of coffee in front of me. "Daire says it's the right color, but if you need more cream, let me know."

I sniffed and dropped my head against Rik's chest, even as I tore off a bit of croissant to nibble on. Goddess, it was fantastic. Warm, flaky, buttery, with just enough chocolate to be decadent, but not too sweet. I looked across the table at Winston as he returned to his seat across from me. "But how did you even know when we'd be up to have all this hot and ready?"

"That's why I'm here," Gina said, smiling. "I figured you'd be up after noon. When I felt you wake up, I let Winston know."

Wait a second. She felt me wake up? Just because I'd given her a few drops of my blood?

What else had she felt this morning? Or rather afternoon, once I woke up?

She smiled wider, her eyes dancing with mirth. "Enough to know that Winston had plenty of time to make a full-service breakfast for your Blood before you'd end up here."

Wow. Okay. That shed a whole new light on how the bonds

worked, especially with my human servants. Poor Frank. And yeah, it made more sense now why all my Blood had come with me last night. They felt everything I did through the bond. They always had.

I'd never really tried to separate out my pleasure from theirs, but I must feel theirs too, though my pleasure was usually so quick to respond and so overwhelming that I didn't realize I was feeling their desire too.

:Pleasure is magnified in the bonds.: Rik used our bond so at least I wasn't blushing at the thought of having this realization out loud with Winston and Gina listening in. *:So is pain, though. It's a strength and a weakness. Even though you tried to shield me, I felt the moment Leviathan broke your arm as if he'd chomped down on mine. I would have gleefully slit his belly, stripped his hide, and nailed it to a wall.:*

I took a sip of coffee, mulling things over. "You said Mayte Zaniyah wants me badly. For what, exactly? I won't be her pawn either."

"She hasn't said explicitly," Gina said. "I grew up deep in Triune politics. I know how consiliari think and act, and I know most of them, or I have my mother's and grandmother's assessments and notes as reference. While I don't know Bianca or Mayte personally, I know *of* them, and I know what the other courts think of House Zaniyah. With that experience only to guide my gut, I think she wants to be your sib."

"*My* pawn? But I don't want to make anyone a pawn either. Doesn't that imply I can't stand alone, independently? That I need an ally to help me hold my own territory?"

Xin's wolf trotted into the room and sat on his haunches before me. It was so strange to see him inside the house, let alone visible. He was usually out hunting and guarding, silent in the woods and only the faintest whisper in my mind. *:I would shift but I won't have clothes. I remember your command to wear pants around other women.:*

My lips quirked. "Thank you," I said aloud. "Do you know Mayte Zaniyah?"

:Not at all, though I know court intrigue inside and out. While she's not weak—or she wouldn't still be independent despite Keisha Skye's best efforts to crown herself the queen of the Americas—she isn't strong, either. She can't be.:

Though my other Blood were nodding, hearing Xin's words in the bond, I repeated roughly what he said for Gina and Winston.

"That's a very true assessment," Gina added. "Mayte has been queen for several hundred years and has managed to retain her independence. She isn't Keisha Skye's sib. Neither is Leonie Delafosse."

I thought about the meeting I'd overheard in my dreams between Keisha Skye and Marne Ceresa. It definitely supported the idea that Keisha wanted to be the queen in the Americas, as well as take a seat on the Triune. "So Skye's been trying to make them hers."

"Exactly," Rik replied. "That's why she finally allowed small groups of us to go out exploring for our own queens, with the goal of pulling more sibs to her."

:That's why Wu Tien dissolved the nest in San Francisco.: Xin said through the bond. *:She refused to offer throat to House Skye but had lost too much of her power base to remain independent. She hoped to reunite with some of the Wu clan to regain strength.:*

"What about the queen who'd been in Dallas? Was that Mayte?"

"Perhaps, though she never established a nest or court, and I haven't been able to get a full report from anyone in the area to be sure."

Thinking a few minutes, I polished off the last of the croissant and started on the fruit. I wasn't a fan of the cantaloupe, but the strawberries, grapes and pineapple were delicious. "Have Leonie and Mayte formed an alliance?"

"They may have an informal agreement, but they're not sibs," Gina replied. "They can't be, not without infuriating House Skye."

"True. Yeah. I could see that. If Skye thinks people are uniting against her, she'll attack harder."

"Which is why she made the move against you in Kansas City." Rik's voice rumbled toward rock troll at the memory. Skye had sent one of her lower Blood, Kendall, who had a blood bond with my first two Blood, in an effort to gain a foothold in my new court. Or betray me. We weren't really sure, and we didn't give Kendall long to show his hand before Xin killed him. "She had to see which way the wind would blow with you before you could connect with any other queen."

"It's a gamble for Mayte right now," Gina said. "She doesn't have any way to know how strong you are. Whether you can help her stand against House Skye. But she knows the Isador name and hopes that even if you're half human, that you'll be enough to defend her against Keisha Skye."

"But she has no idea if I'm any better of a queen, or fairer, than Skye is. Why would she want to be my sib but not hers?"

Rik tightened his arm around my shoulders. "Trust me. Anyone who knows Keisha Skye would run in the opposite direction and hope for the best."

I nestled my head against his chest. "You've never talked about your time in her court."

"For good reason. Thank the goddess Daire and I were too far down her list to worry much."

I wanted to know more, but I was afraid to ask. I didn't want to break down crying—or go off half-cocked with anger. Just the thought that my alpha and cuddly warcat had been unhappy made me want to cut the bitch, and I didn't even know her.

Gina's phone rang, and I knew before she said anything that it was Mayte Zaniyah's consiliarius. She nodded, meeting my gaze. Waiting to see what I would do.

:Taking a queen as strong and independent as Mayte Zaniyah will greatly expand your power base,: Xin said. *:Their power becomes yours. Her Blood indirectly become yours. Some queens even take a few from her sib's Blood, especially if she needs a particular skill.:*

:I don't want her Blood. I have mine.:

:Six Blood are not enough to protect you from the Triune.: Rik said. *:You need more. This is one way to make that gain—without actually taking more Blood of your own.:*

I couldn't imagine making it work. Not really. I liked my small team the way we were. I loved having my Blood so deep and close to me. If I had to gain ten or twenty more Blood to protect us from Marne Ceresa... I didn't want that. Not really.

:Sibs weren't always like pawns,: Guillaume said in our bond, and I felt Xin's immediate agreement. *:Sib is short for sibling. At one time, this was a way to make your family larger. To make connections and share oaths of protection and fealty among the houses. It's a risk for her to offer herself to you, but only because she doesn't know you like we do.:*

That made my throat tighten and my heart suddenly felt like it'd grown too large for my ribcage.

"Tell her I'd like to meet Mayte," I said to Gina aloud. "No promises or pressure though."

"You got it." Gina answered the call. "Gina Isador. Yes, hello, Bianca. So nice to talk with you again." She listened a few minutes, nodding as she jotted some notes on a legal pad. She turned it toward me so I could read it. *New Year's Eve party in Mexico City. 3 day stay.*

That'd give me a few days to mentally prepare. I nodded.

"Wonderful, yes, my queen accepts your queen's invitation. The size of our party?"

I did a quick mental count. Me and the Blood. Gina. If we all left the nest, then Frank should probably stay behind to help with any workers needing access. With all my Blood, I shouldn't need a human security team.

:The eight of us, plus anyone else you think should go.: I thought at her.

"Nine at this time. If that changes, I'll call you again. Yes, thank you. We're looking forward to it." Eyes bright, Gina hung up. "You know what this means, right?"

"We get to use the jet again?"

"True. But more."

Rik pressed his mouth against my ear. "Queen events are generally formal affairs."

Even though he wasn't present, Daire's warcat purred loudly in my mind. *:More shopping.:*

3

DAIRE

When Rik paired me up with Mehen for guard duty, I braced for the man's arrogance and the dark twist of his bond. The oldest Blood, and by far the most grumpy after centuries of imprisonment as a dragon, he could make the simplest of duties unpleasant, to say the least. His hatred and rage leaked through our bonds, and carrying that much negativity took its toll, poisoning our minds with his bitterness.

So it was a very good thing that Rik and Shara had fucked him so hard last night. It'd definitely knocked the mighty dragon down a few pegs and taken the edge off his rage. But what had helped the most was the cuddling after the fact. Sleeping with several warm bodies made it difficult to sulk and plot revenge. Though I'd die of old age before I'd ever hear the man admit that he'd actually enjoyed sleeping tangled up in that big pile of warm bodies.

Listening in on our queen's bond as much as possible at least helped pass the time when I wasn't physically near her. I couldn't wait to take her shopping again, and a queen's court visit would be off-the-chains fun to prepare for. She'd need a formal gown for each night, and we'd need to dress up too.

Her first political challenge had ended in the death of another queen's Blood. Hopefully this visit with Zaniyah went better.

"So why are you banned from her bed?" Even Mehen's voice was harsh and abrupt, slicing through my thoughts like a red-hot poker.

I couldn't suppress the twitch of surprise. I'd totally forgotten he was with me. Stupid. We were supposed to be on guard duty, not listening in on our queen's bond and plotting a wardrobe. "I fucked up."

Since he'd distracted me anyway, I cast my senses out as far as possible, feeling for anything amiss. A few rabbits had braved the fresh snow in search of food. A bird with long green tail feathers sat on a low limb at the edge of the woods, watching as we paced our queen's blood circle. But I sensed nothing else for miles.

Mehen grunted beneath his breath. "That doesn't tell me much."

I shrugged uncomfortably, avoiding his gaze. "I made a mistake, okay? She shifted into a cobra and was hurting Rik. I tried to free him before she killed him. I would have hurt her to save him, and Rik banned me from her bed until he's sure I wouldn't put his, or anyone else's, welfare over our queen's ever again."

Mehen's eyes widened. "She managed to hurt our alpha?"

"She fucking killed him," I said flatly. "Though being Isis's descendant has its advantages. He's got two huge scars on his stomach from where she bit him."

"She loves him."

"Her cobra didn't care. At least when she bit you, she didn't poison you too. Rik's poisonous, but Guillaume said anyone of her blood carries the antivenin now."

"Alpha won't be feeding us anyway."

Probably not, though sometimes I missed the taste of his blood. Though I loved my queen and tasting her blood was fucking fantastic, I loved Rik too, and I'd known him for far longer. I needed my queen's blood for power.

But Rik's...

He just tasted like home. Family. When it'd been just him and me against Keisha Skye's court. I'd never in a million years want to go back to that. But he'd been the best thing I'd known for nearly forty years.

"So how long do I have to put up with all of you being absolute shits to me?"

I snorted. "As long as you were imprisoned."

"You tried to hurt her too."

Wincing, I shrugged and focused on the bird again. It still sat there. Watching. It was strangely colored, too. More tropical than anything I would have expected to find in Arkansas. But it didn't feel like a thrall or another Aima, though I'd have to get closer to be sure it wasn't something magical. "I never would have killed her. I just wanted to stop her from smashing all the bones in his body and suffocating him. Does that bird look strange to you?"

"Yeah, I wondered how fucking long it'd take you to notice it since we're supposed to be on guard duty."

:*There's a suspicious bird watching us.*: I told Rik in the bond. :*But I don't sense anything off or threatening. It's just out of place.*:

:*Show me.*:

Looking at the bird, I dropped my inner shields. Literally letting my guard down. Rik's bond surged inside me and I felt him slide into me, looking out through my eyes.

"Fuck," Mehen whispered beneath his breath. "I didn't know he could do that. You even smell like him right now."

I didn't try to speak, not with Rik in me so strongly. It'd be weird to hear his words come out in my voice. I didn't think Mehen or any of the other Blood would be able to do this. Not as fully as I could. I'd submitted to him in more ways than one, which made this easier. He might have fucked Mehen last night, but mighty Leviathan hadn't *submitted*. Not entirely.

A raucous caw announced Nevarre's raven as he flew past, headed straight for the strange bird. I hoped he didn't kill it. The bird was beautiful and it wasn't hurting anything. Yet.

The giant raven landed on the ground below the limb and cocked its head, watching the smaller bird. It squawked and squeaked, Nevarre bobbing his head and pacing beneath the tree. Then the bird shot up into the air, headed south.

:It was a messenger from Zaniyah.: Nevarre said through our bonds. *:Skye will attack. She said beware the ground.:*

"Beware the ground?" Mehen asked. "What the fuck does that mean?"

Nevarre flew back over the nest boundary and landed on the ground before us. *:She was a true bird, a quetzel, not a shifter, so she didn't have a full vocabulary. She sent me images, though, of something swarming up out of the ground. She pecked at it, like she could eat it. So maybe bugs? Worms? But something coming up out of the ground.:*

I let out a disgusted growl—that sounded way more like Rik's troll than my warcat. "Up through the ground—directly into the nest."

Rik backed out of me so hard and fast that I reeled, losing my balance a moment. Mehen steadied me with a hand on my shoulder.

:Everybody shift. Nose to the ground. Nevarre, use your eyes from above. If you see anything suspicious, even a dark speck against the snow, map it for us. Find this fucking threat before our queen's nest is compromised.:

RIK

I DID NOT RELISH the chore of admitting to my queen that her supposedly impenetrable nest might soon come under attack.

I had sworn she'd be safe here. And within days, we faced an unknown threat from the ground. Worse, she'd owe a debt to Zaniyah for warning us in advance.

But all of those considerations paled in comparison to the very real threat of what would happen to my queen, and me, if Keisha Skye managed to get a hook in Shara.

"How does she know where we are?" Shara asked, turning from her conversation with Gina to look at me.

I hadn't thought she was listening through the bonds, not while planning the trip with her consiliarius. "Kendall wasn't our only sib in Skye court. Any of them could pinpoint our location, though we fed from Kendall the most."

"So she's going to try to break through the nest from below," she mused, staring off into space. "Could one of her shifters fly over at the same time, like Nevarre?"

"No, not to my knowledge. But I've never heard of anyone penetrating a nest through the ground, either."

:If Nevarre wasn't your Blood, he probably couldn't fly high enough to penetrate the nest,: Mehen added, still in his human shape. Now that our queen had taken him as Blood, he couldn't shift into his dragon form unless she explicitly allowed it. *:Your blood creates a magical wall that extends above and below, though the ground is harder for your blood to penetrate. Most winged creatures couldn't get over it, but my beast could.:*

"What kind of shifters would come up through the ground?"

"None that I can think of," I replied. "Especially in her court. She has mostly cats and wolves in her Blood."

"You haven't talked about her court much."

She'd said much the same thing a few moments earlier, but more than curiosity rang in her words. She needed information and if we were under a real and present danger…

Rock hardened beneath my skin, turning my face to granite. "Because I would rather forget."

She could have sank into my bond and dragged the past out of me. She could have viewed my memories like a movie. But my queen only threaded her fingers through mine and hugged my arm to her. "If no shifter can get up through the ground, what could she send against us? What powers does she have?"

"The bird pecked at something on the ground, so Nevarre is guessing some kind of bug." My voice rumbled with rock troll bass, but hopefully she thought it was anger from the threat, not because my heart ached with gratitude. I knew she needed information, desperately, but she wouldn't drag it out of me all at once. Though maybe the rip-off-the-bandage approach would be best in this case. "I wasn't high enough in her court to know her powers, and what she displayed…"

She kissed my shoulder. Only then did I realize how tense I'd become. I made my muscles relax so I wasn't a granite boulder against her.

"There's only two things to know about Keisha Skye." Daire stepped into the room, his usually easygoing personality a vicious snarl, his warcat pacing back and forth in his bond. "She wants a child to replace the one she lost, and she enjoys breaking alphas."

4

SHARA

I'd known Rik and Daire had left Skye's court in search of a lost queen, and that Skye had expected them to reel me in for her to expand her power base. But I hadn't realized that Rik had actually been afraid of her.

My big, bad alpha Blood. Afraid.

That told me all I needed to know about Keisha Skye. Flames licked through my veins, stoking my rage. No one would ever hurt or scare or threaten any of my Blood ever again. So help me goddess.

"You should be out searching the nest," Rik said to Daire, but without the ring of an order behind it.

Daire gave a little toss of his head that sent the tawny fall of his hair rippling down his back. Now well past his shoulders, his hair made me want to wrap my fists in it and haul him close.

Padding over to me, barefoot and shirtless but with jeans on, he dropped to a crouch so he could drape himself in my lap, pushing his head under Rik's arm that I'd hugged to me.

"There's nothing to find yet," he replied. "Nevarre is still scouting from the air and his bird vision is way better than any of ours."

I combed my fingers through his hair, listening to his purr. Waiting. When they were ready, one of them would tell me what Keisha Skye had done that left them both so scared.

"I can confirm some of the basic facts," Gina said slowly, as if hesitant to speak. "Keisha Skye did have a child almost one hundred years ago. It was a big deal at the time, enough that my grandmother made a note of it in her personal records. Breeding queens are rare in this day and age, but queens able to successfully conceive and deliver a child are even rarer. No queen in several centuries had managed to have a child and she was rightfully lauded for it. Other queens were quick to ask her what she'd done to conceive, but she was very closed mouthed about it. Grandma said that could only mean one thing." She dropped her voice even more and whispered, "dark magic."

For vampires that reveled in blood, I was almost afraid to ask what would make Gina whisper. "What's that?"

"Dark magic requires the death of something to raise the power."

"An unwilling sacrifice," Rik whispered, though with his rock troll's graveled rumble.

"She prefers women," Daire said. "Always has. But a queen needs a male alpha to sire a child. The more powerful the alpha, the better. So she always has plenty of alphas in her stable, so to speak, and she… uh… tests them."

"She tortures them," Rik growled so deep and low that my cup rattled on the table.

"Deep down, she hates men, I think," Daire said softly, rubbing his head on Rik's arm to soothe him. "She takes pleasure in hurting them under the guise of testing to find the best alpha to sire a child. When she finally did conceive, she coincidentally killed the alpha in the process."

My mouth fell open. "She killed him?"

"So they say."

"But she lost this child? How?"

"She had a daughter, yes," Gina answered. "Tanza, I

34

believe, though I'd have to check our records to be sure. The whispers started right away though that the child wasn't… right."

"She was gone before Rik and I came to court, and Skye cast a geas to keep anyone in her court from talking about her." Daire said. "But they still whispered about her in hushed, general references. I don't know how many of the stories were true, but if even half of the nightmares they told us actually happened, then I can only say it's a blessing the child died."

"Grandma wrote that the child was possessed," Gina admitted, still whispering, as if we were all afraid that Keisha would somehow sense that we were talking about her. "That she carried a demon in her. The queen went a little mad when she lost her child. To my knowledge, no one outside of Skye's court knows exactly how she died, either."

"She went a lot fucking mad," Daire corrected. "She's still unstable, to be honest, but supposedly better now than she was even fifty years ago. Though she's still obsessed with conceiving another child."

"No one sane would torture people like she does." Rik's voice still rumbled, his muscles rock against me. "She's the one who carries a demon."

"She only tortures alphas," Daire's voice broke and he turned his face deeper against Rik. "I lived in dread that one day he'd get called up to join her Blood. She burned through the alphas much too quickly."

Rik dropped his other hand on Daire's head and leaned into me harder. "There were plenty of alphas in their prime ahead of me, but I was relieved when she finally allowed us to leave."

I closed my eyes a moment, fighting to regain my composure. My eyes were hot and burning, but I wouldn't cry. Not now. Maybe later, when it was just me and him and I could hold him tightly against me, I'd cry at how close I'd come to losing him before he could have ever found me. "How did you end up in Skye's court in the first place?"

"My parents served as sibs in Jarnsaxa's court. She had a long-standing relationship with House Skye to exchange young Aima to keep the blood fresh in both courts. No one outside of Keisha's court knew exactly how bad it was, especially for alphas, and when I did realize how dangerous it was for me, it was too late. It would have shamed both my parents and my mother's queen if I broke their agreement, and so I endured to the best of my ability."

"That's what we do," Daire said softly. "If you don't have a queen of your own, you endure, and hope for the best court possible. I guess we were lucky not to go to Marne Ceresa's court."

Rik grunted softly. "I don't know anything about how she runs her Blood but surely it wouldn't have been as bad as Skye's."

I could feel dark spots in Rik's bond that echoed with pain and fear. Memories of things he'd seen, that he tried to shield me from. He didn't want me to know exactly how terrible it'd been for them both, but him in particular.

Part of me wanted to know, so that I'd be sure and not do anything like it.

He turned to me so fast that I flinched back a little at his intensity before I could catch myself. "You'd never do anything like it. I have no doubt of that at all. If you want to see the torture she inflicted on her Blood, my mind is open to you. It always is. But I'd rather you not see and fear the same way as we do."

I reached up and stroked the hard marble planes of his face until his fierceness eased. "I'll take your word for it. I don't want to see, unless it's something I need to know to beat her."

"You've already beaten her."

"Actually, yes, you have," Gina said, her voice trembling with worry. It made me turn away from Rik to see her face. Her eyes were big, dark, shimmering with fear. "You're able to breed. That means you're able to conceive. From everything I've read about her in Grandma's notes, Keisha Skye will hate you for that reason alone. It'll make a political fight personal for her. In fact, her obsession is probably eating her alive already, wondering how on earth Selena could have conceived you with a human. It wouldn't surprise me if she's kidnapping human men off the street now to try and conceive another child."

"Would it be better or worse if she knew the truth?"

The truth was so much more difficult to believe, even as outlandish as the thought that I might have been half human. The people who'd raised me until their deaths weren't actually my parents. Selena was my aunt, and Alan had no blood relation to me at all.

My mother and Selena were both Aima, a powerful line of vampires descended from the ancient gods and goddesses. My family in particular descended from Isis.

My father…

A long forgotten god. Typhon, the father of monsters like Cerebus. And me. Though I didn't have three heads, I could transform into both a cobra and a wyvern so far.

"Honestly, I don't think it'll matter much," Gina replied. "You can breed, so you're a threat to her personally. The other queens will definitely be more wary if they know you're not half human, but for Skye, it won't matter."

"Let's handle this one problem at a time, then. Keisha Skye is my problem right now. She's planning an attack on the nest, something that no one's heard of before other than Mayte Zaniyah, since she sent the warning. What goddess is House Skye descend from?"

"She's several generations removed from Scathach, the legendary warrior maiden associated with the Isle of Skye," Rik replied. "Though she isn't known for being a warrior like her ancestor. The only power I've ever heard associated with her is controlling the weather, especially storms."

I frowned. "Then what power does she have that might affect or come from the ground?"

"None that I'm aware of. I've never seen her display her power, though, and since we weren't Blood, we didn't feel her directly."

Gina typed on her laptop a few moments and then said, "According to Grandma Paula's notes, the hurricane in 1938 marks the death of Tanza. Over six hundred people died."

I didn't try to think of a solution exactly. I just let ideas well up in my head. Options. Possibilities. Until something crystallized.

I stood and immediately everyone stood with me. "Go ahead and get the trip set up as we planned."

Gina nodded, but her brow was creased with worry.

"Thank you, Winston. That was a delightful breakfast, er… very late brunch."

He inclined his head. "You're most welcome, Your Majesty."

"Shara, please. I don't want there to be formality in my house. As far as I'm concerned, you're all family."

He blinked and pulled out a monogrammed handkerchief to dab at his eyes. "It's an honor to serve, Shara."

I gave him a quick hug and then Gina. "What are you going to do?"

"I'm going to protect my nest the best way I know how." I smiled and her eyes flared, one brow arching with curiosity. "I'm going to bleed."

5

SHARA

I didn't think we'd been in the house too long, but it was already dusk outside. Snow still covered the ground, but tracks marred the white surface. It made me smile to see wolf tracks beside hoof and paw prints.

Rik gave a jerk of his head at Daire. "Go on patrol. I have a feeling she'll attack after dark."

Daire stepped in close to me first, giving me a quick but deep, full body hug. He didn't just use his arms, but managed to drape his whole body on me, even though he was nearly a foot taller than me. "When you're ready, I'd love for you to try and burn her out of me."

In Kansas City, I'd had the idea that I could try and burn their previous blood bonds out of them, so that Keisha Skye wouldn't have any hold on them any longer. No one had been able to break a bond like that before, at least not that we knew of.

"I don't want to hurt you like that."

"Hurt me. I don't care. I hate being a liability, a weakness."

I wrapped my hands in his hair and tugged his head back. He started purring, so I tightened my grip, pulling his hair back to bare the long, sexy line of his throat. "You're never a liability or weakness. In fact, I fully intend to use your bond with Skye court to betray them."

"How? When?"

I smiled and kissed his throat, giving him only a faint prick of my fangs. Then I released him. "You'll see. Don't worry about her bond."

He pouted, but I felt a push in their bond. Rik, exerting his alpha will. Daire shifted immediately, though he bumped his head into my stomach for some scratches behind his ear.

Rik let out a rumbling growl.

Daire twitched his tail, smacking Rik's legs, but obediently headed out into the darkening night.

"So what's this plan of yours to use our Skye bonds?"

My fangs descended, making me shiver. My stomach knotted. Hunger rose. Need burned. Rik rumbled deep and low, his arm sliding around my waist, and yeah, I wanted his blood. But not yet.

I dragged my fangs across my wrist.

Power bubbled up inside me like a pure mountain spring. My senses sharpened. I could feel my other five Blood. Their heartbeats. Each feather in Nevarre's wings. The thud of Guillaume's hooves pounding the ground. The whisper of Xin's fur as he ghosted across the snow.

"You don't have to add blood to the circle." Rik's voice rumbled deep and low in my belly, stoking my desire.

"I know," I whispered, holding my wrist out so blood dripped down my skin and onto the ground.

The first plop of blood on the ground sent a ring of power rippling out like a wave. Primed by my blood circle's sacrifice, the great Earth Mother, Gaia, answered eagerly. The earth absorbed my blood like a starving creature. Frost melted in the heat of my blood. Life sparked in the dirt. A tiny seed sprouted, a faint green leaf unfurling in the snow.

Regret tightened my throat. I didn't want the tiny sprout to die. I hadn't meant to make something start growing in the dead of winter.

The sprout had other ideas, though. It grew quickly for a few moments, green leaves up to my knees. But then it stopped, tender leaves wilting a bit. The whole young stem leaned toward me, leaves straining to stand against the snow and cold.

I held my wrist back out over the young plant and allowed blood to splatter on the leaves. Immediately, the plant started growing again until its tender stem was replaced by a woody stalk taller than me. Leaves and branches stretched up to the sky, but more importantly, the roots sank deep into the ground, spreading like a sensitive network.

My blood pulsed in the tree, deep into the ground. Pumping energy through the soil and rock, the roots cast out a steady radar bleep, searching for anything out of place.

"Wow," Rik said, his voice soft with reverence. "How did you know to do that?"

"I didn't, not exactly. But I felt how much She loved my blood when we set the nest, and I figured that was a way to start."

The lattice of roots stretched a good thirty feet down and out in a wide circle, but nowhere near the entire nest. Trailing blood, I started walking, listening and feeling for another seed to spark. "What kind of tree is that?"

"Looks like an oak."

I glanced back, amazed. The tender green leaves had transformed into gnarled thick branches running low the ground. The tree looked like it'd been here for a couple of hundred years.

I felt a spark in the snow and paused, watching as another sprout broke through the snow, stretching up toward my blood. This one was some kind of evergreen. In a few minutes, a mighty pine stretched into the sky, interlacing its roots with the oak. I sighed, looking at how much ground I needed to cover. It was going to take a hell of a lot of blood.

Rik drew me into his arms. "Then you should definitely feed on me while you grow the next tree."

"I don't want you weakened if we're going to have to protect the nest."

He snorted and walked with his arm around me, waiting until I found the next seed that sprouted beneath the snow. "Feeding you makes me stronger, not weaker. And I want my queen well-fed and pumped with alpha power before Skye attempts to spoil your nest."

6

NEVARRE

Wheeling in slow circles above my new queen's nest, I couldn't still the tumult fluttering like a trapped bird in my chest. Uncertainty burned in my veins, suffocating me.

My fate had already been determined. My time had run out. I was dead. It was too late for me.

Until Shara Isador called me back from the dead and breathed life back into me. But why me?

I still didn't know why I'd been given a second chance. I had already suffered the ultimate failure. I'd lost everything, including my life. I certainly didn't deserve another chance. Let alone a queen.

Though Brigid had been a druid not a queen, I'd sworn my life to her. She'd found me at my lowest point and brought happiness and hope back into my life, rather than the desolation I'd been living. Her court had been a simple three-hundred-year-old cottage on the outskirts of Inverness. She dyed and spun the wool from our sheep and made trinkets that we sold at fairs and tourist shops all over the countryside. They looked like simple wall hangings with Celtic knots and carefully woven scenes, but each piece was made for a specific magical purpose. Ward your house. Increase your fertility or wealth. Heal your sick. Improve your crops.

Certainly a long fall from grace for a Morrigan son.

No queen. No nest. No sibs. No family.

Only a druid witch who'd loved me despite those failures.

Looking back, those decades with Brigid had been some of the best of my life. She'd taught me so much about life and love and family and simple pleasures. A newborn lamb. Silvery moonlight dancing across the moors. The gleam of firelight on her glorious sunset hair. With her arms around me, the missing hole in my chest dulled to an ache that was almost bearable. Until I lost her too.

With night falling fast, my eyesight wasn't as sharp. I turned back toward my queen. The scent of her blood was thick on the air, pulling all her Blood to her side. She'd bled a great deal, though I wasn't sure what she'd done. The air was thick with magic and blood, going straight to my head. Drunk on magic. Drunk on my queen's blood. Drunk on her sex.

She'd tasted me last night and fucked me under the stars. I'd thought nothing could move me again after I'd lost Brigid, but I'd been surprised at how easily and quickly I responded to Shara. How well I fit into her existing Blood. They'd welcomed me without any resentment or strife, even a dead raven. Even her big alpha hadn't questioned my right to serve or cast shadow on my abilities since I'd obviously failed so severely in the past. If they only knew the half of my failures...

I wouldn't survive the loss of this queen.

In the darkness, the woods around her house looked different. By sight alone, I would have said I was lost. The shape and texture of the forest had changed. New trees grew where I swear nothing but snowy gardens had been before.

Trees.

In a circle about her house. A ring in her nest.

I dived for the ground, shifting at the last moment so that I made a running landing on my feet, stumbling to catch myself until I fell on my knees before Shara.

She stood under the spreading branches of a gnarled ancient Norway spruce. A tree that wasn't native to Arkansas or even North America to my knowledge and it certainly hadn't been here just an hour before.

In fact, this particular tree had once grown in Morrigan's Grove in my mother's nest. I'd climbed these limbs as a boy and my first queen had taken me beneath its branches. It felt so familiar that I didn't rise from my knees. I just knelt there, trembling, looking up at the glorious branches.

"Nevarre? What is it?"

"Morrigan's Grove." My voice broke, and I didn't care. "These trees grew in my mother's nest, until her consiliarius betrayed us and the trees were destroyed. We lost them. We lost everything. I saw them heaped in a pile and burned to nothing but ash on the wind, yet you recreated it. How? How is this possible?"

She shrugged. "I offered blood to Gaia, and this is what She grew. I needed something to help us protect the nest from the ground, and now I can feel the roots stretching out fingers deep into the soil, forming one giant network. It's like they're talking to each other, and to me."

My brain said it couldn't be the same grove. The same trees. It was impossible.

My magic was another story. It leaped in my blood, eager and restless, ready to be used. Magic that I'd lost when the last beloved tree had been ripped from the earth and burned.

She cupped my cheeks in her hand and turned my face up to hers. "You're crying. What's wrong?"

"Nothing," I whispered hoarsely. "It's... wondrous. I never thought... I never hoped..." I buried my face against her stomach. "My queen."

She stroked her hands through my hair, holding me close. "Morrigan was your queen's goddess?"

I shook my head against her. "My mother's. My queen was Elspeth White, but she dissolved our bond when we lost the grove. Then I lost Brigid too, the druid witch who took me in when no one else would."

"How?"

The image of the fatal car accident flashed through my mind. I let Shara have it, seeing it like a movie. Our farm truck careened off the road into a steep ravine. "She saved me with her magic, but I never knew why. Not until now."

Shara's doubt was bitter on my tongue. A simple car accident shouldn't have been able to kill me, not a son of Morrigan, even without a queen to power my magic. But the flames had been so intense, the ravine too deep. We couldn't have crashed in a worse place, and I hadn't been able to save us. I deserved her doubt. I had failed to protect Brigid, and now I was alive and she wasn't. "Flames erupted immediately so hot and intense I couldn't breathe. I started to shift automatically, but my wing was so badly broken on impact I couldn't even think to fly. Let alone carry her."

I felt Shara's bond sliding through me, liquid moonlight touching those old shadowed places of pain. Reliving those memories hurt.

I relived them every night.

She paused the memory playing out in my head. We'd run off the road and crashed into the ravine. I smelled gasoline. Blood choked me, dripping down my face. Feathers were sprouting from my skin, the raven starting to emerge. Slowly, she backed up the memory, flashing scene by scene. The truck flying through the air. Veering off the road. The bluest eyes in the world looking into mine, framed by brilliant red hair. Freckles sprinkled across her cheeks.

Brigid.

:She's beautiful,: Shara whispered. :She loved you very much.:

I couldn't answer. I hoped that I'd made her happy while we were together, even though I'd failed her in the end.

Shara backed up the memory a bit more and my eyes watered. Something flashed across the windshield like a lightning bolt. The heat and brightness made my eyes tender, streaming again, even from the memory.

"Ra," she said aloud. "He caused her to swerve off the road."

I tasted blood in my mouth, hard iron and cold hate grinding through me. "The god of light killed my Brigid?"

"I've seen that light before. He tried to kill me too, though not with a car accident. I'm sure it's his signature, though."

The knight managed to make a very disgusted sound even in his horse form. *:I agree. It's him.:*

The trees whispered around us. Leaves and branches speaking the ancient language I hadn't heard in hundreds of years.

Ra. Retribution. Punish him. Ra.

I met my queen's gaze and she nodded. She heard them too. She was part of the grove now. It spoke to her too.

Standing, I slashed my palm open on my fangs and walked closer to the giant pine. My knees trembled, not with fear, but awe. These trees were sacred, impossibly old, and magical beyond even my understanding, and I'd been privileged to grow up in the grove. The sight of these glorious old trees bulldozed into a pile and burned had brought my entire clan to their knees and my mother had died of despair.

Reverently, I placed my bleeding palm on the ancient trunk. *I'm sorry I failed to protect you.*

The bark moved beneath my hand as if the heart of the tree surged, pushing outward. One bough brushed my cheek and the whispering wrapped around me. Not words, but a feeling. Forgiveness. Peace. Fate. Destiny.

We were all connected. We were all brought to this moment for a reason.

Her reason. Morrigan's. And Shara's. They were united in this goal.

My magic pulsed in my blood, dancing with joy and burning with retribution. The heavy beat of my heart was Her war drum. My raven, Her messenger.

The Battle Goddess blessed me with Her shadow and Her wings. I would fly to war with my queen, her goddess, and mine.

And Her Shadow would blot out the mighty sun forever.

SHARA

URGENCY THRUMMED THROUGH MY NERVES. Morrigan still had a great deal of work to do. Her grove wasn't complete yet.

The heart tree was missing.

My knees quivered, though, and hunger burned in me. I needed to feed before I could continue.

Nevarre's blood drew me like a moth to a flame.

Need pounded in me, but I stopped before I touched him. He'd already lost someone he'd loved, and that pain was still fresh. I could feel the memory of Brigid's death throbbing like rusted spikes driven into his heart.

Deeper, I felt betrayal like cracked, splintered bones. So much loss and anger burned in him, eating at him like a cancer.

He turned toward me, but kept his back pressed against the rough bark of the tree. Branches swayed gently around him, his long hair tangled in the limbs. Earth music rose around us, singing in welcome and joy. A beloved son who'd been lost, now home.

Though he was worn and weary, he'd been welcomed with open arms.

"Not weary," he whispered. "Broken."

His sadness and pain tightened my throat. Finding the grove again was bittersweet for him. I hadn't known the trees' significance, but I couldn't change what Gaia had given back to us. I needed to protect my nest and my Blood. The network of roots still dug deeper into the earth below, now interlacing with the surrounding forest. Trees spoke to each other, whispering of creatures moving in the night, the cold of snow on bare branches, the promise of spring.

A sense of wrongness miles away. A thrall, I thought. No, a pack of them. They smelled my blood on the air. Mindless hunger pulled them closer, even though they knew what waited for them. They could smell my Blood too. Yet they'd come. They'd linger outside the nest like scavengers.

"Let them come," Rik growled. One big arm came around me, drawing me back to his chest. He lifted his other wrist up to me, silently offering up his blood.

But if I bit him…

I'd rather he be inside me first.

"Your wish is my command, my queen."

I turned and draped my arms around his neck. "Would you be up to feeding two of us at once?"

His nostrils flared. "Of course, if that's your wish."

I loved that he didn't question my motives. If I wanted or needed something, he'd take care of it. No matter what it was.

"Daire," I whispered, holding my hand out to him without looking away from Rik's face.

His eyes softened. *:You heard his silent wish today.:*

:Of course.:

The warcat rubbed against my legs and Rik's, twining around us, his rumbling purr like thunder.

"I need you to shift so you can do the biting," I told him. "I don't want to get distracted yet. I still have too much work to do."

I'd never cease to be amazed as I watched him shift back to my sexy Blood. The warcat folded up, rolled inside, until he was Daire again. No bones popping, pain, or effort. Easy.

"You make it easy," he purred, rubbing against me. "You make it possible."

I moved to the side a bit, making room for him against Rik.

With my left arm around Rik's neck and my right tucked around Daire's waist, I settled between the two of them.

My first two knights. The ones who'd saved me at my darkest hour.

"Where should I bite him, my queen?" Daire whispered in that rumbly purr.

"Hmmm." I pretended to think about it a moment. "If you bite his neck, I'm too short to reach. You should probably bite him lower."

Daire waggled his eyebrows, making me laugh. "How low, my queen?" He dropped to his knees and rubbed his head against Rik's abdomen, looking up at me through his tousled hair. "Maybe here? They say that blood drawn from the groin is more potent and hot."

But Rik wasn't amused by our game. He bent down, snagged an arm under my butt, and hauled me up high against him. "My queen never goes down to her knees. Let alone in the snow."

Pressed up against him, I was starting to regret my decision not to bite him.

"Later." his low voice crashed like falling boulders.

"Promise?"

"You know it." He gave a hard look at Daire. "Get on with it. She hungers."

Daire slid in beside me, still purring as he sank his fangs into Rik's throat. He groaned deep in his chest and took several swallows before lifting his head.

"Thank you," I whispered, remembering our first night together.

How they'd had to help me, bite for me, because I didn't have fangs.

Now, I had huge fangs—with a serious side effect. So they still had to help me, and I didn't mind one bit. Not anymore.

How could I, when I loved them so much?

Locking my mouth over Daire's bite, I drank Rik down. So

good. So strong. I couldn't imagine his blood being any hotter or more potent, even if I'd sunk my fangs into his femoral artery. His blood settled me, my rock and foundation, unshakable.

Still purring, Daire curled up beside me, licking the trails of blood that I'd missed. Rik held us both to him. Taking care of us. Loving us. And I could cry at how beautiful it was.

Daire licked at my mouth, wanting me to share. Normally, I wouldn't have minded in the slightest. Tasting Rik's blood from Daire's mouth was a heady, erotic act that would quickly have me dragging them both to the guest house. But tension still coiled inside me, my nerves tight like a drum. Keisha Skye was going to attack, and we weren't fully prepared yet. Not until the heart tree was done.

:No,: Rik said before I could move. *:Make your own bite.:*

Daire did as he was told, sinking his fangs into the other side of Rik's throat. *:You taste different. Stronger. Fuck me sideways, but that cobra bite made you taste even better.:*

Rik made a low noise like distant thunder, his arms tightening on us. Listening to his bond, I kept a careful sense on his health. I couldn't risk weakening my alpha, no matter how good he tasted.

He snorted, dropping his head so his chin rested on me. *:You could never weaken me. Even if you drained me until I couldn't stand, all you'd need to do would be to give me a few sips of your blood and I'm stronger than ever. Take what you need, my queen.:*

I sensed movement to my left and smelled Nevarre's blood. He didn't interrupt, but made himself available to me by leaning against Rik, his arm coming around me too. Then Mehen, of all people, pressed against Daire and me both, a silent offering. He couldn't shift, not until I allowed it, though in his bond, all I felt was eagerness.

He wanted me to feed. He wanted to fuck. All of us. It didn't matter who, as long as he was part of it. Though the vibration from Daire's purring was doing some serious arousal for my oldest Blood. So of course Daire purred louder and shoved his butt back against the other man.

If I didn't hurry up and grow the heart tree, we were going to have another orgy under the stars.

Not that I'd mind in the slightest…

But I had some serious work to do first.

Lifting my head, I looked up at Rik as I licked his blood from my lips.

His eyes smoldered, heavy and intense. :*I think Daire has been punished long enough, my queen.*:

My heart leaped and I smiled, blinking back tears. Finally, I'd have my cuddle buddy back in my bed.

Daire, like a little shit, purred so loud and so hard that I could probably come just from leaning against him. Though he might have done that as much to torment Mehen as me.

Instead, I turned to Nevarre. Before I could say anything, he lifted his hand to my mouth, offering his blood. Before, he'd tasted like ancient Celtic magic and wind-swept moors, at least that was what my mind thought. Now, he had a darker, subtle edge in his blood. The clang of swords. The raucous call of war ringing in his bond. A slow, insidious shadow that crept across the land, obliterating even the strongest and mightiest of warriors.

:*Morrigan has returned my gift.*: He whispered in my mind. :*I am Her Shadow once more.*:

:*What does that mean?*:

His mouth hardened in a grim slant, his eyes the hard, stone-cold glint of a brutal sword. :*Not even the god of light can stand against Her Shadow.*:

:*Good.*: I licked his palm but then lifted my mouth, taking his bleeding hand in my own instead. Our blood dripped and mingled, trailing down our wrists. :*Let's grow the heart tree now.*:

Lowering our hands so our blood dripped onto the ground, I started walking, slowly, waiting for Gaia to tell me when to stop. I hadn't realized exactly what She'd led me to do before, but it

looked like the grove completely surrounded my house, a tighter
ring inside the blood circle I'd laid to create the nest. My manor
house wasn't perfectly center, but set back toward the rear of the
grove. I walked toward the center, listening to the earth music.
Trees whispered, swaying gently, calling to the creatures of the
night. A few birds already roosted in the ancient branches that
hadn't been there an hour ago. A fat squirrel scurried beneath a
gigantic oak, scooping up a fresh bounty of acorns that had
fallen from the mighty tree.

The ground itself pulsed with life, feeding roots water and
nutrients. Worms and beetles loosened and primed the soil,
responding to the fresh leaves that had dropped onto the melting
snow. The ground seemed warmer with the trees, as if their life
force was so strong that they could change the very temperature
of the ground and air around them, bringing a thaw in the dead
of winter.

Something like icy water dripped down my spine, making
me gasp. I stopped, letting our blood feed the soil. My scalp
tingled, my hair flaring up around my head. My face throbbed
with each beat of my heart, and my fangs descended. Something in the ground called to me. Urgently. Hungry. Desperate.

:*This one will be painful,*: Nevarre warned, his tone soft with
regret. :*My mother did this when she moved her clan from Ireland to Scotland. I was only three or four years old, but I still remember.*:

I'd endure anything if that meant we'd be safe. Especially if
Rik's former queen thought to try and break him. I took a deep,
steadying breath and slashed my other wrist. Holding out my
arm, I let my blood gush like some kind of grisly fountain.

Sprouting vines writhed up out of the ground and started
climbing my legs. I let go of Nevarre's hand and held my arms
out, palms down, letting my blood fall as it would. I tipped my
head back and stared up at the full moon, huge and silver in the
sky. Had it been there before? I couldn't remember. But now it
looked like it was close enough to touch.

I felt the first prick of thorns, scratching my calf beneath my jeans. A small pain. Though the vines began to twine more eagerly around me. Pinning me. Trapping me. My heart rate accelerated and my stomach quivered, but I made myself stand firm. Bigger thorns dug into my thighs through my jeans. I bit back a soft cry. Shit. It hurt. Up my stomach. Cloth tore. Even heavy denim was unable to stand against the thorny branches. Thorns sank deeper. Instinctively, I flinched away, only to be gouged by others. My skin burned from hundreds of pinpricks. Thousands. But it still wasn't too bad.

Until the thorny vines snaked around my wrists and yanked me off the ground. A startled cry escaped before I could prevent it. Thorns pierced my wrists, sliding under my skin. Burning, so hungry, like dozens of fangs feasting on my blood. Steam rose from my skin as my blood hit the air. My clothes ripped away, shredded by voracious vines, baring more tender skin for them to mark.

Tears dripped down my cheeks but I tried not to make another sound. I tried to think of Xin's fog, like I did when Leviathan broke my arm, but I couldn't concentrate. The pain was too intense. Everywhere. No escape. Relentless. Fire. Blood. Pain.

I screamed.

7

RIK

I'd do literally anything my queen asked of me.
I'd kill anything or anyone who threatened her. I'd die for her. Gladly.

But I couldn't bear to stand aside and feel her pain, hear her scream, and do nothing.

Fuck. Her pain was so intense I couldn't see or breathe myself. A Blood was dedicated to his queen's wellbeing, so one aspect of the bond meant that any pain or discomfort she felt was magnified a hundredfold. If my queen was hurting, I'd know it, because I'd feel it a hundred times worse than she did.

We all did.

Daire retched beside me. Guillaume was on his hands and knees, head down, groaning miserably. Xin stood, but he stared up at the silvered moon and red tears trickled down his cheeks, his face drawn and hollowed with pain. Mehen thrashed on the ground, raking his fingers through the frozen packed snow. Red stained the white, his hands bleeding and torn from ice. He threw his head back and bellowed, so much like his dragon, even though she'd chained his beast.

Nevarre plunged his hands into the thorny patch, shredding

his arms up to his elbows. "Take my blood. Not hers. Spare her, Morrigan. I beg you."

If his goddess heard, She didn't stop our queen's torment. Instead, Shara was jerked off the ground and lifted high into the sky. Her scream of agony cut through me like Guillaume's deadly blade. I tried to shift, determined to wade into those vines to get to her. Surely thorns wouldn't be able to pierce my rock hide. But for the first time since she'd given me her blood, I couldn't shift.

I could only kneel there in the snow and listen to her scream.

The vines started braiding together, forming some kind of giant tree. The limbs shook, raining down droplets of blood.

Her blood.

Every drop sprouted another vine. Another torturous plant loaded with spikes. Buds formed on the branches and opened to the full moon. Roses, so dark red they were nearly black. They covered the towering tree and the ring of thorns around it. I'd never seen a rose tree, but that was the closest way to describe it. The sweet perfume lay thick in the air. It smelled like Shara. The soft, sweet scent of her skin, as if I'd buried my face in the hollow of her throat behind her ear, her hair falling down over my face.

She lay stretched out on her back across the crown of the tree, vines wrapping up her arms and legs, making her a part of the tree. Her clothes hung like tattered rags in the lower branches. The full moon hung low in the sky, aimed perfectly to illuminate her and the tree like a spotlight. I strained to see if her chest was moving. If she was still alive.

The ring of deadly thorns parted enough for Nevarre to squeeze through, though the plants took their toll from him in blood. He looked back at me. "I think we can get her now."

I pushed after him, ignoring the scratches that burned like fire on my thighs and stomach. They were nothing, like fireflies against the fireball of agony our queen still bore.

The tree itself towered well above our heads. The only way to get her was to climb up a prickly trunk of braided rose branches fused together.

"I'm lighter." Nevarre paced beneath the tree, looking for the best way up. "Throw me up as far as you can and I'll lower her to you."

He found a good spot to squeeze through, a thick branch nearly ten feet above my head. I took up position below it and he scrambled up my body. The other Blood joined us, bleeding from scratches on their arms and faces, as though the branches had fought them hard. Mehen grabbed one of Nevarre's arms and Guillaume the other, steadying him until he could stand on my shoulders.

"It'd be a hell of a lot easier if you'd shift and fly up to her," Mehen grumbled beneath his breath.

"I find myself in your unenviable position," Nevarre replied in a voice as hard and cold as chipped ice. "We all do."

"You can't shift? Fuck." Mehen blinked, then scowled back at all of us glaring at him. "How the fuck was I supposed to know? I can't ever shift without her."

"Don't you think I'd be up there with her, shielding her from the thorns with solid rock if I could?" I retorted, fighting back the urge to punch the arrogant bastard. I wouldn't need the rock troll to flatten him.

My patience was gone. My control dried up in the blistering heat of rage that pulsed like hot sludge inside me. But I wasn't angry at Mehen, not exactly. I was angry at whichever goddess had made my queen scream.

"The price—" Guillaume started to say but I cut him off with a fierce growl.

"I know. I don't have to like it." I worked my hands beneath Nevarre's feet, waiting until he steadied himself in my grip. "Ready?"

"Throw me as high as you can."

I took all my rage at her pain, my irritation with Mehen,

57

and my own frustration and helplessness, and shoved my arms up as hard as I could with a roar. I'd fucking throw Nevarre to the moon if that meant we could end her pain.

He grabbed hold of the branch above and yelped, but didn't let go despite the thorns.

"Get her the fuck out of there!"

NEVARRE

AT LEAST THE thorns helped me hold on to the branches despite the blood slickening my palms.

I didn't allow myself to think. I just climbed as quickly as I could, straight to the top of the tree. It had to be nearly thirty feet high, even taller than the one my mother had grown. Which meant Shara had bled so much she must be near death. My mother had been weak for days after growing the heart tree, even with ten healthy Blood to feed her back to full health. My queen only had six, and she faced an external threat from Skye, and an unknown queen, Zaniyah.

We had to get her back up to full strength quickly. Or everything she'd managed to restore would be bulldozed one way or the other all over again.

I poked my head up out of the canopy, ignoring the scrape across my forehead, though the blood dripping in my eye was annoying.

I'd seen my mother's trial. I thought I was prepared.

But the sight of my queen, trapped and bound with massive spiked thorns driven through her flesh, made my stomach heave. Looking at her, I didn't know where to start. Vines as thick as my wrist wrapped around her arms, legs, and waist, as if the torturous tree was determined to hug every inch of her into its branches. Thorns dug into her flesh, piercing completely through her wrists. But the worst...

A giant thorn had pushed through her back and punctured

through her chest, poking up between her breasts. It had to have gone through her heart.

"Get her down!" Rik bellowed up at me.

My hands shook. I didn't know where to start. I didn't want to hurt her more than she was already suffering. Pulling those thorns out of her...

Goddess. I don't think I can do this.

Shara made a low sound and her eyes opened. Blood dripped from her eyes, nose and ears, but she smiled. She fucking smiled. At me. "Nevarre."

Blood dripped down her chin, her fangs distended painfully long. Her bond roiled with too much pain for me to sense her hunger, but as drained as she was, she must be ravenous.

She tried to lift her head, but her hair was tangled in vines too. She gasped with pain and Rik roared something again, though luckily I couldn't make out his words.

"Band-Aid approach," she whispered, meeting my gaze.

Rip it all off at once, quick and smooth. My stomach pitched queasily, but I nodded. "We have to get them uncurled first."

I found the corkscrewed tip of the vine tightly wrapped around her leg closest to me. I pulled on it, as hard as I dared, trying to unwrap it from her thigh. At least the top. Her breathing quickened to a frantic pant, but she didn't cry out again. Rik would probably have ripped the tree out of the ground and beat me with it for being so slow. With the vine peeled back, I could see the damage it'd done to her skin by the red, angry welt.

One leg free. At least her upper thigh. But as soon as I let go of it to work on the ones tightly coiled around her calf, the upper vine quickly snaked back around her in a new place, making her cry out.

"NEVARRE," Rik roared like a category ten hurricane.

"I'm trying my best but these fucking vines..." I growled my own wordless curse. "Morrigan, please, let my queen go so—"

The vines quivered and released her at once, though the spiked thorns were still pinning her in place. I pushed up to my feet to gain some leverage. Balanced precariously, I had to lift her straight up off the thorns to do as little damage as possible. She met my gaze, her eyes solemn, braced for pain, but not afraid.

Gripping her forearms firmly, I counted out loud, taking deep breaths. "One. Two. Three."

I pulled her straight up against me. My fearless queen didn't make a sound though I felt the slide and pull of those wicked thorns grinding against bone and tendon and muscle. Blood should have fountained from her chest, but she didn't have much left. She flopped, lifeless and heavy, almost toppling us both out of the tree. I knew exactly which one of us Rik would catch and it sure as hell wouldn't be me.

"Jump," he ground out. I could see him pacing back and forth beneath us, but there were a lot of branches in the way.

I gathered her closely to me, tucking her arms beneath mine so she didn't accidentally catch on a branch. Then I closed my eyes. "Great Queen, Goddess of Shadow and War, move Your branches out of our path so I may get my queen to safety."

I didn't look to see if She heard my prayer. I jumped, clutching Shara tightly to me. My hair snagged on a branch, pulling my head sharply to the side and likely yanking a good chunk out of my scalp. Another branch swiped me slightly on the shoulder. But otherwise, we slipped straight through the vicious branches and dropped into Rik and Guillaume's arms.

Rik already had his bleeding wrist pressed to her mouth, cradling her against him. A massive hole gaped in her chest and blood ran from so many wounds I couldn't even begin to count them. Yet she lived.

"Of course she lives," Guillaume said softly. "She's Isis's daughter, and she's feasted on the headless knight's blood. The tree could have ripped her head off and she'd still find a way to come back. But my blood can't do anything about the pain she must endure to survive."

My knees quivered and I sagged against Guillaume. Surprised, I looked down at myself. I too bore many punctures and tears and scratches, and while no massive thorn had spiked my heart, I'd lost enough blood to be wobbly.

Guillaume offered his wrist. "Feed, my friend. She needs us all prepared for Skye's attack, and she's not going to be up for feeding any of us tonight."

Grateful, I carefully bit into his wrist. My eyes fluttered shut as the first soothing, rich flow hit my tongue. Sharing blood was such an intimate thing. We already shared our minds through her bond, but this would deepen my sense of only him. It was like our souls brushed together.

He was so old and weary. Not as old as Mehen, but the great king of the depths had his rage and thirst for retribution to sustain him. For hundreds of years, Guillaume had nothing but his honor. While he'd served Desideria, that honor had weighed him down like a massive chain around his neck, dragging him slowly to hell. Something so treasured and valued had become the sole source of his torture.

Even now, I saw him in battered armor, bloody, dirty, dented. But Shara's blood had wiped away the tarnish from his armor and cast the chains aside. She'd freed him, just as she'd freed the king.

Just as she'd freed me.

I lifted my head. "Thank you, Sir Guillaume. I'm indebted to you."

"There's no debt among Blood." A corner of his mouth twitched slightly, the closest thing to a smile I guessed his face ever got. "*Her* Blood, at least."

Rik groaned, drawing our attention to him. She'd recovered enough to sink her own fangs into his wrist. Though he'd made a wound for her to drink from, sometimes instinct took over and you buried fangs in the one you loved. Something I had missed sorely with Brigid. Ropes of come spurted onto the ground, some onto the heart tree's trunk itself.

"Sorry, Morrigan," he panted, eyes closed.

A gust of wind whipped my hair back from my face, carrying with it a hint of a woman's sultry laughter. "I don't think She minded. At all. In fact, She'd probably love it if we all made such an offering."

The breeze twirled my hair back into my face and I smelled the roses again, thick and sweet and heavy. The roses Shara had grown with her blood. Ghostly fingers brushed my cheek and trailed down my chest. Powered up with Guillaume's blood, I intended to offer myself to Shara with the hopes that she'd sink those brutal fangs into me too.

She opened her eyes and looked directly at me, though she didn't lift her mouth from Rik's wrist until I stepped closer. "Are you sure?"

Dropping to my knees beside her, I tipped my head to the side, offering my throat. "Without question."

She started to sit up, but didn't have the strength yet to make it on her own. I pulled her close while Rik lifted her, holding her between the two of us. She sank her fangs into my throat and my back bowed, every muscle straining with release. My come dripped onto the ground and my head buzzed with the whisper of Her trees. *Too long, son of Morrigan. Shadow walks again. Call to war. Danger is coming.*

I forced my eyes open. "Danger," I forced the word out, meeting Rik's gaze. "The trees sense it coming."

My alpha's hard eyes drilled into me. "What is it?"

Guillaume pressed against us now, and Shara turned to him, sinking her fangs into his throat too. I scooted away enough to press my hand to the thorny trunk of the heart tree, ignoring the immediate stings on my palm. Closing my eyes, I sank into the tree, letting it pull me down through the trunk, pulsing with our queen's blood, deeper into the earth. Cold, rich earth, dark and fertile though stony. The tree was happy to be here, even though it wasn't Ireland or Scotland. New dirt, new organisms, new life. Root fingers dug through the soil, deeper, tiny wires that connected the heart to the grove, and the grove to the surrounding woods.

Through that network, I felt the disturbance in the ground. Something forced its way up through an underground cavern. Millions of tiny creatures, working together seamlessly. Their queen was in the back, protected by her soldiers. The trees sensed her like a malignant cell, marking her for elimination, because she carried a drop of Skye's blood.

They marched with determination. Pushing aside dirt and debris, climbing through miles of rock and soil and, most importantly, thick roots, to reach us.

I opened my eyes. "Ants. A huge army of them. They're..." I closed my eyes a moment, trying to gauge how far away they were. It was hard since they were so deep, but the trees helped, echoing one by one to help me mark the distance. "An hour away, probably. Close—but not ready to explode up out of the ground yet."

"Fucking ants?" Mehen retorted. "That's the great trap Skye is sending against us?"

"Millions of them," I replied grimly. "And they're not just normal ants. Each of the soldiers are nearly an inch long and they have large cutting jaws. I'm pretty sure they could devour a corpse in a matter of minutes. Their queen is the one we need to worry about though. Keisha Skye marked it with her blood. I'm guessing the queen is supposed to get to Shara and sting her, injecting her with whatever spell Skye has worked into that blood."

"So how do we kill them as quickly as possible?" Rik looked at each of us one by one. "If we're talking millions, we don't want to waste time."

"I say you let me shift into the dragon and I'll light the fuckers on fire. I'll just blast them with continuous fire as they try to crawl out of the ground."

Shara lifted her head from Guillaume's throat. She looked better for the most part, but the wound in her chest was still ugly. She still looked… dented and misshapen. Blood still dripped from punctures she hadn't been able to close yet. "Fire should kill them. I'd throw fire on them too, but I don't know that I'll be up for that in an hour or less."

Daire squeezed in between her and Guillaume, rubbing himself against her. "You should ride on one of us, just to be safe. If we keep you off the ground, you'll be harder for them to get to. I'm game, but G's hell horse would probably be the best bet. It's not like either of us are going to be very good at killing something as small as ants."

"Agreed," Rik said. "Take turns if you need to with Xin too. If Mehen's able to roast them as they emerge, I'll smash any that escape, and Nevarre can attack from the air."

"The trees will help." Rik looked skeptical, so I added, "they're voracious. That's why they make such good defense. Their roots can ensnare anything in the ground, and they can change position as needed."

"Trees. That move." Mehen smirked, shaking his head. "That I'll have to see to believe."

"It's pretty… creepy," I replied, shrugging. "I can't explain how they do it, but one moment, the tree is paces away, and the next, you're surrounded by trees you didn't even notice."

"We may get the chance to see them in action sooner than later." Shara turned to Rik, giving him her hand. "We've got company."

"What?" He stood, pulling her up into his arms. "Who?"

"I'm guessing it's another one of your sibs. The trees say there's a man walking through the forest about two miles away."

I didn't wait for Rik's order. I leaped into the air and called my raven to explode out of me. It was going to be one busy fucking night.

8

SHARA

I felt pretty good considering that I really should be dead. I didn't know if it was Isis's heritage that kept me alive, or Guillaume's blood, or both. I hurt, yes. Badly. But I wasn't scared of dying. Not today.

Especially not from one of Keisha Skye's plots.

I was able to stand, but walking was beyond me. I just didn't have energy, or balance, or control of my body yet. Rik swept me up in his arms, but I didn't want to appear too weak. I wanted to make an impression on this Skye sib, especially if his queen was watching through his eyes.

I turned to Guillaume. After the Christmas Day news footage from Venezuela, they knew the great headless knight who could shift into a hell horse was with me. "Feel like putting on a show for them?"

The corners of his eyes crinkled and he shifted without hesitation. Daire rubbed up against Rik's legs, head to tail as long as the hell horse, but Guillaume stood taller at the withers. :*Should I fetch you some clothes?*:

Normally, I would have leaped at the chance for some clothes before meeting a stranger. But honestly, I was beyond

65

caring at this point. I wanted them to see me bleeding, hurt, but alive, and better yet, unafraid and unshaken. I wanted them to think harder about what I'd done to be so hurt before their attack—and doubt that they could do the same.

"No," I finally said. "There's so much blood on me that he won't be able to see much anyway. Xin, stay hidden, as before. They don't know about you yet."

My silver wolf touched me with his nose. *:May I feed you first, my queen?:*

I ran my hand over his head and ears, smearing him with my blood. "After we deal with this sib, absolutely. Nevarre, they don't know about you either, so stay high and out of sight."

The raven cawed agreement as he flew in slow circles overhead.

"And me?" Mehen stepped up into Rik's space aggressively, earning a rumble that rattled his chest against me.

I gathered my strength and struck hard and fast, sinking my fangs into Mehen's throat.

He roared loudly enough the approaching stranger probably wondered what the hell was happening before he could even make his threats. Come spurted on me and Rik both as Mehen shook with release.

I needed his older, powerful blood. In all honesty, I should have fed from him first, but—

:Always feed from me first, my queen.: Rik whispered for my bond alone. *:I am yours, heart and soul.:*

Ancient blood flowed through me, soothing the hurts deep inside me, though I still felt feverish. My eyes blazed hot in my skull, which the dragon's blood did little to alleviate.

In fact, his blood only fueled all the fire in me. My emotions flared. Anger, that Skye was going to attack us. Fury, that my alpha had seen enough in her court to be terrified of her. Rage, that she would continue to come after us as long as Rik and Daire still had sibs in her court.

Which made me lift my head from Mehen's throat. "How

many sibs do you still have in Skye? Can you tell who's coming now?"

Daire's giant head tipped to the side as he listened. *:Ezra. Huh. That's a strange one.:*

"Why?"

"I never fed from him," Rik said. "Only Daire."

:He was the first one to feed me in Keisha's court.:

"Who else? I guess what I'm asking is how many more times can she send someone after us because she knows exactly where we are?"

Neither answered right away. I looked from Daire to Rik, surprised at their reluctance to answer.

"Not reluctance, exactly," Rik finally said with a sigh. "In hindsight, we made a huge mistake. It never occurred to me that Skye might use those bonds to hunt my future queen."

:We fed on many in Skye's court,: Daire added, hanging his head. *:A new one almost every time, though Kendall more than any of the others.:*

Well fuck. That dashed my initial plan of targeting any of their remaining sibs to stop these attacks. I was going to have to deal with Keisha Skye directly once and for all. "I guess it doesn't matter now anyway. She knows where the nest is, so it's not like she can't find it again. We'll spend most of our time here. Though will it be safe to leave it for a few days to visit Zaniyah's nest?"

"A few days will be fine," Rik replied, his jaw still tight with regret. "You can remove all access you've given to outsiders while we're gone, or entrust Frank to handle the comings and goings of visitors."

I reached up and cupped his cheek. A muscle twitched beneath my palm. "It's not a big deal. Now I know that I have to hit her directly, rather than eliminate your sibs first."

"I should have—"

"How could you possibly know that you'd find a queen at all? Let alone that Skye would hunt us like this?"

Setting me on Guillaume's broad back, he grumbled beneath his breath. "I still hate that I've weakened you."

I smiled, trying to make it mysterious and sexy even with a thousand thorn-holes in me and coated in blood. "It's not a weakness if I use it against her. I probably would have taken the fight directly to her anyways." I met Mehen's gaze. He'd said nothing while I talked with my alpha, but his eyes were bright and eager. He wanted his beast. He wanted to kill. Even if it was just ants.

Without saying a word, I drew back the magical leash I'd looped around Leviathan's neck. As soon as he was free to shift, Mehen threw his head back, arms open wide, and welcomed his dragon. Leviathan roiled up out of him with claws and scales and wings. The mighty dragon gave me a glare with emerald green eyes, but didn't roar to announce his presence to our enemy. Instead, he took quietly to the air, his massive wings no louder than the soft flap of a large owl on the hunt. He immediately soared up into the night sky and disappeared from view.

Guillaume's hide twitched beneath me. It was so strange sitting buck naked on a horse.

:It's so strange to be a horse and have my buck naked queen's pussy pressed against me.:

I squirmed against him for fun. He lowered his head back and nickered, a low, deep rumbling horse sound I'd never heard before.

"I think we'd best go see Ezra now." Rik grinned with amusement and started walking toward the edge of my nest. Guillaume automatically moved with him, keeping pace so that Rik could keep a hand on my thigh in case I started to fall.

"He's still a few minutes away. What's the hurry?"

"That was the sound a stallion makes when he smells a mare in heat."

Oh. Crap.

:My queen,: Nevarre said in my head. :I have an idea, but will need to leave briefly.:

Without hesitation, I replied, :*Go. We have time.*:

Purring, Daire rubbed against my calf and Guillaume's side. :*When do I get to give you a ride?*:

Guillaume twisted his neck around and snapped viciously at the warcat. Daire dodged away and flicked him with his tail. I couldn't help but laugh, even though it hurt my ribcage. Never in a million years did I think I'd have to say I'd take turns riding a hell horse and a warcat.

Mehen snarled in our bond. :*And a dragon.*:

9

SHARA

My knights' former sib slowly slipped through the trees toward my nest. When he stepped out of the woods at the far edge of the woods behind the guest house, he jerked to a halt, surprised as fuck to see us waiting on him.

Maybe that's why Keisha Skye had sent this particular sib as her messenger this time. She'd wanted to be stealthy, and if Daire had only fed from him once, and Rik not at all, they wouldn't have likely felt him approach.

A good plan. If I didn't have other ways of tracking threats to my nest. Although maybe he was merely surprised to see me sitting on top of a massive hell horse. Even standing still, Guillaume's hooves smoked against the ground and all the snow had melted in a ten-foot radius from where we stood.

Ezra looked like he'd just climbed down a mountain where he'd been living off the grid in a cabin he'd built with his bare hands. Big and burly with massive shoulders and huge hands, he looked like he could pull up a tree and snap it like a toothpick. The full beard and bushy hair only added to his wild-man look.

Somehow I couldn't picture him living in a New York City court.

I asked Rik, *:Is he her Blood? Or just a sib?:*

:Sib only.:

Daire added, *:We grew up together in Christabel Devana's court in the Ukraine, which is why he deigned to feed me once I came to Skye.:*

I wanted to ask so many questions. There was still so much I didn't know about my Blood. I had no idea if their mothers had been queens or not. Which goddesses they'd descended from. If they'd served other courts before Skye.

:None of that matters, honestly,: Rik said in our bond, and Daire nodded. *:We were never famous like Guillaume or Mehen.:*

:It matters to me. I want to know everything about you.:

"Your Majesty." Ezra's voice was just as rough as his appearance. "I'm—"

"Ezra Skye," I cut in, nodding. I didn't have time for pleasantries. I especially didn't have the patience, not when I was still bleeding from dozens of thorn punctures. "Let's skip to the threats, yes?"

"I prefer Ezra Ursula Devana because Skye did me no favors," he retorted. "You've only got three Blood. Want another?"

Daire bristled, his fur rising along his spine. *:I forgot how belligerent he could be.:*

I didn't think Ezra meant to be rude, exactly. He just didn't give me the impression that he liked people, or had any patience for conversation. Same as me at this point. I could actually admire skipping the bullshit small talk. "Sure. But not you."

He drew his head back, shaking his heavy hair off his forehead so he could see me better. "Why's that?"

"You carry Keisha Skye's blood."

His eyes narrowed. "So. Do. They." He jerked his head at Rik and Daire. "The cat can vouch for me."

With a low hiss, Daire turned his back, winding around Guillaume's legs, ignoring this old friend entirely.

"You little fucker," the man growled. "I need help. You'd turn your back on family?"

Watching the stranger, I frowned. I was braced for all-out war and threats, not a plea for help. Despite the man's lack of finesse, I sensed desperation. Though I still highly doubted his sincerity. He might be desperate to escape Skye. Or desperate to do his part in whatever dastardly plan she'd concocted. But did he really want help? My help? That, I couldn't be sure of.

Daire didn't look at the man, but I felt reluctant concern in his bond. :*We did grow up together, though I didn't know he counted me as family. I don't know why he'd need help.*:

"What help are you asking for?"

Ezra looked from me to Daire and back. "You don't know?"

The trees murmured in the crisp winter air. *Threat. Close. Many.*

The invading ants were close, slowly climbing up from the underground cavern and approaching the roots, and yes, my nest. The trees swayed, leaves rustling, even in the stillness of the night. I sensed eagerness. Hunger. They were ready to defend their forest, their grove, and yes, my nest.

Feast, I told them. *Kill as many as you can before they even reach us.*

The trees rustled louder. Ezra cocked his head, noticing the noise despite the lack of wind. He suddenly reminded me of a bear, rising up on his hind legs, looking for food or danger. A big burly bear. Yes.

The sense of… rightness… surprised me, and my Blood too. Rik narrowed his gaze on the man, sizing him up. Daire sat on his haunches and started licking his giant paw, razor-tipped claws unsheathed. Guillaume lifted his head and blew out a hard breath, nostrils wide. Even Xin paused, nose in the air, my silent ghostly wolf.

Reluctantly, I closed my eyes and brought up the tapestry in my mind. I didn't want another Blood. Let alone one with this kind of complication.

But his red glow blazed on the outside of my nest, a giant grumbling grizzly bear.

:Fuck: Daire growled disgustedly. *:Do you know how much trouble he got me into as cubs?:*

Rik groaned silently in our bond. *:Great. Just what we need. Another mischief maker.:*

"No," I said slowly. "I guess I don't."

"Skye." He spat out her name like a curse, which I could highly approve of. "She's trying to force Devana to support her bid for the Triune, by using me, and indirectly Daire, as hostages."

Daire slowly lowered his paw, staring at his friend. *:Fuuuucccccck. Not good. At all. Huge breach of protocol.:*

Blood loss made my brain too sluggish for court politics. I remained silent a few moments, trying to trace the convoluted threads of alternatives and options in my head. At first, I'd assumed he was sent by Keisha Skye with another ultimatum. But maybe he'd come of his own volition. To be *my* Blood, though? Another from Skye's court? Despite his promising red glow, I just couldn't see it. For all I knew, she'd probably allowed him to leave as a dupe to cover up her own approaching attack. Then she could eliminate Ezra without repercussions, assuming that I would kill him, like I'd killed Kendall.

My head hurt. My entire fucking body hurt. And millions of ants were descending on my nest in minutes.

Unobtrusively, Rik slid an arm around my waist and supported me against him. At least then I didn't have to use my muscles to stay upright. Blood dripped down Guillaume's withers, chest, and down his legs. He hadn't fed, and now I was tormenting him, them all, with all this blood. I sagged a little more against Rik. I really needed to feed again so I could get these wounds sealed off. As long as I was still bleeding, I wouldn't feel much better.

:It's a heavenly torment,: Guillaume said in our bond. *:Imagine*

his torment. A queen, bleeding, in obvious need, a possible salvation in his darkest hour, or his greatest danger.:

:Do you believe him?:

Guillaume bobbed his head slightly, *:He smells sincere. That doesn't mean Skye isn't using him, though.:*

Ezra let out a deep, low grunt. "I'm too late. She already hurt you."

I lifted my gaze to his. "You came to warn me?"

He jerked his head in affirmation. "And Daire. He ought to know."

"You want me to believe that Keisha Skye didn't send you."

"Nope."

Rik growled. "Don't ever fucking lie to her, Ezra. Your queen could command you back to New York City with a thought."

Ezra humphed out a laugh beneath his breath. "You think so? First of all, she's stretched too far to use one drop of her blood to force me to do anything against my will. I've always been strong in that regard."

Daire rumbled in my mind, part exasperation and part laughter. *:It's true. Our queen often despaired of making him do anything he didn't want to, even when we were cubs.:*

Rik groaned and Guillaume humped his back slightly, enough to convey his disgust at the thought of having two troublesome Blood in our nest.

"Second of all, she's got bigger fish to fry than an obstinate unruly sib with the penchant for roaming. Besides, few in her court would ever feed me. I've probably got less of her sib blood in me than those two."

I weighed my alternatives, letting my senses roll over this man and the surrounding forest. The trees liked his sense of wildness. They burned with hunger and eagerly stretched their roots down into the ground, waiting to entrap the approaching ants, but didn't twitch a single branch his way. They had no interest in devouring him. Because he was mine? Or because he was innocent in this plot?

My fangs ached. I needed to feed. A lot. I'd tapped several of my Blood already, just to be up and moving somewhat normally. How much blood would it take to heal the rest of my injuries? Would I incapacitate them all to heal myself? I didn't dare risk it. Not with Skye's attack coming. In that regard, another Blood would be welcome.

:More than welcome,: Rik added sternly. *:You need to feed many times before you travel to meet Zaniyah. You should be at full strength, and right now, you're barely upright and can't control your bleeding.:*

I blew out a sigh. I knew he was right. "Did you ever feed from Keisha Skye directly?"

"Fuck, no. The males who feed from her throat die quickly. You know the truth of that better than anyone, Rik."

Rik's arm tightened around me, his big body sliding toward granite. "Things are different in the Isador court."

"I should goddamn hope so," Ezra retorted back.

Growling deep in his chest, Rik squared his shoulders and lowered his head. "You won't be leaving this nest on a whim and wandering around the countryside causing problems."

"Who says so?"

"Me." Boulders crashed and tumbled in his voice with that single word.

They stared at each other. Long moments passed by. The trees murmured with excitement as the first of the ants came up into their main root system. I felt ants popping and snapping in the ground, devoured like movie popcorn by the voracious roots. Tendrils grabbing, curling around tiny bodies. Smashing them. Nutrients to feed the earth. Roots snapping into place, entrapping huge pockets of ants in a corral of their design. The trees gobbled them up as quickly as possible, but thousands upon thousands were still marching relentlessly to the surface.

I tried calling up my power, even a small fireball, to gauge how long I could last.

Agony. My ribcage ached like it'd split open, pain slicing through me. I couldn't hold back a soft cry.

Rik whipped his head to me, already tearing his wrist open to give me blood yet again. That didn't surprise me, though I tried to tell him not to bother. I'd already fed from him deeply just a few minutes ago, and with an attack imminent, I couldn't risk him. What did surprise me was the ruckus Ezra made on the outside of my nest.

Roaring, he pounded on the invisible barrier of my blood circle. "Let me in! Daire, you little bastard! Get that furry ass over here and bring me through! She needs me!"

Rik lifted my wrist and gently licked my blood from one of those brutal punctures. *:Better? Don't worry about me, my queen. A few swallows of your blood and I'm good as new.:*

The new man roared louder and I felt his pain. My circle did not like him trying to break through. At all. But he wouldn't stop.

:Let him in,: Rik told Daire with a mental sigh. *:Though I'm holding you responsible for him.:*

:Then I don't want him in.: Daire grumbled, though he did head toward the circle. Instead of brushing or pressing against the man to bring him through my blood circle, Daire clamped his jaws around Ezra's beefy forearm and dragged him through and directly to me, refusing to let him go until he stood before Rik.

Rik didn't say anything. He held my wrist, tenderly licking my blood from the many wounds the thorns had made, his other arm wrapped around me, his wrist pressed to my mouth. Slumped against him, I watched their interaction, not letting go of Rik's wrist. Not until he was ready.

They stared at each other for what seemed like an eternity. Ezra was almost as tall as Rik and nearly twice as wide. But this time, I wasn't worried for Rik's safety. I knew one hundred percent who my alpha was. And if Ezra wanted to stay...

He'd know too.

Finally, he said gruffly, "Alpha." Then he looked at me, his eyes softening. "Queen." He dragged his gaze away, wincing as if it hurt to do so, and gave a look at Guillaume. "Stud." But when he looked at Daire, he growled. "Pussy cat. You didn't have to bite me so hard."

:Wait until Shara bites you,: Daire said in our bond, even though Ezra couldn't hear it yet. *:Nobody warn him.:*

I let go of Rik's wrist. "The ants. They're close."

Loud caws and bird sounds had us all jerking our gaze up to the sky. A huge flock of crows and other birds swarmed into the trees, led by my huge raven, Nevarre. *:I roused as many birds as I could. They're grateful for a nighttime feast. Winter's a lean time.:*

"Crow," Ezra said, slowly turning back to look at me, one brow arched. "Four Blood. Or more?"

"More." My lips quirked. "But he prefers raven."

:Wait until Mehen gets to meet Mr. Surly.: Daire cackled in our bond.

Rik shifted into his rock troll, his colossal boulder form slowly rolling out of him. Fully shifted, he made my other Blood look like toys a kid would play with.

Ezra whistled, soft and low, but didn't say a word.

"Guillaume, Daire, our queen's life is in your hands." He didn't say Xin, even though my wolf prowled in a slow circle around us, invisible. He wouldn't be able to do much against ants either. I thought we could trust Ezra, but I wouldn't know for sure until I'd had his blood, and then it might be too late. I felt better knowing my assassin Blood was close, an unknown threat Ezra wouldn't know to guard against.

Cold and silent, Xin hovered just paces away, ready to pounce. He wasn't thinking about whether or not he'd be able to kill his target. I had no doubts. I knew he'd defend me in a heartbeat, silent or not.

Ezra moved closer, wrapping an arm around me so Rik could leave. My alpha gave him a long look.

"You don't have to tell me to feed her long and well," Ezra muttered. "She'll be fit as a fiddle in no time."

"They're here," I whispered, my stomach quivering. Not with fear, exactly, or even dread. Just… anxiety. I didn't want my Blood hurt in any way. Three. Against a marauding army of vicious ants.

Rik kissed the top of my head and lumbered toward the center of the grove as quickly as he could. I watched him go, straining to keep my head turned, even though it hurt. Everything hurt. I needed…

Guillaume shifted his weight and I started to slip. Ezra stepped closer, bracing me against him. I knew my hell horse had done it on purpose, a way to distract me from the battle. It still irritated me. I didn't want to be distracted. I didn't want…

Ezra's neck was warm against my cheek. His beard tickled my face. Wiry, but strangely soft, too. Very much like what I expected his bear to feel like. He smelled like warm cinnamon and sweet tobacco, utterly masculine, yet also soft and rich and soothing. Despite his belligerence, I suspected he was a big old marshmallow on the inside. With Daire watching, ready to tease the man about the side effect of my fangs, I took pity on him. "You may want to tear open your wrist for me, like Rik did."

He nestled me closer against him, making sure his throat was pressed to me. "Nah. I like fangs. Sink 'em deep, sweetheart."

:You heard the man,: Daire practically chortled.

I pressed my lips to Ezra's throat, pressing soft kisses to his skin until I found his biggest vein. I gave him a good long lick to let him brace, and then I sank my fangs into his throat.

His back bowed on a bellow that made Guillaume twitch slightly beneath me, an ancient flight instinct that kicked in despite being a hell horse. Or maybe he had to catch his balance, because Ezra's knees sagged and he sank against Guillaume's side. But he didn't let go of me, and he didn't let me fall off.

Ezra tasted as good as he smelled, and just as soft and gooey on the inside as I'd imagined. In fact, he tasted like a snickerdoodle cookie. Slightly crispy on the outside with spicy cinnamon and sugar, but soft and fluffy on the inside. I sucked him down, absorbing his bond. He'd led a lonely existence in New York City. He'd never fit in. A mountain man at heart, the city had been a prison for him. He wasn't alpha, so Skye had no real use for him, and he'd had no friends, even once Daire came to court. Everybody loved Daire. He was playful and fun, the life of the party, amiable and easy to get along with. Where Ezra was crusty and gruff and had no patience for fools or pretenders. He didn't care what you thought, and he couldn't give a fuck about your feelings or playing nice.

While it'd cost him dearly, his solitude made it easier for him to slip away, giving him more freedom. Especially when he realized what Skye was up to.

In fact, for all his standoffish ways, he had the uncanny ability to sniff out secrets, always in the right place at the right time to hear the soft whispers and clandestine meetings. He'd just happened to be sitting on the stoop of the servants' backdoor entrance of an ultra-modern high-rise condo when Keisha Skye had stepped out onto her balcony dozens of stories above to make her threats regarding Christabel Devana's fosters in her court.

He shifted back upright after the initial shock of my bite forcing him into climax, taking his weight off Guillaume and cuddling me against his big barrel chest. For all his gruff ways, his big hands cradled me like I was a baby bird that had fallen out of my nest. He didn't take my blood for himself, though he certainly could have. I was still bleeding from so many wounds he could have swiped his fingers across my skin and had his power.

He didn't know for sure that he'd be a bear as so many Ursula males before him, though he hoped to honor his blood, his queen mother, and most especially, me.

I lifted my bleeding wrist to his mouth and he still hesitated. "You've been hurt, my queen."

I couldn't send him my thoughts, not without giving him my blood first, but I wasn't letting go of his throat. I pressed my wrist harder to his mouth, insisting. The pressure felt good on the wound, helping stop some of the blood flow.

He swallowed and pulled me back in time to his childhood mountain. Tall pine, thick carpet of needles, snow on the air, his breath frosting in his beard, heavy fur boots and coat, muffling his steps and giving him that broad bear look. Then he was a giant grizzly, standing on his hind legs, big paws draped around me, holding me up. His fur pressed against my face, soft and thick, still smelling of cinnamon and a hint of tobacco, but now with added pines and mountain air and the deep, wild Ukrainian forest of his homeland.

:Thank you, my queen.:

:Thank you, my bear.:

10

MEHEN

I would never admit it under the most dire torture, but I had finally found peace with losing control of my beast.

I coasted in slow, silent circles around the perimeter of our nest, watching for any sign of invasion. Though how she thought I could blast millions of ants without harming the trees, I wasn't sure. Hopefully I didn't turn them into a bunch of glowing torches accidentally. Though I would continue to bitch about losing the ability to shift whenever I wanted, it was actually quite freeing. I didn't have to worry about who I'd slaughter now. My queen would use me to slaughter her enemies as she saw fit, and she'd make sure she leashed me before I could harm those she didn't want roasted or torn apart.

Simple.

She pointed. I would blast with fire and rend limb from limb. Perhaps she'd send me after Skye directly now that Xin felt like he couldn't assassinate her. The thought made smoke puff out of my nose. A giant dragon flying over the sprawling hub of New York City. It could totally happen.

Nevarre made a gods-awful screech and dived toward the

ground, hopping around like flames scorched his tail feathers. Bullseye.

I focused on that spot. *:Got it.:*

He hopped up into a nearby tree, its limbs heavy with all kinds of birds. More crows, a dozen owls, several hawks and a million or so little ones. I had no idea what kind they were. As long as they were hungry and fast, I didn't give a fuck what they were.

I couldn't see much. Even in broad daylight, my vision wasn't as sharp as the crow's would be. I hunted by my nose. But what the fuck did fucking ants smell like? Dirt? Fucking bugs.

Through our queen's bond, Nevarre shared a sort of underground map with me. The new trees above ground that Shara had grown with her blood were already impressive, but the underground network of roots was astounding. A sensitive lacy web of roots covered the entire nest now and reached at least thirty or forty feet deep. I felt the horde coming up out of the ground like an oil geyser. In fact, they smelled like some kind of chemical that reminded me of raw petroleum.

That, I could definitely track if they tried to change course at the last moment once they realized we were ready for them.

:Are they commanded directly by Skye?: I asked Nevarre. *:Can she change the plan when she sees us ready and waiting?:*

:Unknown.:

I drew great gusts of air into my lungs, powering up my internal bellows. I wanted liquid fire, hot molten rock level heat. Crispy critters. No chance for escape.

The smell intensified. The birds all leaned closer to the ground, focused intently, ready to feast. I waited until the stench of petroleum was strong in my nostrils and the ground started to move. Then I let my hottest fire blast, lighting up the ground like an inferno with controlled, long, blasts. I wouldn't singe the trees my queen had suffered so much to grow. My fire trickled to smoke and I shot back up into the sky, hauling in air for another strike. The birds descended immediately, swooping in to pick at the crispy ants and the live ones still kicking.

Goddess. The ground was crawling with them. Bugs. Wings. It was definitely the stuff of nightmares. The burned ants smelled more like roasted popcorn now.

I sensed movement several feet off to the side. Nevarre's underground map flared in my head, showing the dark mass trying to slide through roots to a new safer exit point. Heavy-duty snappers were trying to cut through roots, but it was taking time, and the roots were doing a damned fine job of lassoing ants and crushing them. Fuck. Never in a million years would I have imagined going to battle with fucking trees and random birds. I blasted the ground again, making it steam and smoke, hopefully killing them before they could even emerge, or at worst, keep them down with the vicious roots.

In our bond, Shara felt stronger, a flood of fresh energy surging through us all. Holy fuck, a new Blood. :*Find their queen.:*

The trees responded so loudly in her head that we all felt it. *Queen. Here. Danger.*

One tiny ant among the horde. The trees marked her, though she looked no different as far as I could tell. She was still below ground and pushing hard toward Shara, well-insulated and surrounded by her soldiers. While the birds were busy feasting on the ants escaping to the surface, Nevarre tracked the queen ant, scratching at the ground, digging with his beak, trying to find a way down to her.

I circled back around and checked the main group of ants. The ground still teemed with bugs and birds, but the birds had them well in hand, cawing and tweeting at each other in a bedlam of excitement. They'd probably never eaten so many bugs at once.

Nevarre felt me sweeping back toward the queen's group and flew up out of the way, making room so I could blast the ground again. I got the top layer of her soldiers. But not the queen. Some of the group swept closer to a tree, sensing that I wouldn't burn it. The oak had a split in its side, an ancient rotted hole that had probably made a great squirrel or raccoon nest. The ants swarmed up into that crevice, shielded from fire. Old and dry and rotted, the tree looked like a big pile of kindling. Of all the other trees in the grove, it didn't stir as the ants crossed its roots.

I thought it was dead, and so did the ants. Until the crevice snapped shut like a giant mouth, trapping thousands of ants in the hollowed center.

The ground rumbled, drawing my attention back to the group of ants making a beeline toward our queen. Shifted into the rock troll, Rik pounded the ground with massive fists, shoving layers of dirt and rock tight, smashing ants by the hundreds.

Yet the queen marched on.

Dragons didn't sweat, but I didn't like how close this thing was getting to Shara. Rik didn't either. He tore at the ground, heaving up giant pieces of sod and roots. Trying to expose the queen where either Nevarre or I could get to her.

:Blast this area again.: Rik ordered me. *:Your fire won't hurt me.:*

I wasn't so sure, but did as he told me, bathing the entire area with fire. Flames licked the ground and up his calves as he stomped and thumped the ground. Ants scrambled up his stony body, snapping uselessly at giant boulders. It looked like some kind of apocalyptic scene, with a giant monster slapping at his body and the ground, killing the ones fire didn't consume.

"Where's the queen?" Rik roared aloud. "Find her."

The trees lost track of her. That told me she had to be above the surface. Sweeping low over the ground, I scanned the heaving carpet of ants. Many were smoking or damaged, legs twitching uselessly as Rik plowed through them. But no queen.

We were dangerously close to where Shara waited now. Too close for me to risk burning her or one of the guarding Blood.

I landed, joining Rik in smashing with my huge feet as many as I could.

With a low rumbling roar, a gigantic grizzly lumbered over and started scooping up pawfuls of ants and eating them. Xin's wolf materialized and he hopped and smashed ants beneath his paws, making the bear sit up and twitch his ears a moment, before scooping up another pile of ants to munch. Daire joined him, but the disgusted twist of his warcat's mouth proclaimed that ants were not to his personal taste.

Guillaume swung around to face the approaching threat, carefully so she didn't slip, though she was stronger and steadier now. Head low, the hell horse scanned the ground.

"She's not dead," Shara warned. "I can feel her close."

:There.: Nevarre cawed and dove straight down to the ground just feet away from our queen.

I couldn't even see what the fuck he was after. Urgency hammered through our bond. Rik scrambled toward her, his fists slamming into the ground in rapid succession, but he was too far away. Smoke puffed with each breath I took, but I didn't dare stream fire at her. She might be able to stand unharmed in my flame, but I wouldn't know until it was too late.

The hell horse lifted one platter-sized hoof and slammed it down on the ground with a satisfying crunch. *:Done.:*

I landed, chuckling out puffs of smoke. We came to her, automatically forming an arc of protection before our queen, mounted on a hell horse, and surrounded by a dragon, rock troll, warcat, wolf, raven, and now, another fucking furball.

:That's grizzly, lizard..: The new Blood snarled in our queen's bond.

I rolled my slitted eyes and puffed smoke in his direction, making Daire cough and the bear sneeze. Guillaume made a wheezing whinny that startled us all, until I realized he was actually laughing.

Crouching, I snapped my jaws, my tail lashing the ground.

85

I'd never eaten a grizzly before, let alone a hell horse, but I was pretty sure they'd both make a tasty snack. At least a hell of a lot tastier than those nasty ants.

Rik strode between us. He wrapped one rock-hard hand around my gullet, right below my bottom jaw, and squeezed, locking off my air. Fuck, when did he get so big? So strong? Even as a rock troll, he hadn't been as big as Leviathan, but the dragon had serious doubts about escaping unscathed.

Which reminded me exactly how he'd pinned me last night. How hard he helped her fuck me. And yeah, my mood shifted mercurially fast to lust.

Shara slid down off Guillaume, holding onto his mane and leaning against him a moment to make sure she was steady. Daire pushed his head under her arm, and she leaned on him as she walked slowly toward us.

Toward Rik. Naturally. She always went to him first. I shouldn't care. He was alpha. She ought to go to him first of all her Blood. But my tail snaked restlessly on the ground and I jerked my head up, trying to dislodge his grip. Impossible, really. Though I had to try.

She paused, leaning against my side. Concerned, I searched her bond. If she really was so weak that only walking a few paces exhausted her, she'd never be up for taking out another much-older queen. The kind of power she'd need to master Keisha Skye, let alone Marne Ceresa...

But her bond felt fine. Much better than before. Her skin was coated with dying, flaking blood, but the awful wound in her chest had finally healed.

She leaned. Against me. Leviathan. King of the depths.

For comfort. Safety. Affection.

All things I felt in her bond.

Mixed with a healthy dose of amusement, granted, but compassion and understanding as well.

Her alpha released my throat so I could return that affection.

I curled up around her and lay on the ground, using my tail to lift her up off the dead ant carcasses and shredded earth. Rumbling deep in his chest, Daire hopped up beside her. Uncaring that he lay on top of a mean, vicious, terrible dragon.

And somehow I was completely okay with that.

11

SHARA

For all their immense strength and protective instincts, each of my Blood had a vulnerable side. Mehen didn't allow any weakness to show. In his mind, hopes and dreams and hurt feelings were only weaknesses that he refused to admit to anyone, certainly himself. He might be the biggest, oldest dragon in history, but he was still shaken at having a new Blood make an appearance. Even if he didn't quite realize it himself.

As Daire had needed some reassurance when Guillaume first came to me, so did Mehen. Only he acted like a fucking jerk instead of letting me see that he needed some affection.

:I wasn't a fucking jerk,: he retorted in my head, though he made no move to dislodge me or Daire from resting on his side.

Still purring, Daire had his head in my lap, pretending to be asleep, though every now and then his tail tapped the dragon's hide playfully.

:So you didn't threaten to eat two of my Blood?:

His side rose beneath us with his breathing. *:I was joking:* His side sank down, a gentle rocking motion that would quickly put me to sleep. *:Mostly.:*

Nevarre hopped closer, still in his raven form. Before he could give me an update, I said, *:Thank your friends for us. They've been immensely helpful.:*

:They're the ones who're grateful.: He replied. *:Many of them would like to stay in the new trees you've grown, if you don't mind.:*

:It's up to the trees, but I'd love to have any of the birds stay.:

He bobbed his head and leaped up into the air, sleek black wings lifting him off to check in with the birds. Many of them were roosting on the lower branches now, fat and sleepy, though some of the smaller birds still pecked at the ground in search of ants.

Rik shifted back to his human form, and the rest of my Blood quickly followed suit. Even Mehen, though now he had both Daire and I sitting on his very human form. He didn't seem to mind and still didn't push us off.

My former Blood naturally congregated near me, leaving the newest Blood on the fringe. On the surface, he didn't seem to be bothered. He'd even say he preferred his solitude. But deeper, I sensed an aching loneliness in his bond. Especially when he looked at Daire.

"Everybody, this is Ezra Ursula Devana. Ezra, this is Mehen, formerly Leviathan, king of the depths. Rik and Daire, you know. Wu Tien Xin, Guillaume de Payne, and Nevarre Morrigan," I added as he came striding back to join us.

"Isador," Ezra drew my house name out slowly, looking at us one by one. "Are there any more of you hiding around invisible or flying around in the night sky?"

I smiled slightly. "Nope."

"Seven." He looked at me, shaking his head. "You think to stand against Skye with seven Blood. Don't even get me started on Ceresa. I don't know if you're a damned fool or just stupid."

Guillaume narrowed a hard look on the man. "Respect our queen's honor, or I'll teach you a lesson you won't soon forget."

Ezra humphed with disgust. "I hate to be the one to tell you this, sir knight, but honor isn't worth shit as far as Skye is concerned. We won't win any battles because we're honorable."

I stroked one hand lazily through Daire's hair. I wasn't upset by Ezra's words. For the most part, they were true. I was a fool for hoping to defeat major houses like Skye and Ceresa with only seven Blood. We all knew it, and they'd already tried to convince me that I should call many more Blood, or even take a sib and her Blood.

I just didn't want to.

"Peace, Guillaume," I said softly. "I'm not offended."

"You should be," Ezra muttered. "We're all going to die."

"Maybe." I started to stand, and immediately Rik lowered a hand and Daire and Mehen both scrambled to their feet to help me up. "Or maybe I've got a few plans in the works that you don't know about."

"I should hope the fuck so." With another disgusted grunt, he turned and headed off into the woods.

Rik didn't move a muscle, but his bond rumbled with alpha irritation. *:I told you no wandering off into the forest alone.:*

"Fuck off," Ezra growled, not stopping. "Or send someone with me if you don't trust me to fetch the bag I stashed about a mile back in case she was already dead."

Rik narrowed a hard look on Daire. "Go with him and keep him in line."

Pouting, Daire trudged after his childhood friend. "I told you I didn't want to let him in."

Ezra hollered back over his shoulder, "I'll be ready for dinner when we get back!"

"What a delightful personality," Mehen drawled as he turned to the other Blood, shaking his head.

Guillaume slapped him on the back as we started toward the guest house to get some clothes. "Yeah, he makes you look about as friendly as a smiling crocodile."

Mehen flashed his teeth in a vicious grin. "Well, at least I'm fucking smiling."

DAIRE

"So…" I drew the word out, not really sure what to say. It'd been a long time since Ezra and I had been alone, walking in the woods.

He didn't say anything, but slowed his step so I could walk beside him. He didn't make conversation easy. He never had.

"How are our queens back home?"

"Worried as fuck, thanks to Keisha Skye. As soon as I slipped out of her territory safely, I called our consiliarius and let her know we were both out of House Skye's control, though I wasn't sure where you were yet. My link to you was pretty fucking faint. She promised to let our mothers know."

I winced. I'd left Skye's court at least a year ago. Not once had I thought to call home and let Mom know. Or to let her know that I'd found my own queen, and was now Blood to House Isador. She'd be thrilled. "If someone from Skye's court came to find us, I'm glad it was you. Thanks for letting Mom know I'm all right."

"The shit is going to hit the fan on both sides of the pond. Keisha Skye lost her leverage. Our queen's pissed that threats were made. It's gonna get ugly."

"And Shara's in the middle of it."

Ezra made a low sound, softer than his normal grunt of disgust. Almost a hum. I hid a grin. He already had a soft spot for Shara, and no shit, who wouldn't?

"When you came after us, did you know she'd call you to be Blood?"

"Fuck, no. But as I got closer, I felt her more than you, and the urgency kept hammering through me like Rik was using my skull for an anvil."

He'd come after me, not to be Blood, and he'd called me family.

Guilt churned in my stomach. I had pretty much turned my back on him when I came to Skye... and I hadn't ever treated him like family either. Even after he'd fed me.

Fostering young Aima with other houses was a carryover tradition from the medieval period. It was supposed to assure that political alliances were upheld, but also to keep the blood and power fresh. If a house only ever fed on their own bloodlines, the magic got stale over time, or so the general thinking went. Some scholarly types even theorized that was why queens didn't conceive very often any longer. The magic was too thin, the bloodlines too tired, weakened over the generations ages ago.

But no one ever really acknowledged that you could have a seriously difficult time in a new court as a foster. Primarily, finding someone willing to feed you the first couple of times in order to give you the queen's blood that made you part of her court. When I first moved to New York City, I'd never expected to be an important member of Skye's court. My home court wasn't extremely powerful, though old and respected, and my mother only one of our queen's minor sibs. But I had displayed enough promise and worked hard enough at political etiquette, that our queen had made arrangements for me to join Ezra in House Skye.

She hadn't wanted me to be alone. Looking back, I wondered why Ezra had been sent. Alone. How difficult a time he must have had.

It'd shocked the hell out of me when no one cared whether I fed or not. Here I was in this new politically powerful court, eager to learn, ready to please, and not one single fucking person would even think about offering throat. Maybe new fosters weren't looked upon with suspicion at other courts, but in House Skye, no one trusted anyone else. Relationships were slow to develop. Without Rik...

Guilt twisted harder in my gut. Because once I had Rik, I'd

never spared a second thought for Ezra. I'd never made sure he was well-fed, or had a place of safety if he'd needed it.

"Um—"

"Don't," Ezra bit off the word. "The past is the past."

"But—"

"Do you ever fucking listen to a word anyone says to you?"

"Nope," I said lightly, though my eyes burned. "You should know me better than that." In fact, other than Rik, Ezra probably knew me better than anyone, which made my betrayal all the worse.

"It wasn't a fucking betrayal, you imbecile," he retorted gruffly as he bent down under a fallen log and dragged out a rucksack. "You did nothing wrong."

"The fuck I did nothing wrong. I did everything wrong." He stared up at the moon, avoiding my gaze. But he listened, and so I was going to have my say. "You took care of me when I came to Skye, and then I fucking forgot you the first chance I had."

He shrugged, still not meeting my gaze. "You had a great opportunity. I would have gotten the fuck out too if I could."

"Then I should have taken you with us."

He huffed out a laugh. "Yeah, right. Big and tough would have loved dragging my obstinate, grumpy ass around. I never faulted you for seeking out a promising young alpha to be your protector. Though the chances of any alpha surviving long in that court were nil."

"I'm sorry," I whispered, my chest aching. "I fucked up."

"Don't be sorry on my account. You were smart. You did what you needed in order to survive. I could have been smarter. I could have been nicer to people. I could have tried to make friends. But that's not my style."

"Why did our queen send you to House Skye in the first place?" He started walking back toward the nest without answering, faster than we'd come out this way. I hurried to catch up. "Ezra?"

He jerked to a halt. "To get me away from you."

I couldn't have been more surprised if he'd pulled a shotgun out of the rucksack and blasted me with a full barrel right in the stomach. "What?"

"Our queen called our mothers together and decided it'd be best if I fostered sooner, rather than later, to give you time to develop on your own, without my influence."

Bewildered, I searched the craggy lines of his face. "But we were best friends. We got into some trouble, yeah, but nothing bad enough to get you sent away. Why would they do that?"

He jerked his head toward me, eyes blazing. "Because I fucking loved you, Daire. I was getting obsessed with you, and an obsessed Ursula without his queen to help control his urges is not a good thing. They were afraid I'd maul you accidentally if we didn't get some distance."

I didn't know what to say. It'd been so long ago. We'd been young. Friends. Roaming the mountains and woods, skipping out of the nest when we weren't supposed to like wild hooligans. I'd been fifteen, maybe sixteen, when Ezra left. He would have been eighteen or twenty—I couldn't remember our age difference exactly. For Aima, we'd been babies.

I hadn't gone to foster with House Skye for another ten years.

He'd endured ten years alone in New York City in a nest of vipers.

I still remember how glad I'd been to see a familiar face when he'd come to pick me up at the airport. He'd made sure I got settled, though he hadn't offered to feed me right away. Nothing had seemed forced or strange between us, though we'd both changed and matured over the years.

I'd gone to him after months. Upset. Alone. In fucking tears because no one had fed me the entire time I'd been in New York City.

Aima could go a long time without blood, if they weren't

depleting their power by actually using it. I certainly wasn't Blood, then, and had no power of my own to give anyone. But for sibs, feeding was a way to network and make connections. Plus, we simply liked to feed. It felt good. Damned good. I wasn't going to die without it, but I was fucking sick of being the low sib on the totem pole.

I'd whined that no one liked me. I wished I'd stayed at home. And he'd put his arm around my shoulders, pulled me in against him, and offered throat without another word. And yeah, as Aima tend to do when they feed, we'd fucked too. It'd been good, too. Good enough I stayed with him several days, sharing blood and his bed.

He'd never once said anything about loving me or being glad I'd come to him. Nothing.

That wasn't Ezra's style.

Then I'd traipsed out into Skye's sibs and sought another, and another. I had to build my network, prove my worth, gain their confidence. It'd still been tough going. Though I carried a bit of Skye blood then, Ezra sure hadn't made it easy on himself. While he never begrudged me feeding elsewhere, he refused to make friends. Other sibs saw me having an association with him, and it only made them more wary of me. When I stumbled, literally, into Alrik Skye and his bed, I'd never looked back. Not once.

I turned away again now, unable to bear the emotion blazing in his eyes. "Fuck, man. Why didn't you say something?"

"Why should I? We had a good time. You moved on. If you'd wanted to stay, you would have stayed."

"But I didn't know!"

"Do you think I would've wanted you to stay out of guilt? Because you owed me? Fuck that shit. You knew where I was and if you'd wanted me, you would have come to me. Then you left, and I started paying more and more attention to what was going on with Skye herself. It didn't make sense to let a young alpha with Rik's promise out of her sight. Not with her obsession. I watched. I waited until I had proof. And then I hightailed it straight to you."

Ezra wasn't much for grand displays of affection, but I grabbed a handful of his beard and pulled his head low, tucking myself up under his chin. "How can I ever repay you?"

"Are you fucking kidding me?" He growled, but he didn't pull away. "I don't want your pity thanks. Just feed me a bit until I figure out how this court's going to work. I'm fully prepared to hightail it to the badlands if Rik decides to bash my head in because I won't follow his bullshit rules."

I snickered, nuzzling deeper into his throat. I'd forgotten how hairy he was, and how much I liked it. His chest was covered with a thick mat, his hair and beard wild and shaggy. He'd always been more bear than man, even before Shara revealed his power. "You won't have to worry about getting fed here. Shara's different."

He rubbed his nose into my hair and breathed deeply, pulling my scent into his body. I remembered him doing that before, but hadn't realized why. Now I knew and it fucking shredded my heart like a cheese grater. "Do the Blood feed each other mainly?"

"No, hardly ever. We feed from her."

"All of us?" He didn't say it out loud, but I knew exactly what he was thinking. *Even me? The new (low) guy? The one nobody will like?*

"All of us. Nearly every night too. Though she'll about drain you dry in exchange. Her power is fucking incredible."

He huffed out a breath. "Yeah, I got that. With that bite of hers…"

He hesitated, too polite to come right out and ask. It made me laugh again, shaking my head. Because when it didn't matter, he was polite. But when he ought to be polite… He was crude and blunt as hell. "Yeah, she fucks us too, usually several at once so we can keep her fed."

"Huh."

I raised my head, meeting his gaze with a wicked smirk. "Suddenly eager to get back to the nest then?"

"Lead the way, you little shit."

12

SHARA

I pulled on the robe Nevarre had brought to me. I'd asked for *clothes*, but when a man wore a kilt and little else, I couldn't complain that he'd brought me something similar to put on. At least it was comfortable, and I could sit down at the table with Winston and not be embarrassed.

Rik squeezed my hair in a towel, taking off some of the moisture so I wouldn't drip everywhere. I hadn't wanted to call the blood to me, because I didn't know what it'd do to the trees my sacrifice had grown. If they could use the crazy amount of blood on the ground, let them have it. I preferred a hot shower anyway, though I couldn't wait until my new bathroom was ready, complete with the biggest tub Gina could find.

Since we hadn't had dinner yet, I'd decided to take a quick shower in the main house. The spare bathroom was perfectly serviceable (though Winston thought the master bathroom needed too much work to use before it was renovated), and I hadn't felt like tracking back and forth to the guest house.

I caught a glimpse of myself in the mirror and couldn't help but stare a moment. A scar the size of Rik's fist lay between my breasts, the skin still pink and fragile. A reminder of what I'd endured to protect us. Something I would gladly do again when the time came.

"Goddess," Rik whispered, pulling me back against him with a shudder. "Let there never be another time that you must suffer like that again."

I turned in his arms and lay my head on his chest. "Now I have a scar to match the one I gave you."

"What you did…" He breathed deeply, his big hands gentle on my back. "It was impressive. I mean literal goddess-level shit. Growing Morrigan's Grove, here, in America, in the middle of fucking Arkansas of all places…"

I blew out a sigh. "Yeah. I didn't know that's what She would do. Only that if I was willing to make a sacrifice, She would use it. I didn't know that I'd basically die, stabbed to death by a gazillion rose thorns."

Even if Gaia had forewarned me… I still would have done it. I couldn't imagine anything getting up through the ground into my nest again. Evidently ant carcasses were almost as good for fertilizer as my blood and the trees had made good use of both, towering both above and below the ground.

"I didn't know about the new Blood, either. We could have won without him, but one of you would have had to feed me again to get me upright." I watched Rik's face in the mirror, listening to his bond for any concern about the new man. "I guess he and Daire were a thing."

One of Rik's eyebrows arched and he shrugged a little. "Maybe. It would have been before we became sibs."

"Does it bother you, having Ezra here now?"

His eyes widened even more. "Because he's with Daire? How could it?"

"Ezra still cares for him, though I get the impression Daire doesn't have a clue."

Rik snorted. "Typical. Winning hearts left and right without a care, never even realizing it."

I turned in his arms so I could press against him, soaking in his body heat. His strength. My rock. Unshakable. "It's just getting complicated. I don't want to offend anyone by taking one to bed but not another. I don't want to have to think so hard about it, you know? I just..." It seemed silly but I had to say it out loud. "I just want to love everybody. I want everybody to feel loved and happy and included."

He tightened his arms around me and pressed his lips against my forehead. "And that is why we love you so much, my queen. There can be no mistakes when you call one or many of your Blood to your bed. All will come to you gladly, eager to experience and share any desire you may have. The only combination I would hesitate to suggest right now is Mehen and Ezra together, though as long as I'm there, I'll keep the two of them in line."

I tipped my face up so I could see his reaction. "So if Daire and Mehen fucked for me, you wouldn't mind? Or him and Ezra?"

Rik's eyes smoldered, his lips curling in a sublimely arrogant smile of a man fully confident in his ability to constantly blow my mind. "How could I, when you'll be fucking me at the same time?"

I leaned up on my tiptoes so I could brush my mouth against his, letting my words become a caress. "Would Daire mind?"

"You don't really need to ask that question."

:I'm mortally offended that you even thought I might mind,: Daire whispered in my mind, sending me an image of his delectable bottom lip in a pout. His warcat rubbed inside me, wicked fur winding around my heart. *:Which one would you like to see first, my queen? Big, mean Leviathan, pounding me to a pulp? Or the grouchy, obstinate no-good bear who's actually the biggest softie you've ever met? He's so hairy and rough, it's sometimes hard to tell when he's a man and when he's a bear.:*

Um. I couldn't think. My brain had turned to mush. My nipples ached and I pressed harder against Rik, groaning at how hard he was. Everywhere, not just his dick. He was rock-hard muscle from top to bottom and I suddenly couldn't wait to have his weight on me, crushing me into the mattress.

:I think her answer is both.: Rik's bond rumbled like an avalanche.

:Sounds good to me.:

"You need to eat first," Rik said, pulling me up tighter against him. "You lost too much blood tonight. And while we eat, you can decide how you want to arrange your lovers tonight."

"It seems ridiculous to waste time on something as mundane as eating when I could have you. Or Daire. Or Xin…"

"You'll have us." He set me firmly aside, though he tucked my arm around his and kept me close as we walked downstairs to join the rest of my guests.

Sitting down at the formal table in the dining room dressed only in a robe was strange to say the least. All my Blood stood as I came to join them, including Ezra, complete with a scowl leveled at the room in general. He'd even cleaned up a bit. His shaggy hair was pulled back into a trendy man bun, his beard tamed with a comb. He'd put on jeans like the rest of my Blood, but had gone with a flannel shirt instead of a T-shirt. Not unexpected, given his wild man preferences.

But he'd left the shirt unbuttoned, tucked into his jeans, but gaping open.

Which revealed loads of chest hair, a thick curly line that naturally led my gaze downward. I wasn't sure if Ezra had left the shirt open to tempt Daire…

Or me.

Because I had a hard time looking away.

"Two can play that fucking game," Mehen retorted, drawing my attention to him. He jerked his T-shirt over his head and tossed it over his shoulder. "Problem solved."

And yeah, I liked looking at him too. All those iridescent scales across his shoulders and down his arms reminded me of his formidable power as Leviathan.

Daire tossed his shirt and his fingers settled on his fly. "Awesome, naked supper."

Rik growled and jerked his head at Gina standing in the doorway, covering her mouth as she laughed.

"Oh. Right." Daire winked at me, quirking his lips to show off his dimples, but he kept his pants on.

Nevarre only wore his kilt. Though he did have the long tail of his plaid wrapped around his shoulder, most of his chest was bare. Leaving Xin and G, daring each other to keep their shirts on, or take them off.

"No more stripping, please," I said as Rik pulled my chair out for me. I'm pretty sure I was nipping badly with nothing but a thin silky robe on, but oh well. I sat down and watched as my Blood then took their seats too. Rik sat on my right, close enough our shoulders touched. Daire sat on his other side, far enough up the table that he could give sultry looks to both Mehen and Ezra, though luckily, they weren't sitting close enough to do more than glare at each other.

Gina sat on my left with a leather case that she discretely set down on the floor beside her chair. She caught me looking though and smiled. "It can wait until after dinner."

Lines about her eyes and mouth concerned me. She looked upset. Or ill. "Are you sure everything's all right?"

She nodded and patted my hand. "Of course. What I felt was a mere fraction of what you endured. I'll be fine after some sleep."

Oh shit. I never thought about what my human servants would feel. "I'm so sorry! I should have warned you, but when I realized exactly what was going down, it was too late. Is Frank okay?"

"I'm fine, honestly. It just feels like I had the worst migraine of my life and I still feel fragile, like my skull is an eggshell. Frank texted me that he was going back to his room and lie down awhile, but would be back at five in the morning."

I wasn't bleeding, so I couldn't heal her, but I listened unobtrusively to her bond a moment, trying to feel if there were any internal injuries or lingering problems I could fix. Other than weariness, I didn't feel anything else wrong.

My stomach growled, which my Blood took as the "let's eat" command. Rik immediately grabbed the large wooden bowl of salad greens in front of us and started loading up my plate. Lasagna and garlic bread were passed around, making my mouth water. Winston had also made seafood alfredo, spaghetti with a simple tomato sauce, and some kind of stewed or roasted meat that I wasn't familiar with.

I tried some of everything and was not surprised that it was all fantastic. "Winston, you've outdone yourself again."

"My pleasure, my queen, but I did have some help. Until we hire a few more staff, we have an arrangement with a caterer in town. Their osso bucco is fantastic."

"How many people should we hire?"

Gina picked up a wine bottle and offered me some. I nodded and she poured us both some white wine. "We're still talking about that. Winston thinks he only needs one or two people, but I keep insisting we need at least five to manage such a large house."

With Winston's age, I fully agreed with Gina. "I'm not even sure that five is enough. I mean, look at how much these guys eat."

Guillaume paused with a huge mound of spaghetti headed toward his mouth, and Daire had an entire loaf of bread torn apart, half in each hand.

"Pass that meat back over here," Ezra bellowed.

Mehen grabbed the platter before Winston could pass it and dumped the remaining meat onto his plate. "Sorry, it's all gone."

Ezra growled, rising up partway out of his chair.

Mehen only grinned at him. "Bring it on, big man."

Winston laid his napkin down and pushed his chair back. "Now, now, not to worry, there's another entire pan in the kitchen. I know how Blood eat."

He popped into the kitchen and when he returned, Ezra took the whole pan from him and started eating out of it.

"Hey, I wanted some more of that," Daire said.

"Come and get it, pussy cat."

Daire let out a rumbling purr and started to get up. I could only imagine what kind of show that could get us into, so I quickly changed the subject to something that would definitely distract him. "So, where are we going shopping?"

Turning back to me, his eyes lit up. "Rodeo Drive? London?"

Gina said, "I was thinking Dallas on the way to Mexico. There's a beautiful boutique shop that has some of the most unique designer gowns in the country, as well as men's clothing. I thought we could stop on our way down, without worrying about spending the night outside a nest's protection. Dallas is one of the few cities we don't currently own property in and I doubted Rik would be willing to deal with a hotel, even a super nice one."

Rik shook his head. "Security would be a nightmare, and they're not going to have rooms large enough to accommodate us all near her."

Gina nodded. "That's what I thought. I'll set up an appointment with the boutique so we have the place to ourselves, well before dark."

"Good. There will likely still be thralls in the area, even though the queen left."

"I wish we knew if she was Mayte or someone else," I said. "Has Zaniyah always had a nest in Mexico City?"

"According to our records, yes."

"So if it was Mayte in Dallas, why did she leave her nest? How long did she stay?"

"There have been reports of thralls off and on for a year or two. Enough to show up on my map. Since we didn't have a confirmed identity, I actually thought it might be you, and sent several private detectives to the area with your picture. Of course they never found the queen, since it wasn't you."

I pushed my plate away and picked up my wine glass, settling back against my chair. The guys were still eating like a pack of starving wolves, and they'd need all the energy they could get. After the ant battle and growing the trees, my hunger went deeper than food. A dull ache spread across my cheeks, my fangs throbbing, even though they hadn't descended yet. I was going to need blood. A lot of blood.

I had a feeling that my hunger would be insatiable. My stomach quivered, remembering how I'd drained my Blood when it'd been just the three of them, to the point that they couldn't walk. I was afraid I'd get my fangs in one of them and not let go until it was too late.

Rik's bond gleamed like molten lava in my mind. Red hot liquid rock. *:You would never harm us.:*

:I fucking killed you once already.:

He dropped his arm around my shoulders and pulled me in close. I turned my face against his chest, breathing in his scent, even while fear gnawed through me. This hunger...

:You've got seven Blood eager to give you every drop of blood in their bodies.:

:That's what I'm afraid of.:

:Trust me to help you control it. I stopped you when you'd drained Daire before, remember? You need. We'll provide. Gladly.:

Gina reached down beside her and pulled a folder out of the bag she'd set down. "Ready to go over a few things?"

"Of course."

"I've been talking with Bianca and we've set out an itinerary for your trip." She opened the folder and pushed it over to me so I could read the pages inside. She'd neatly typed out the dates and times. "I know you're not an early riser, but if at all possible, we need to leave by nine, so we have time to stop in Dallas and still make it to Mexico City by dark. House Zaniyah will have cars pick us up at the airport, and we'll drive out of the city a short ways to the nest."

Inwardly, I groaned. I didn't think I'd been up by nine since Rik and Daire found me.

"We'll have a formal dinner with Mayte Zaniyah each night and will need to dress accordingly."

"How formal?"

"Black tie. Her consiliarius will introduce your Blood one by one. Each will walk in with one of Mayte's Blood."

Guillaume scooted his chair closer. "In the old days, a visiting queen was never allowed to bring more Blood into the nest than the host. If anyone stepped out of line, there would always be a home Blood assigned with the sole duty of eliminating their assigned target. So there's an art to assigning Blood to Blood. It'll be interesting to see who she pairs with each of us, though since you're relatively unknown, she may not have enough information to build a file on each of us."

"How many people will be there?"

"No idea, honestly," Gina replied. "I don't believe Zaniyah has a large court, but conservatively I'd guess at least fifty, maybe one-hundred people."

Great. Just the thought of walking in front of one hundred strangers all staring at me…

"At least it's not Desideria's court," Guillaume added. "She always made visiting queens approach her court naked and refused them a single Blood when introduced. She wanted that queen as vulnerable as possible."

Gina patted my arm again. "I know it seems strange, but formal processions are a holdover tradition thousands of years old. If you're ever called to Marne Ceresa's nest, you'll be presented to at least five hundred of her court. Every queen is different. Some will use it as an opportunity to intimidate a new queen and reinforce the host queen's power. Mayte Zaniyah will want to show you her power and prove her worth, if we're right about her wanting to be your sib. She'll want to know how much she can trust you, too."

"Marne Ceresa uses formal presentation to prove her power, the same as Desideria," Guillaume said with a scowl. "The old queens make their halls long and narrow, forcing the visiting queen to walk seemingly miles through hundreds of watchers."

"Not just the old ones," Daire snorted. "House Skye's formal court is the length of a few football fields."

"The first dinner will be formal and very structured," Gina continued. "Every queen's court is different, of course, but generally the queens will sit together at an elevated table overlooking the rest of the court with their consiliari. Usually the queens sit side by side, so they can talk, and their alphas will be close, usually standing behind them the entire dinner."

I frowned. "The alphas stand the whole time and don't eat?"

"Usually, no, they don't eat," Guillaume said. "Some queens won't let any of the Blood eat for fear they'll be distracted. This is all about the queens and their security. We'll eat after, usually in shifts. Both her Blood and yours will be on high alert the entire time. A twitch at the wrong time can be deadly. Bloodshed before questions."

With a sinking feeling, I looked down at Ezra, who was still glaring at Mehen across the table. The more wild bear Ezra acted, the more indolent lord Mehen became. The two of them were going to be insufferable.

"Don't worry about those two." Guillaume didn't raise his voice or even look at them, but there was an edge in his voice that made everyone at the table stop talking and look at him. "We'll be on our best behavior for you, my queen. One word or look out of place before your host's court, and I'll have the man's head. Whoever it may be."

"I can hold my tongue when I must," Ezra muttered darkly, his cheeks turning red. From anger? Or embarrassment? I wasn't sure. His bond roiled like an angry bear who'd been roused too early from hibernation, but he'd felt like that since he'd shown up.

"The rest of her court will be seated on the main floor in smaller tables," Gina said. "They will all be watching you and your Blood, evaluating your power and your stature. Watching the way you interact with Mayte. If she's unhappy, her court will be displeased. Everything from your clothing to the way you eat will be judged. If you send an offered dish away, for example, then Mayte could be offended. It will say her best efforts to entertain you are insufficient."

Geez, talk about pressure. "I'm not so great in social situations. I mean, I know better than to eat with my fingers or belch loudly, but other than that, formal table etiquette is beyond me."

"We'll practice," Gina promised. "And Zaniyah's a small court. The pressure won't be as immense as you fear."

"Oh, the pressure's there," Guillaume said, nodding. "But for Mayte, not you. She needs you. Remember that. She wants to impress you. She wants to make sure you're willing to protect her from other queens. Anytime you're worried about something, just remember that her alternative is Keisha Skye, the queen who would have tortured your alpha before he could find you, and you'll be fine."

Indeed, just the thought of how close I'd come to never having Rik at all made my power rise. Goose bumps flared down my arms and my hair fluttered slightly about my shoulders, as if someone had cracked a door.

"What's the worst thing that could happen?" I asked. "Honestly, I want to know."

"Honestly?" At the end of the table, Mehen kicked back with a beer in his hand. "We're killed. Every fucking one of us."

Guillaume sighed. "The snake's right. Worst case, she seals the circle, locking us inside. We'll be out numbered. It's been done before under the guise of diplomacy."

I took a deep breath, my mind racing. I didn't want to go

into this if we didn't have a Plan B. Some back door way to get out if we needed to escape. "I couldn't break her blood circle?"

Gina spluttered on her wine and set her glass down. "No."

I arched a brow at her. "No? For sure?"

"It's never been done before. A blood circle, made by a queen, is impenetrable."

"So you've told me, but then ants tried to crawl up from underneath my circle."

Mehen took a long pull of his beer and then said, "I could fly you out. But no queen's circle can be broken."

"Unless the queen's killed," Rik said. "Here's my orders to each of you so we're absolutely fucking clear. If this meet goes badly, we get Shara out. No matter what. Kill your assigned Blood and get her to Mehen. He flies her out. Guillaume, your main priority will be to kill Mayte. Only you will be able to do it if she's well protected."

Guillaume nodded coolly. "Understood."

Rik looked at Xin. "You will use your gift of invisibility to reach Shara and get her to Mehen. I don't care if you kill anyone else, even your Blood. Just get her to the dragon so he can fly her out."

"Understood, alpha."

I shivered, looking down at my men, now grim and hard as they contemplated killing our way out of Zaniyah's nest. I wasn't scared, just... On edge. Nervous. Adrenaline already pumped though my veins and we hadn't even left for Mexico yet. I didn't doubt our ability to win. Not in the slightest. How could I after tonight's battle with the ants? After Gaia and Morrigan and Isis worked together to grow a formidable grove of magical trees to protect us?

I wouldn't have my trees or my nest in Mexico.

I would have something better.

My Blood.

13

SHARA

H and in hand with Rik, we slowly walked toward the guest house. Slowly, because that was all I could manage. My legs still felt weak, but I didn't want him to carry me. It was early, not even ten o'clock, but sleep was far away. My mind raced with plans and questions I needed to remember to ask Gina. We had little time to prepare for this meeting.

I needed to practice using complicated sets of silverware for all the various courses. The polite ways to greet a queen and her Blood, as well as the less warm and fuzzy ways. So many nuances were built into life at court—something I had never known. I didn't have any idea how to insult with a smile or charm with a touch.

Three days to teach me a lifetime of court etiquette, when I was so weak I couldn't walk from the house to my bed.

Rik drew me to a halt outside the guest house door. "You've got an innate sense of how to play the game, whether you know it or not. You handled Kendall perfectly."

"But that was only a minor Blood, not his queen. I don't

care what Keisha Skye thinks of me, but Mayte may be more important."

"She will know what we know." Rik's eyelids were heavy, his voice a deep rumble. "I have no doubt."

My Blood formed a loose ring about us, waiting for their orders.

From me.

I looked up at the sky a moment, letting the silver moonlight glow on my face. The moon seemed smaller now, normal sized rather than huge and mystical. Softly, I said, "I'm going to need a lot of blood tonight."

"Take me first," Daire said immediately, sliding up in a hug behind me.

"I'm ready," both Mehen and Ezra said at the same time, and then they glared at each other.

Guillaume didn't say a word, but he casually flicked his wrist and a blade gleamed against his palm. Standing beside him, Xin rolled up his sleeve and offered his wrist, though G didn't cut him. Not yet.

Nevarre was the only one I really wasn't sure about.

He immediately came and dropped to his knees before me, slinging his hair back in an effortless, practiced move. He tipped his head to the side so his throat gleamed in the moonlight. "Take what you need from me, my queen. My sincerest apologies if I gave you any reason to doubt my willingness to serve."

"I know you'll let me feed. But I'm not sure how you feel about everything else."

"My queen?"

"I didn't give you much choice last night, and for that, I'm sincerely sorry."

Tiny crinkles formed at the corners of his eyes and his lips curled in slow, wide smile that made me sag with relief, leaning a bit harder on Daire. "You're worried about that? Surely my enthusiastic participation in your Christmas evening orgy was full indication of my willingness to do everything you could ever desire."

I reached out to stroke my fingers through the long black hair that fell over his shoulders. "You're still grieving for Brigid and what you lost."

He nodded, but leaned closer to press his face against my stomach. I wrapped my arms around his head and continued combing my right hand through his hair. "I'll always grieve for the woman who took me in when no one else would. I loved her. I died with her. But she was not my queen. If anything…" He pressed his face tighter to me, leaning in harder. "I'm guilty of not loving her as much as I should have. She often said our love was quiet and kind, not wild and passionate, but sometimes I saw a wistful look on her face when she thought I wasn't watching. Or I'd leave, and I'd see a look come into her eyes. The doubt that I would actually return to her side. It hurt, so badly, because it was true. I'd loved her more than my first queen, chosen by my mother to solidify her power, but not enough. Never enough."

Tipping his face up so he could see me, he still kept his mouth pressed to the thin silk barely covering me, his eyes burning with dark emotion. "When I felt your call, nothing, absolutely nothing, would keep me from you. Nothing would ever make me leave your side. There is nothing kind and gentle about what roars through my body when I look at you or touch you or smell your blood or feel your magic. I already love you more wildly and passionately in a day, than I ever loved the woman I lived with for decades. That's my guilt to bear, my queen. Not yours."

"Am I to feel guilty for loving each of you?"

His eyes flared with shock. "Of course not, my queen. I'd never make that judgment of anyone, let alone you."

"I don't love you the same as I love Daire. Does that make my love for you less? Should you leave, then, because you're not Daire?"

His hands closed around my hips, his fingers digging into me. "Please don't make me leave you, my queen. I'd rather you suck my life out of me and let me die here in the grove than live one moment without you."

I cupped his cheeks in my hands and leaned down, holding his gaze. "Then why do you punish yourself for having different kinds of love for more than one woman?"

He swallowed hard, his throat working, and when he spoke, his voice was as raw as his words. "Because if she'd still lived when I felt your call, I would have left her without a moment's hesitation and flown straight to you."

I brushed my lips against his. "I'd rather think that I couldn't have called you if she'd still lived, because I'd never want to take a man from someone he loved, no matter how badly I needed him as Blood. I won't take a Blood I don't love, and I won't call a Blood when he loves another."

The moon shone brighter and I could almost feel the pearly beams sinking into me, sliding through the lava-hot bonds of my Blood. I felt the surety in my bonds, the moon binding my oath into my magic and my Blood.

Nevarre's shoulders relaxed and he melted against me. Daire started purring. Nevarre nuzzled my stomach, his lips tugging on the belt of my robe.

My eyelids fluttered, my skin sparking at their soft touches. Daire's mouth moved on my neck, while Nevarre kissed my stomach. My knees quivered and Rik swooped me up against him. "Daire, Nevarre, with me. Ezra, Guillaume, stand by. Xin, Mehen, take the first watch."

I expected Mehen to bitch about having to take watch when Ezra didn't, but he stalked off into the night without a word.

Rik carried me inside and lay me on the bed.

But he didn't join me.

My eyes flew open and I pushed up on my elbows.

Before I could say anything, he snapped his fingers and

Daire and Nevarre slid in on either side of me. Blissfully naked. Hot flesh. Soft mouths. Slow, stroking hands.

"Soak them in, my queen," Rik whispered, a deep yet soft rumble that thrummed my spine. "Let their touch wipe away every sting the thorns gave you this evening."

I'd had several men in my bed at once for many nights now. But I'd never had two at once who made it seem like they were in absolutely no rush to do more than stroke me with their hands and mouths. All my Blood wanted to give me pleasure. But these two made me believe they'd be perfectly happy giving me endless pleasure with just their mouths. They didn't attack the most obvious areas either. Neither of them touched my pussy or my breasts at all.

Nevarre cupped my left hand and kissed every fingertip and then my palm. He paid loving attention to the pulse in my wrist, stroking his tongue over my skin as if he could taste my blood without ever biting me. While Daire did the exact same thing to my right hand. Using their bond, they coordinated their touch, drowning me in waves of exquisite sensation.

Kisses in the crooks of my elbows. Soft nibbling lips up the curves of my biceps. My shoulders. My throat.

I reached around them both and pushed my hands up into their hair, tangling my fingers in the long strands. Daire's wasn't as long as Nevarre's yet, but it'd easily grown six inches since he'd come to me.

Then Rik joined them, and my brain had a nuclear meltdown.

He was just as gentle... but with a firm grip. He massaged my right foot, rubbing his thumb firmly in my arch to loosen up kinks I wasn't even aware of. Then my left received the same deep massage. Both hands squeezed and kneaded my calves. His mouth teased the tender skin on the inside of my knees. He worked my thighs, stretching and loosening every muscle, his mouth a slow torment. He didn't tease and flutter like Nevarre or Daire. The higher he got up my legs, the more firmly he gripped me with his jaws. Not a bite, exactly, but he worked his teeth up and down my thighs until I trembled beneath their slow assault.

Nevarre's hair trailed over my breasts. Daire's rumbling purr a steady, deep vibration. If he laid between my thighs, I'd come just from feeling him purr against me.

He whispered against the hollow of my throat, "Could we make you come just from kissing your breasts?"

I didn't have to answer. We all knew they could. Climax already hovered inside me, a fluttering, eager bird ready for the cage door to open.

He licked my skin like I'd dribbled blood all over my chest, his tongue firm and rough like his cat's, but slow and tender. Nevarre's lips roamed over my breast like butterfly wings, soft and dreamy. Rik kneaded my thighs in those big, powerful hands. Two mouths finally closed over my rock-hard nipples and my back arched on a soft cry. Climax pulsed through me, as gentle and tender as their touch. Pleasure rippled through my body, a sweet, soothing salve to the internal nerves and muscles that remembered suffering and bleeding on the thorns.

Rik's palms slipped under my buttocks and he lifted me up to his mouth. He flattened his tongue against me and licked firmly up my entire slit. A low rumble tore out of his throat. Hunger.

If their come could be addictive and intoxicating, it made me wonder what my juices would do to them. Only Daire had ever licked between my thighs that I could remember, and most of those times I'd been bleeding, which had been a whole other fire to play with.

Rik's bond blazed inside me. The hottest forge fire, melting me into iron he could hammer and meld into a new shape. *:You'll see.:*

As if they had all the time in the world, Daire and Nevarre continued to lick and suck and bite my nipples. Endless pleasure. Torment. Delicious agony. A hint of fang. Rik kneaded my buttocks, keeping my pelvis tipped up to his mouth. He licked my outer lips, the tender curves where ass met pussy, dropping tiny, gentle bites that made me quiver. My clit throbbed, so sensitive and swollen it'd only take a touch to send me soaring again. But he waited until I trembled on the edge of orgasm, muscles wrenching tighter. My breath caught in my throat. I fisted my hands in their hair, helplessly tugging, pulling them closer. A silent plea.

Rik closed his mouth over my clit and I flew apart at the seams. I dragged Daire up by his hair and sank my fangs into his throat. He let out a guttural cry and came with me. Rik sucked me firmly, drawing out my climax. Wave after wave of pleasure throbbed through me, and only when my hips jerked in his grip did he finally relent and slide his tongue deeper to taste me again. Groaning with pleasure himself, he sought out every crevice to lick every drop. His bond seared me like a branding iron, a molten sun that hurt to look at. So it surprised the hell out of me when he pulled up to his knees and backed away.

"Nevarre, our queen needs to be filled."

Nevarre immediately slid up over me. I tightened my hand in his hair, but didn't let go of Daire's throat, either. He tasted too good. Thick and sweet like warm, slow honey. I kept my fangs buried in him, even though it slowed the blood flow, just because I liked being inside him. Nevarre pushed into me, making me groan against Daire's throat. I wrapped my legs around Nevarre's waist and he started to move inside me with an unhurried continuous stroking, just as he'd done with his mouth.

With Daire's blood flowing into me and pleasure rippling through me, my need had eased a bit. Nevarre wasn't a big, powerful man, but he moved with the same lithe grace that he had in the air. Sometimes a bird flapped its wings frantically to gain altitude, but other times it coasted on the wind currents, gliding effortlessly on the breeze in a dreamy cruise. That was how he moved in me. As if we had nowhere to go. No rush. No hurry. No urgency. Just the ceaseless stroking of his body in mine.

I thought a good long drink from Daire would steady me, but his blood only stirred my hunger for more. I finally pulled my fangs out of him but kept a firm grip on his throat, gulping him down as quickly as I could. His purr a constant rumbling drone, he worked one arm beneath my neck to help support my head, but his other arm looped over Nevarre's shoulders. It was the most natural and sweetest thing in the world when Nevarre turned his head and pressed his lips to Daire's. The three of us. Wrapped together in black silk hair and a warcat's purr.

Even though I drank Daire's blood, Nevarre's bond whispered to me, drawing me deeper into his shadows. Where Rik was volcanic lava and Daire was playful feline, Nevarre was the dark stillness of a moonless, starless night. Not dark-evil. Just the absence of light. Something fluttered nearby, heard but not seen, his raven rustling its wings. I sank deeper into his bond, mentally feeling my way toward his core.

In the darkness, it was his scent that had me turning and gliding closer to the giant raven of his gift. He smelled like brilliant green fields. Thick fog hanging low over ancient stone monoliths. A warm, smoky hearth after tromping across windy moors sprinkled with sweet purple heather. Music floated through his bond, not the earth music I'd heard before, but a high, soul-piercing wooden flute. That sound brought tears to my eyes. It was so sad, and yet glad too. Full of hope. Warm with love.

Letting go of Daire, I pressed my face to Nevarre's throat. Though I felt hot skin and man on top of me, in the bond I touched feathers, soft as down.

He gathered me close, fingers spread against my nape and we flew through the night with whisper soft wings, moonlight dancing in the air, and that brutally haunting flute.

His need rose, powerful shoulders moving beneath my hands. No longer silent, he let out a low groan with every thrust and he added a little twist at the end, lifting at the end of his stroke to change the angle inside me so I gasped. My nerves sang with sensation. I wouldn't have thought I could come again, not so quickly, but the wave of pleasure crested inside me. I sank my fangs into his throat and he shoved deep with a ragged groan.

I could taste his pleasure in his blood. He'd tasted like magic before, but now his blood was deeper and richer as he spurted into me, both his blood and his semen. My body eagerly took his offering, soaking him in. Soaking them all in. I'd had them all one after another before, except Ezra. The remnants of my human sensibilities insisted that should be disgusting and degrading and most of all, messy, but I never had much mess after sex with them, unless it was blood.

A queen's body must have use for all that semen, even if she wasn't breeding.

Blood and come and pleasure made for some goddess-level magic.

14

RIK

My lips and tongue tingled, the taste of my queen's desire burning in my mouth. But I only watched as she took her first two Blood of the evening. She needed me to ensure their safety with her thirst so intense. Daire was barely conscious but unharmed, so fucking glad to be back in her bed that I'd probably have to shift to the rock troll and forcibly drag him out when he was needed on guard duty. I knew exactly how I'd do it too. One hand in his hair. The other on his dick.

Amusement skated through me briefly, but I ached too much to be distracted for long. My time would come. I had no doubt. But my balls would probably be the size of watermelons before I ensured she tasted the others.

Nevarre never made a complaint as darkness closed in. None of us would. I'd never served a queen before, so I didn't know if it was common for her to be able to drain powerful, healthy Blood, in their prime, to unconsciousness. Not just one, but several, and many of them uncommonly old and powerful in their own right.

And still not be sated.

:It's very uncommon,: Guillaume said as he joined me, sensing her continued thirst before I needed to call him. *:She's still coming into her power, and that's a fucking frightening thing, Rik. I've never seen a queen with raw power like her. Desideria and Marne Ceresa don't even come close, though Marne's got hundreds of years of experience in wielding her power, which makes her a formidable threat. She couldn't stand toe-to-toe with Shara and fight raw power to raw power and win, and our queen's still growing.:*

It should have thrilled me that Shara was so strong, but I met Guillaume's solemn, worried gaze and nodded to show my understanding of his concern. She was vulnerable. All the power in the universe couldn't protect her if she didn't understand how to use it. If she was tricked by another queen, she could be manipulated, entrapped by her growing power, just as the knight had been imprisoned by his honor. The more powerful she became, the harder every queen would work to tear her down in order to protect their own courts. If they all united against her… Or even just the Triune queens…

Shara couldn't stand alone, no matter how fucking strong she was.

Guillaume had already stripped except for a single blade harness strapped to his left forearm. As he moved to the bed, he drew the blade and made a cut on his throat, giving her a generous amount of blood. She watched him, gleaming eyes locked on him, but she didn't let Nevarre go until Guillaume planted a hand and knee on the bed. Then she attacked.

Watching, I was pretty impressed. She shoved Nevarre's dead weight off her and rolled the knight beneath her without even grunting with effort, even though he had to outweigh her by a hundred pounds of sheer muscle. She surprised G a bit, not that he cared being beneath her, as long as she took him. She locked onto his throat first, gulping down several swallows before she even thought about anything else. Groaning against his throat, she wriggled on his abdomen, silently asking him to help her. Guillaume was too big for her to get inside her by herself, unless she was willing to let go of his throat and sit up. And that wasn't happening anytime soon.

He clamped his hands on her hips and lifted her up into position. He tried to control his penetration, taking it nice and easy, but she'd have none of that. She jerked in his grip, working her hips until he let her sink deep with another rough, muffled cry. G leaned up, bending in toward her so she didn't have to fight to keep her mouth over the cut. He didn't try to move in her. I don't think he could have. He'd filled every inch of her, stretching her in ways even I, her alpha, couldn't do.

And yeah, that stung my ego a bit. The alpha should always have the biggest dick of the pack.

:If you were as big as G, then I couldn't ask you to join us.:

She didn't have to make any further requests. I knew exactly what she wanted. What she needed.

Striding to her, I tore my wrist open and dribbled blood all over her and Guillaume both. Her back. Her hair. Her buttocks and hips. Guillaume sat up, shifting her knees to an easier position on either side of him. But I didn't jump right into the fucking yet. I'd hoped she'd wait until later to invite me to bed, because after tasting her cream, when I blew this load, I'd be done for quite awhile. Hopefully the other Blood would be able to rise quickly enough if her desire wasn't sated.

:More.: Her bond tugged on me like a powerful ceaseless tide. *:Coat me in your blood. I want to wear you. You too, G.:*

Guillaume bit his wrist and let blood run down his arm, dripping off his fingers. Then he started smearing his blood on her breasts. Up her throat. Down each side. Her flanks. Her thighs. I rubbed my blood into her back, using both hands, massaging my blood into her skin. And she drank me in, her skin absorbing my blood like I was using massage oil. I'd never seen anyone feed like that before but I could feel the alpha hit in her bond. She arched her back and pushed down harder on G, grinding her clit against him, jamming his big dick so deep inside her I felt the thud in our bond. A pain that was so good she groaned and did it again and again.

Her climax rose like a dark, monstrous shape from the deepest part of the ocean. Slow, silent, but massive. Unstoppable. Devastating. She let go of G just long enough to sink her fangs into him. His back bowed and he groaned with release, spurting deep inside her. Her climax gripped him hard, working spasm after spasm out of his dick. When she finally raised her head and let go of his shoulders, Guillaume slumped back to the bed, eyes closed, but with one hell of a smile on his face, he mumbled, "Thank you, my queen."

Then he buried his face in Nevarre's hair and passed out.

15

SHARA

Three men lay in my bed.

Passed out. Gone. Dead to the world. Because I'd fed so long on each of them that they'd fainted.

My stomach quivered a moment, and yeah, I was pretty fucking scared. I didn't want to hurt one of them seriously. Surely losing so much blood—

"You know we love it," Rik said in his troll voice that sounded like a landslide tumbling down a mountain.

He knelt behind me, his blood thick on the air. I didn't stop to think. I twisted like a snake in his arms and flipped him around so he lay on his back across the other Bloods' legs. I hesitated a moment, as surprised as he was. Did I just take my alpha down? Without even trying? Of course he'd never resist me, so it wasn't really a take down. More of an invitation to take him down, anytime, anyplace, as often as I wanted. I knew full well that he'd *allowed* me to move him, but it still made him arch a brow up at me.

"Building a pyramid of bodies in your bed, my queen?"

Daire stirred, stretching each muscle in his incredible body, his purr like a snoring bear in hibernation.

"Fuck me," Ezra said disgustedly. "Bears don't snore."

I looked up at him, eyes narrowed. He'd entered my domain. My den. And I hadn't called him.

I thought about being pissed, but he looked too good standing there for me to be angry for long.

I'd almost say he was fluffy. He wasn't cut. He wasn't lean. He was one burly, barrel-chested man with thick arms and thick legs and no washboard abs to be seen, but I didn't doubt for a second that he was as powerful and strong as my other Blood. His cock wasn't as long, but he more than made up for it in girth. Thick hair ran down in a dark line to his groin. Even his thighs were fairly hairy. I wasn't sure if I'd like that or not.

But by the goddess I was definitely willing to try. "Get over here."

He sauntered over to the opposite side of my bed like he was taking a Sunday stroll around a lake.

"What are you willing to do?"

His mouth fell open and he gaped at me. I'd finally rendered the grouchy bear speechless. "Whatever you tell me to do, my queen."

I snorted and rolled my eyes. "Oh yeah, right, because you're such an eager and obedient Blood without a single complaint."

He slammed his mouth shut and narrowed a hard look on me. "I can't help the disposition Ursula cursed me with, but may the Great Bear devour me here on the spot if I'd ever refuse my queen. I might grouch and complain but I'll do it. Without fail. I don't give a fuck what you ask of me."

Rik's big hands kneaded my thighs, reminding me of exactly where I sat.

On one of his tree-trunk thighs. With my willing and eager Blood's dick ready to cut diamonds. I rose up and took him inside me. My head fell back, my breath sighing out on a long sigh with bliss. My alpha always felt incredible, but tonight, he seemed even harder, and his blood burned on my skin. He knew it, too, smearing his wrist down my thigh to my knee. I didn't even have to move on him and my body was singing with pleasure.

Ezra cleared his throat roughly, drawing my gaze back up to him. He'd do what I wanted... but he was quickly running out of patience just standing there.

"Daire, are you fully coherent?"

He didn't answer me with words, but rolled up from beneath Rik to give me a kiss that turned into a teasing nip on my bottom lip.

I fisted my right hand in his hair, pulling his head back to arch his neck. Hunger burned in me, a need that I hadn't managed to slake even by feeding deeply on three of my Blood already. I was tempted to bite him again. And yeah, he would have let me, gladly. I knew Rik would keep an eye on how much I weakened him, but I didn't want to risk hurting any of them. Especially when I had plenty of Blood to taste tonight.

Daire melted against me with a thunderous purr. "Does the bad kitty get to be punished by the mean bear now?"

I looked back at Ezra and let a smile curve my lips. "If he's up to the challenge."

His eyes widened and a small, soft sound escaped his throat. Fucking priceless. "You would let me... let him..."

That tender, ragged look in his eyes made my heart bleed for them both. Ezra had answered my call, fully expecting to join the ranks of my Blood where he'd see Daire and smell him and touch him—but never in a sexual way ever again. Because Daire was already mine, he could never be Ezra's.

He hadn't realized that this queen would share her love with all.

"I don't know if he can manage you," I said softly, giving Daire's hair another tug. "You can be quite the handful."

Ezra swallowed in a loud gulp and growled deep in his chest, though his eyes still gleamed with softness. "I can handle the little fucker just fine. If that's what you want, my queen."

I settled deeper on Rik, and naturally, he pushed his hips up with a little swirl so the head of his dick rubbed inside me. Meeting my need, as always. My breath caught in my throat, making my voice husky. "I want, Ezra. Very much indeed. I don't want to risk feeding on him again, so come in close. Be warned—I will sink fang into you before we're done tonight."

"You sure you got room up there for another?"

"The bear has a point." Nevarre's voice was slurred and drowsy, but at least he was awake. He worked himself out from beneath Rik and jabbed Guillaume in the ribs a few times until he stirred too. "Let's go find some food."

All the shifting around made my eyes roll back in my head. So of course Rik made sure to jostle and rock me harder.

Both Blood leaned in for a lingering kiss. And another. I couldn't keep my fingers out of Nevarre's hair. Not to be outdone, Guillaume unsheathed his knife and stroked it down my throat and over my breasts.

"Yes," I groaned, arching my back.

"Both of us?"

"Of course."

"Small cuts only," Rik warned him, his voice echoing like drawn steel. "She's lost too much blood already tonight. I won't have you sending her back downhill when she needs her strength."

Guillaume made two quick cuts, one on each breast, and they dipped their heads to my blood. I cradled their heads to me, my eyes drifting shut. Daire licked my lips, pulling my bottom lip into his mouth.

The bed dipped and I felt Ezra moving closer to us. "You keep on kissing our queen, D. No matter what."

"Enough," Rik told the two Blood tasting me. "Run up to the house and see if Winston can send down some sandwiches and plenty of fluids. Once you've refueled, relieve Mehen and Xin. Four hour shifts tonight. I want us all close and ready to feed her again."

They licked the small cuts thoroughly, making me shiver deliciously. Guillaume kissed my breast, throat, and jaw before murmuring, "my queen."

Nevarre closed his lips around my nipple firmly enough I squirmed on Rik, but it was Daire who rumbled a warning. *:Don't make me lose her mouth or you can join me for whatever punishment Ezra will do.:*

With a final but thorough tracing of his tongue around my aching nipple, Nevarre lifted his head and he and Guillaume headed for the door.

I smelled Ezra's blood, spiced with fresh pine needles and fur and thick fluffy snow. I opened my eyes and stared into Daire's. Now that he had my full attention, he traced his tongue over my lip, silently begging.

I knew what he wanted. For all his strength and power and teasing fun, Daire liked to be taken, and I had a feeling Ezra was going to show me exactly how forcefully and rough my warcat liked to play.

I fisted my left hand in his hair at his nape and twisted his head to the side. Making him slant his mouth for me. His mouth opened against mine and I stroked my tongue deep, earning a groan of approval. Or maybe that groan escaped because Ezra was bleeding on him, lubing him up. With Daire's head twisted to the side, I watched as Ezra smeared his blood on Daire's buttocks. His big meaty hands stroked and squeezed, kneading him good, and Daire melted, his head weighing heavy in my hands. Ezra worked his fingers into him, stretching him, making him groan again, his back arching, lifting into the caress. Despite Ezra's rough threats of punishment, the big man touched him reverently, almost like he truly was stroking a beloved pet.

With a loud snort of disgust, he met my gaze, his mouth quirked. "He's always been a kitty, even before you brought out his gift. Though I have to admit, I love that fucking purr of his."

Naturally Daire rumbled louder and wriggled between us.

127

"Me too," Rik said, his own voice a thunderous vibration of shifting Teutonic plates.

:*Me too,:* I said through the bond, sucking Daire's lush bottom lip into my mouth.

Ezra shifted closer, tucking his knees up next to Rik and my knee on that side, so all Daire really had to do was sit back on his thighs. He pushed back, working the man's cock deep, and his purr caught, rattled a few times, and then lowered to a deeper vibration of pleasure that I felt in my bones. He wasn't as loud, but deeper, almost beyond hearing. Caught between us, he sagged with complete trust. Ezra gripped one hip and slid his other hand up around Daire's nape, his fingers sliding in over mine so we were touching too.

Something resonated deep inside me, acknowledging this moment. Three Blood and me, connected by touch. Connected by my blood. Connected by my love.

This is how it's meant to be. Always.

Ezra didn't pound him like I expected, certainly not like I'd seen Rik do. Maybe because Daire had his mouth to mine. Or because there were two other people Ezra was trying to be mindful of. Or maybe he just didn't have the room, because yeah, this king-sized bed felt like a twin with the four of us in it. But I suspected he didn't need a lot of thrust to blow Daire's mind. Not with that girth, and certainly not after it'd been so long since he'd been able to show Daire exactly how he felt.

All growl. But pure sweet gooey marshmallow.

Ezra cradled him on his lap and rocked him, slow and steady. The same way Rik was rocking me. At first I didn't even feel our movement, too absorbed in watching them fuck. Too entranced by the slow rub of Daire's lips on mine and the way our tongues entwined. Rik rubbed up against something in me that made my head fall back on a deep groan. My hips pressed down harder, absorbing that sensation, involuntarily asking for more.

"Now you've gone and done it," Ezra muttered, his voice rough but soft, just like his personality.

Daire groaned, reminding me that he'd been told to keep his mouth on mine.

"That was my fault," I said a little breathlessly. I shifted on Rik, trying to back off a bit, get some space, but his grip tightened on my thighs, just above my knees. Holding me firm. Keeping his dick rubbing on that spot that made stars explode behind my eye lids.

"Doesn't matter," Ezra replied.

Daire's breath came out on an *"oomph"* though he didn't move that much. It wasn't like Ezra was rocking and rolling. So...?

Then my breath came out on a similar sound, and Rik wasn't moving me that hard either. Something zinged up my spine to the top of my skull.

"He's got a hook," Rik finally said, tipping up into me a bit further. Harder. I jerked in his grip like a live wire shot a million volts of electricity through me.

I forced my eyes open and glared down at him. "I don't know what that is. What's with you tonight? You've never felt so... so..."

He rolled his hips again and a sound escaped my lips that would have embarrassed me if anyone but my Blood had heard it. Somewhere between a squawk and a squeal.

A low growl rumbled from Ezra's chest. It took me a second to realize it was a laugh. "Don't tell me this is the first time you let your alpha drink from that sweet pussy."

"Daire's done it before," I replied, trying not to sound like every muscle in my body was vibrating with tension.

"D isn't your alpha though, is he, sweetheart." He tugged Daire's head back toward him, bowing his back, seating himself deeper. "Though it doesn't surprise me in the slightest that he'd be licking that cream every chance he gets. He always was a licker."

129

Sensation screamed through me, making me twitch, gasp, and jerk in Rik's grasp. I couldn't stop it. It didn't feel bad. In fact, it felt pretty fucking fantastic. I just didn't like that I couldn't control my own reactions in the slightest.

If he actually started thrusting...

I was pretty sure I'd lose my ever loving mind.

"Biology is a pretty fucking amazing thing." He pushed up again, sending another earthquake quivering through my body. "A queen wants a strong alpha to continue her line, and if she's breeding, she wants him to empty himself thoroughly, ensuring as good a chance as possible that she'll conceive. So your cream tastes extra special and will make me empty everything in my balls at once. I'll be wiped out for at least a couple of hours. Even more, my dick has a little extra power now, too, because it's to the alpha's advantage to please his queen well and long, so she'll not only want him in her bed, she'll want him to taste her again and again."

"But I'm not—" My eyes flew open. I needed to talk to Dr. Borcht again and run some more tests so we could pinpoint my reproductive cycle. I'd thought I bled every month because I was doing the normal human menstruation thing. But if I wasn't even half human... Had I really been breeding? Or would I ovulate in a few days like a normal human would?

"You would know if you were pregnant," Rik said, breaking the frantic chain of thoughts crowding my brain.

I focused on his face. "Are you sure?"

He nodded, eyes solemn. "You'd know. We'd all know. We'd feel it. You're not pregnant."

"Hold on," Ezra said. "She's already been breeding? This young?"

"Just days ago," Rik replied. "Though we haven't figured out her biology yet."

"Fuck me," Ezra muttered. "Too bad I didn't hoof it a bit faster through the mountains."

Daire wriggled in his grip, making them both groan. "What

he failed to mention is that she says she breeds every month without fail."

"Fuuuuuuck," Ezra groaned again. "Yeah. I'm no alpha but I'd tap that."

Rik didn't make a sound, but his bond swelled as if he was shifting to his rock troll.

"Uh, after you, of course, alpha," Ezra added hurriedly in the most polite tone I'd ever heard him use.

I met his gaze, irritated, yeah, because he didn't care what I thought about being *tapped* at all, let alone on my period. I didn't say anything, but his cheeks blazed red and he ducked his head. "No disrespect intended, my queen. Please forgive my rough and oafish habits. I'm not used to caring what anyone thinks about the fool words that come out of my mouth. I'll do better."

Not surprising anyone, it was Daire who managed to break the ice and ease the straining tensions between us.

"He fucks better than he talks, my queen. Maybe you'd better hurry up and show her, Griz."

16

DAIRE

The three people I loved most in this world were here. Together. Made possible only by Shara fucking Isador, my queen.

I'd forgotten how sexy Ezra could be. Rough and crude on the outside, yet behind closed doors, amazingly tender and gentle. Shara might not realize how rare and special it was to see him like this. While I loved the shit out of Rik and would follow him anywhere…

I loved this big old grizzly bear too. And I was right. He could fuck like no one else.

"I guess you're wanting to put on a good show, huh, D." Lazily, Ezra reached around my waist and wrapped one of his beefy hands around my dick. He didn't stroke or even squeeze me. That wasn't why he took hold of me.

It wasn't about pleasure, though I loved his touch.

It was about control.

Which was why I always wanted alphas or at least big, powerful dominants. I wanted to be wild and silly and out of control and bratty and even dangerous. I wanted to scratch, wrestle, fight, and still know that my partner had control of the situation. That if I fell, my partner had me. Even if I fell *apart.*

I braced my hands on the mattress, though I managed to slip one hand up beneath Shara's lower leg so I was at least touching her a little. I let my head drop down, my hair falling in my eyes. Then I gave complete and utter control of my body to Ezra.

He used my dick like a steering wheel and a gear shift. Revving me up, slowing me down, making me change gears. He pulled me back deeper into his lap, shifting so I basically sat on his fat dick with my knees barely touching the bed. And he rocked me. He stroked me. He pulled me back by my hair and nuzzled my throat and bit my ear hard enough that I hissed at him.

"Ah, there's the bad kitty. Look at our queen while I fuck you."

I groaned, because I knew seeing the heat in her eyes would only make me crazier. I squeezed my eyes shut, tight, refusing to look. I wanted him to make me.

Goose bumps raced up and down my arms, waiting for him to set the hook. He'd only teased me a bit earlier.

"The hook?" Shara asked, picking up my thoughts in the bond.

Her voice stroked over me like thousands of fingers. I knew she was watching. I knew she was turned on. Fuck. I wanted to see that heat in her glorious eyes, the flaming destruction of thousands of falling stars streaking across a midnight sky. But if I looked at her, it'd be over. I'd fight to touch her, and Ezra would pop that hook, and I'd be done.

"Some species' males are equipped with another biological miracle that improves their odds of reproduction." Fuck, Ezra even sounded gruffly sexy when lecturing like a college professor. "The Great Bear gave her male descendants a hook to maximize my mate's pleasure and keep her entertained long enough to ensure my swimmers get to their destination. But oddly enough, the hook works fucking great on guys too. Doesn't it, D?"

I didn't answer. I didn't open my eyes like he'd said. He didn't have to see my face to know I'd disobeyed him. He knew me too well to actually expect me to meekly do as he said.

"Though it's not really a hook with a pointy end," Ezra continued in that gruff, lazy voice, slowly rocking deep inside me. "It's more of a ring that flares off the head of my dick. So what's already stretching our fine purring kitty will suddenly grow and press on new territory. And won't let me pull out at all. Not until I'm done. Or nature's done."

I tried not to whimper as the memory of what that hook felt like washed over me. Heat prickled up and down my arms, making me shiver.

"There's a damned good reason there are plenty of Ursulas left in this world. My goddess sure knew what the fuck she was doing when she created us."

He pushed deep and released the hook. My back arched viciously and I pierced through my lip to keep from bellowing at the top of my lungs. Fuck. It felt like the tip of his dick suddenly blew up a hundred times larger.

And being a big, strong grizzly bear with plenty of dominance, he squeezed me down hard on that swollen dick and wouldn't let me move an inch to relieve the pressure.

I thrashed in his arms. Tore at the bedding. Strained to break his fierce grip.

"You're scaring our queen," he barked out against my ear. "She thinks you're scared, or that I'm hurting you. If she blasts me to save you, I'm going to be fucking pissed."

"Not scared," I panted, forcing my eyes open. I could only imagine what I looked like. Eyes glazed over, lips swollen, cheeks red, sweaty and frantic and twitchy. Like I'd taken a massive snort of cocaine. "Or hurt. Shara."

Staring at me, she licked her lip, showing the fangs that had descended again. It made me twitch and fight again, because I wanted those fangs in me. If she bit me, I'd at least come and he couldn't squeeze my dick any more. "You're okay?"

Ezra shifted beneath me, making me yelp and scramble frantically again, my arms windmilling desperately. I wanted something to hold onto. I lunged toward her, but he sensed my intention and dragged me back tight against him, refusing to let me get even a finger on her.

"Oh no, you don't, D. You're going to sit right here and watch her squeeze every drop of come out of our alpha. I hope and pray she'll sink those glorious fangs in me and make me come inside you. Then I'll let you go but not before."

Rik lifted his hips in a slow, circular swirl that made her eyes roll back in her head. She groaned deep in her throat and smoothed her palms over his chest and shoulders. She leaned forward, changing the angle so she could grind her clit on him. Her pleasure rose, a punishing wave that rode the fine line between too much and too fucking good that made me insane. I was right there with her, tiptoeing down that razor blade edge. So fucking good it was impossible. Too much. No one could absorb so much sensation without losing their fucking mind. It was more than I could endure, and it went on and on.

"Give me some of that kitty cat blood," Ezra murmured.

I turned my head, craning my neck so he could run his tongue in a wide swath across my jaw and chin, licking up my blood from my bleeding lip.

"You taste damned good, D. But not as good as our queen."

Fuck, yeah, nothing tasted as good as her. I wanted to agree. I wanted to tell him to wait until he had a taste of her when she was breeding. The rush of power that had flooded me every time she let me taste that dark, rich blood flowing from her pussy. I'd lick her eagerly every day and love the hell out of it...

But I'd do just about anything to get my tongue on her when she was breeding. Anything at all.

"Yeah," he whispered against my ear. "I see your head between her thighs while I'm fucking you."

Evidently she picked up on that image too because she jerked against Rik's grip, and this time, he let her go. Head back, hands braced on his stomach, she rode him hard, plunging up and down as much as she could without his help. Her pleasure rained down on our bonds, sweet and cool like the first spring rain, but quickly darkening with thunderclouds and lightning. She burned. She needed. Her fangs throbbed so hard that mine ached in sympathy, her thirst an insatiable wildfire.

I leaned toward her, eager to feel her fangs again, but Rik growled, "no," at the same time that Ezra planted a forearm between my shoulders and pushed my head down out of his way so he could offer his throat instead.

I would have bitten the crap out of him, if I could have gotten my mouth on him. She'd fed on me already, but I was still fucking pissed as hell.

He leaned on me harder, bending me in half, his weight on my back, his dick impossibly thick inside me. Stuffed and bent like a pretzel, I was starting to feel a little sympathy for Mehen after the way Rik had fucked him last night.

Her voice broke on a soft cry that made me writhe and heave, but I couldn't get free. Not even to put my mouth on her skin.

Ezra suddenly jerked beneath me and I felt her fangs sinking into his throat. I had a half second to brace, and then he exploded inside me. He roared with release, his hand clamping down on my dick so hard the last brain cell I possessed worried a second that he'd break it in half. Then I was coming too, and Shara and Rik like dominoes. Only when Rik came, he let out a deep bellow like a volcano had gone off inside him. His body jerked so hard that the bed shook and thudded against the wall, spurt after spurt emptying into our queen. Her body drank him down as eagerly as she sucked blood from Ezra's throat. Gulp after gulp after gulp.

When he started to sag toward her, I finally worked free of

him and cuddled around her waist, easing her off Rik and down to the mattress.

Our alpha was sweaty and barely conscious, his chest still heaving for air after such a mighty climax. His instincts still drove him hard. Protect the queen at all costs. He tried to roll toward her, but he could barely lift her arm.

:It's all right,: I whispered for him alone. *:We've got her. Rest.:*

:She.: His eyes flickered, his mighty muscles slowly sagging into the bed. *:Hungers.:*

:I've got her,: Ezra whispered in our bond. *:With my bulk, I can tide her over until Mehen and Xin come.:*

We shifted her down between us, Ezra's throat still in her mouth. I pressed against her back and did what I did best.

I purred. Slow and deep and steady. While she fed so long that even the mighty grizzly sagged unconscious in her arms. She made a soft sound of disappointment, but her bond felt relaxed and sleepy. I kept up that steady purring, easing her to sleep. She needed as much rest as she could get in between feedings. It'd help her strength return.

Now that I was back in her bed, I wasn't ever fucking leaving again.

17

SHARA

I wasn't sure who came and went the first few hours. Daire picked me up at one point and they changed the sheets on the bed. I was too sleepy to look, but I figured after I'd fed and fucked so many of them, the entire room probably would have glowed like a nuclear detonation.

Rik pressed a glass to my mouth and I drank it all. Then I drank from Mehen and Xin while Daire and Rik wolfed down some sandwiches. Rik tried to make me eat one too, but I didn't want food.

I had what I needed.

They all fed me again in the wee hours of the morning. It was a strange feeling, this hunger. It tormented me in my sleep, but I was too tired to even consider sex or biting one of them. I kept wandering in my dreams, searching for one of my Blood, my fangs throbbing. It was horrible. Like dreaming about trying to find a bathroom all night, only to finally wake up and realize your bladder was about to explode.

I woke again when they switched guard rotations. It felt painfully early and my body was still heavy and sluggish, but I made myself get up.

I had too much to do to lie around in bed all day. Though Rik glared at me as I shambled around the room, trying to find my other shoe. That I was already carrying in my hand.

"Even you are not invincible. The stronger you are, the more energy you expend, and you've completely depleted your reserves. You need to rest and feed and rest some more."

"I will," I insisted, holding on to Daire's shoulders as he helped me pull on a pair of jeans. "But I've got to learn as much as I can about court life before this trip."

"Etiquette lessons won't help anyone if you're falling down into a faint because you're too weak."

Goddess, he was so sexy standing there, frowning so fiercely. My big protective alpha. He'd completely depleted his reserves last night, too. All inside me. I could still feel the hot splash of his semen deep inside me. Maybe he was right. If I took him back to bed…

My stomach growled and that decided it for him. "We'll get you some breakfast and talk with Gina for an hour. Max. Then you really should take a nice long nap if you can."

"Deal. And a bath, if we can find a tub big enough."

He tugged on some pants and then tucked my arm through his. "I'm sure we can find something big enough for at least two."

I barely recognized my own property when we stepped outside. A massive oak tree with sweeping branches sat just off the path to the main house. Roots had pushed up through the ground in places and though the branches didn't have many leaves, I could easily imagine the shade in the summer. The bare limbs were heavy with a large murder of crows. Nevarre's friends, I guessed. "Good morning," I said to them with a nod. I didn't know if they could understand me, but what would it hurt? "Thank you for your help last night. I hope you enjoyed the feast."

One of them opened its wings and hopped off the branch to glide down toward me. I didn't move or duck, but it did freak me out a little. I'd seen what these birds were capable of and I didn't care to have my eyes gouged out…

But the crow settled on my shoulder and squawked.

"Hello."

It hopped up my shoulder, closer to my head, but I didn't get any bad vibes from it. Its talons tangled up in my hair and then it nestled in close to my neck. "Aw, look. I made a friend."

Daire snorted. "Wait until it craps all down your back."

The bird on my shoulder didn't move or make a sound, but half a dozen up in the tree suddenly dive-bombed at Daire. Wings flapping, talons reaching for his hair. He waved his arms around and yelled until they settled back on the branch above, but he kept a wary eye on them.

The crow on my shoulder was surprisingly heavy. Its talons dug into my shoulder, though it made a low chirp and rustled its wings in apology.

:Nevarre, can you talk to the birds?:

:On my way, my queen.:

I hadn't meant to order him back from his duty, but I was interested in what the crows had to say. Or what they wanted, if anything. They were on my property now, in my nest, and after they'd helped me, I felt responsible for them. If they were hungry… I needed to know what kind of bird seed they'd eat.

As we reached the back door, Nevarre swooped down still in his gigantic raven form. He cocked his head to the side, lifted a wing, then the other. His tail feathers flipped up, down, in a complicated greeting. Or maybe that was their language. I wasn't really sure.

:She's the equivalent of their queen.: Nevarre finally replied in our bond. *:She likes you.:*

"Aw, I like you too." Gingerly, I reached up with my hand, not wanting to frighten her. I stroked my index finger over her wing and she made that soft chirp again. "Are they hungry? Do they need us to build birdhouses or anything?"

:They're not hungry and appreciate the offer of a house, but they much

prefer their own nests. They're building new ones now. She will swear her clan to you in exchange for a token.:

I'd always heard that crows liked sparkly and shiny things. I didn't have much in my bag that might interest her, other than my pocket knife, and I didn't want to give that up. Though I would if that was what she wanted.

:All she wants is some of your hair to line her nest. She believes it will protect her eggs and help her hatch healthy babies in the spring.:

"Of course. She can have some hair."

He cawed a fairly long bird sentence and she sprung up into the air, the sudden flap of her wings startling me. She yanked out a few strands of hair and flew back up into the tree.

"Hey," Daire yelled after her. "You hurt her!"

"It's all right." I rubbed the stinging spot in my scalp. "I told her she could. Let's eat. I'm starving."

As if he heard me coming, Winston opened the door. "That's music to my ears, Your Majesty. I'm glad to see you up and about so early today. I'm hoping that means you're recovering from your ordeal quickly?"

"He'd be better off asking if *we've* recovered from helping her recover," Erza muttered. Daire poked him in the ribs. "What? We all gave her blood twice already. I've never seen a queen drink from seven able-bodied Blood twice and still need more."

:You've never seen a queen build Morrigan's grove before either.: Nevarre didn't sound angry in the bond, but the raven hopped toward the big man and flashed his pointed beak. It reminded me of the way Guillaume always had a blade ready in his palm when he needed to flash a threat. *:My mother had a dozen Blood and she barely survived. You arrived after our queen's suffering. So count yourself lucky you only felt a fraction of what she endured.:*

"Even more impressive, this is America," Mehen said with a sour twist of his lips. "A land so far removed from Celtic magic, that they can't even say it correctly and named a basketball team after them. There are barely any ley lines to pull from, and certainly no Stonehenge or standing stones of any significance. This was all blood. All Shara. And if she needs to drain us all three or four times a day, then I'm game."

Ezra huffed. "I wasn't complaining."

Mehen snorted but thankfully let it go. These two were going to drive me nuts if they didn't stop harping at each other like two old men, fighting over their prized secret fishing hole.

"I'm moving a bit slowly this morning," I told Winston as we entered. "But I'm grateful to be up. Is Gina here yet?"

"She's on her way," Winston replied. "She called a few minutes ago. She's bringing some pastries and fresh bread from a bakery in town."

My stomach rumbled as loudly as Rik's rock troll and Ezra's grouchy bear combined. Rik hustled me to the table and Daire brought me a cup of coffee while Winston started pulling food out of the fridge. "Sorry to drop in on you so early today."

"Not a problem at all, Your Majesty. We'll always have plenty of prepared food for your Blood, even if it's just sandwiches."

"These sandwiches fucking rock," Daire said around a mouthful. "I should know. I'm the sandwich king."

"Knock, knock," Gina called from the front door as she came inside. "I'm glad I stopped for some more of those chocolate croissants."

Rik set a bowl of fruit salad before me and I stared at it a moment, my eyes burning. It was the same as yesterday... except Winston had removed the cantaloupe. He'd noticed how I'd picked all them out yesterday and immediately adjusted it. I flashed a wobbly smile at him and picked up my fork as Gina set a croissant by my cup. "You guys. Thank you."

Winston bowed slightly, his cheeks pink and eyes sparkling. "Our pleasure, Your Majesty."

"Shara."

"Of course, Shara, Your Majesty."

"Give up," Gina patted my arm as she sat down beside me,

her leather satchel bulging with all the things she needed to go over with me. "He's a stickler for propriety. Most Brits are."

"I thought of a whole list of things I wanted to ask you last night. Hopefully I can remember everything."

"We have plenty of time."

Anxiety tightened my stomach despite the delicious breakfast. "Not really. Not considering how much I don't know."

"Again, don't worry about all the formalities. Zaniyah's court won't be nearly as formal as Skye's, let alone the Triune. Look at this as practice. She's inviting you, and she's not known for that. She's the one who needs to impress you."

We spent two hours going over general Aima formalities. A queen rarely ever did anything herself, and it took skill to read through all the intentions and meanings behind something as simple as who sat by whom at the table, or who came to greet us at the airport. The more I learned, the more I realized how much Keisha Skye had insulted me when she'd sent such a low Blood to me. She'd completely misjudged my strength, for one thing, and she'd compounded that mistake by sending someone so weak on Skye's prominence ladder to represent her entire court's interests to a new queen.

It was a major lesson for me when I thought about my Blood and how I would send them, if needed, to communicate with another queen. I would have considered only their personalities. Like it'd be stupid to send Ezra on a political mission. He'd only piss everyone off and end up causing a war. So would Mehen. But worse, Mehen was known for his destruction and hatred. So if a queen saw him innocently standing outside her nest…

She would assume I meant to raze her court to the ground.

And if Guillaume went…

Her Blood would react like Rik had the first time Guillaume walked into my house in Kansas City. He'd be sweating, expecting his head to roll.

Even more care would be going into the seating arrangements on Zaniyah's side.

"I've already sent a brief listing of our party, including each Blood's name," Gina said, her brow crinkling. "I hope that was all right?"

It made me a little twitchy to know the complete list was in another queen's hands. They had to know about Guillaume now after that television footage, but did they know about Leviathan, king of the depths? Or Xin? All Zaniyah's consiliarius had to do was pick up a phone and call the Triune. "I trust your judgment."

"It's polite to do so, but not required from a guest. Our list lets them plan better, but negates your ability to surprise them with who's on your Blood already. I thought it would establish open communications up front if we exchanged our full list without any secrets, so they can fully prepare for your arrival."

I could see how showing up with Mehen in tow without preparing them might cause a bit of a scramble. Incredibly old and powerful, he'd be hard to match up with another Blood, unless Zaniyah had a few secrets of her own.

"She will have secrets," Gina agreed. "No one knows much about Zaniyah. She's worked hard to remain cooperative to an extent—but completely unknown. She might be significantly more powerful than anyone's giving her credit for. She may have a hundred Blood for all we know."

"Or an equally old and pissed off Blood like Leviathan," Daire added, winking at Mehen, who stood glaring at the room in general.

"Maybe I should fly over for a reconnaissance mission," he said.

Gina winced and shook her head. "That would be highly rude and suspicious of us."

"And your point is…?"

"Do we even have a map of her nest?" Rik asked, giving a quelling look at the older Blood. "We should have our own exit strategy in place in case things go south."

He and Guillaume studied the maps Gina spread out on the

table. "Nothing of her direct court, but we have the general area."

By the time they were done asking for emergency cars stationed down the road and horses in case we had to go cross country, my eyes were getting heavy. I forced them open, surprised to find Mehen carrying me with Xin and Daire on either side. "Where…"

"Shhh." Still holding me, he lay down in front of the fireplace on a bunch of pillows and blankets someone had tossed on the floor. A warm, cheery fire crackled in the stone hearth. With Xin's arm around my back and Daire cuddled against Mehen's side so I could feel his purr, I drifted off to sleep on my dragon's chest.

18

SHARA

My days of planning flew by too quickly, probably because Rik insisted I sleep most of it away in order to rebuild my reserves. The day before New Year's Eve, we were on the jet headed to Mexico City, with a quick shopping trip in downtown Dallas. I didn't even know the names of the small yet luxurious shops, but Gina had paid them enough to shut down the entire building just for us. We had access to designer everything, at insane prices that made my eyes bug out of my head. So Gina refused to even let me look at the tags any longer.

I'd never cared about having much money, as long as I had a safe place to hide from the monsters and enough to eat.

But seeing what the Isador wealth could do for my Blood...

I was very grateful for my immense legacy, because I'd never seen anything finer in my life than my seven men dressed in black-tie formal wear. A small army of tailors swarmed over the guys, pinning and measuring, nipping and tucking, until sleek black pants and jackets hugged their impressive bodies perfectly. Each of them picked out a slightly different style, but stuck to simple black and white. Mehen and Nevarre both chose tails, though Nevarre refused to exchange his kilt for pants. The tailors even managed to get Rik's impressive tree-trunk thighs and massive biceps encased in a slick double-breasted suit that made me drool.

While the tailors sewed the adjustments to the guys' suits, it was my turn.

At first, it was chaos, because all of them but Rik wanted to pick out the winning dress. I'd never seen so many guys dragging formal gowns up and down the aisles, yelling jokes at each other. When Mehen and Daire somehow made it a competition to see who could pick out the raciest dress, Gina put her foot down. "This is getting us nowhere. They're overwhelming you with too many options, and ninety-nine percent of their selections are inappropriate."

She might be human, but my consiliarius knew how to throw her weight of position around. With Rik's help, of course. He snapped his fingers and gave an alpha tug on the bonds, and all the guys turned at once to look at him.

"Sit down," Gina pointed at the chairs and ottomans scattered throughout the dressing area, and they did, at once.

She turned to the woman who'd welcomed us to the store. "Shara, this is Alice Wong, owner and designer. We're looking for something for several very important dinners, but one specific gown to make an impression, without making the other guests feel as though she's trying too hard. Red-carpet worthy, but we don't need to stop traffic completely." Gina winked at me. "That kind of dress will be used another day."

She didn't have to say it. I'd need a traffic-stopping dress if I ever had to make a Triune appearance. My stomach clenched with dread at the thought.

Walking around me in a slow circle, Alice asked, "Short or long?"

"I don't really have a preference."

"Your favorite color?"

I had to think about it. It'd been so long since I'd stopped to think about something as trivial as color when I had to fight for my survival every minute of the day. I wasn't a child any longer, but even as a kid, the pretty pink room and frilly dresses hadn't been my kind of thing. Dad had decorated a room in our house for me, and I'm sure it'd broken his heart when I couldn't sleep in there with all those windows. Not with monsters outside. "I don't really have a favorite color. I like all colors."

"Try this," Alice said, her voice a gentle, soothing lilt. "Close your eyes. Picture being happy. Glowingly happy. You can't remember a time when you felt so beautiful."

I did as she asked. Immediately, I was in the grove, staring up at the full moon. The ancient trees whispered around me, dancing and swaying in a gentle breeze. But instead of my house, I saw Isis's pyramid in the center.

"What colors do you see?"

"Not color, really. Moonlight. Shadows. It's dark, nighttime."

"Very good. You can open your eyes now."

I did, and Alice smiled at both me and Gina. "I have a particular gown in mind. I'll be right back."

"She should have more than one," Rik said with a scowl.

"I completely agree," Gina replied, giving me a wicked smile that made my brows arch with surprise. "This is the most important one, which is why I asked for Alice. Her associates are already pulling other outfits from the racks for our approval and will be here shortly."

I groaned. Great. More trying things on.

"Alice took one look at you and knew your sizes and body shape. There should be very little trying on, unless you want to, of course. They'll present the racks and you simply select what you like."

"Or we can nod and take the whole store," Daire added. "That's my vote."

"I don't need the whole store. Where would I wear even a fraction of this?"

"I don't mean to frighten you…" Guillaume said softly, drawing my gaze to him. "But your star is rising fast. Mayte is only the first queen to approach you for assistance or protection. Soon enough, all the queens will know of Shara Isador. The invitations and requests will stack up quicker than Gina's entire team can sort them."

"And then there's the Triune," Mehen said with a grim scowl. "Eventually they'll demand your presence."

My eyes narrowed. I didn't like that word. *Demand.* Let them try and make me do anything or go anywhere I didn't want.

"A Triune audience gown makes everything in this store look like something you'd wear to a picnic," Gina admitted. "Which is one reason I wanted you to meet Alice and see if you like her designs. If so, we'll commission her to make you a formal presentation gown."

Formal presentation. Just the thought made me itchy, like I was breaking out in hives. "What if I refuse?"

Everybody stared at me, jaws dropping, eyes widening in horror.

"You can't refuse the Triune," Gina finally said.

"Why not?"

"They have ultimate power over all Aima. If the sitting queens take a vote to execute you, it's done. No trial, no excuses, no chance to explain your side of the situation. You, your Blood, and all your court will be put to the sword."

I shivered, hugging myself. Rik made a low rumble and came to me, wrapping his arms around me and pressing his solid heat against my back, but I still felt chilled, deep inside. "The nest wouldn't protect us?"

"For a time," Guillaume said, staring down at his broad, scarred hands. It made me think about his years as Desideria's executioner. How many queens—and their Blood—he must have killed over the centuries. "I've heard the formal order go out for execution, though it's been years, before Desideria died. It's hard to keep everyone inside a nest indefinitely, especially in this day and age. No one's self-sufficient any longer. Eventually the nest will run out of food or water. Or they'll let someone in who's in danger, or who promises to help, and they're betrayed. Or, more often than not, the queen will negotiate with the Triune to allow her court to live if she surrenders peacefully."

I tried to imagine what would happen to us if the order came down from the Triune to execute House Isador. Rage bubbled up inside me, a dark shadowy miasma that burned like acid. I didn't know how I'd protect everyone, but I would. I'd find a way.

And if I couldn't...

:We would never allow you to sacrifice yourself for us,: Rik whispered, though his whisper cut like razor-sharp steel. *:Never. If you die, we die. I refuse to live without you.:*

Alice stepped back into the dressing area with a long linen bag draped over her arm, but she hesitated a moment, sensing the dark mood in the room. "Everything all right?"

I forced a smile. "Yes. We were just discussing the possibility of someday needing an even grander gown than anything you may have in the store."

Her eyes brightened and she gave me a wide, charming smile. "Now that sounds like quite the challenge."

"Let's see this gown first," Gina said.

Alice used a small stepladder to hang the bag on a hook high enough the dress wouldn't touch the floor. She unzipped the bag and carefully pulled the linen back to reveal the gown.

The skirt was long and full, made out of some kind of flowy material that drifted in the air like a cloud. The bodice looked fairly simple in a traditional corset princess style. It didn't have any jewels or ruffles or sparkles. What made it unique was the dyed ombre effect, from a dark midnight purple on the bodice that slowly faded to lavender-gray and silvery white at the very bottom.

Alice lifted the skirt and let it flutter back down, showing how it would move as I walked. "What do you think? I call it *Midnight Sonata*."

"It's incredible," I answered, looking to Gina. "What do you think? Is this fancy enough?"

"With the appropriate jewels, yes, I think this will work." With her arms crossed, Gina studied the dress a moment, drumming her fingers on her elbow. "Yes, I think I brought that set. Let me have Angela bring the case in so you can try it on together."

"Wait, you brought jewelry? Not even knowing what gown we'd end up with?"

Gina gave me a smug nod and said on the phone, "Could you bring in the red velvet case and the other I showed you in from the trunk, please. Yes. Thanks."

Nevarre stood. "By your leave, my queen, I'll walk her in."

I nodded and he immediately headed for the limousine. I was still trying to figure out how Gina had brought down a bunch of jewels. The last I'd heard, all the Isador jewels were locked in a safe in Kansas City. Even if she'd stashed them on the jet, we'd only rented the car. Maybe that was why Angela had stayed in the car instead of coming inside with us. She'd been guarding the jewelry that I hadn't even known about.

"It's my job to think ahead and plan out everything to the last detail," Gina reminded me. "As soon as you made the move from Kansas City, I had a majority of the jewelry transferred nearby so we can access it at a moment's notice. Angela's sole job on this trip is to keep track of your jewels and make sure they're secure."

"Should I always have one of the Blood help her guard them?"

"It's up to you, but really not necessary. Angela is armed and is more than capable of dealing with anyone thinking to steal them."

Dressed in a navy suit and elegant heels, Angela walked in with Nevarre, a large red-velvet case in one hand and a larger black case in her other. I glanced over her, trying to see where she'd hidden the gun, but it wasn't obvious to my untrained eyes.

:She's carrying a semi-automatic weapon in the small of her back in the waistband of her skirt.: Guillaume said.

:How do you know?:

His face didn't move, but I felt him grin in the bond. *:I can smell it.:*

"If you'll step behind the curtain, I'll help you into the gown," Alice offered. "The corset bodice can be difficult alone."

"Gina, can you help too? That way you'll know how to get me into it for dinner tonight."

"Of course."

We stepped behind the large dressing curtain and my mouth fell open. A huge selection of underthings were laid out on shelves. All varieties of panties, from thongs to full-coverage briefs. Dozens of different kinds of bras. Garters and stockings. The lower shelves contained glorious shoes of all types, from break-my-neck stilettos to dance-all-night flats.

Wow. I'd seen stuff like this advertised before, but had never really pictured myself wearing it. But yeah, I couldn't wait to try some of these elegant things on. Even more, I couldn't wait to see the guys' reaction to seeing me in such finery. Though I'm sure they'd rather see me in nothing at all.

:You know it,: Rik rumbled.

Alice hung the gown reversed, so she could start loosening the ties. The bodice really was a corset, not just made to look like one. "This particular gown has plenty of support built into it, but a woman can't have too many pretty things to wear."

I could barely remember a time where I owned more than one bra at a time, and certainly never anything as fancy as these. Before I could change my mind, I said, "I'll take them all."

"Perfect," Gina said. "That's what I hoped you'd say."

While Alice showed her the best way to loosen and tighten the corset, I stripped down to my skin and then pulled on a pair of barely-there white lace panties. Then they carefully dropped the skirt over my head and pulled the bodice down.

I watched in the mirror while they tightened the corset back up.

"She already has a lovely shape, so I wouldn't recommend tightening it too much. Especially if she's going to be eating or dancing at all. The boning is incredibly strong and will make it difficult to breathe."

The corset was heavy and snug, but it felt really good. The midnight purple velvet made my eyes shine like jewels. The skirt fluttered about my legs, floating effortlessly about me.

"I have some light crinoline you can add underneath for more volume if desired."

Even more volume? "Actually, yeah, I'd like to see what that looks like."

"Of course. I'll be right back."

I twirled in the mirror, loving the way the color flowed from dark to light. *Midnight Sonata* was a beautiful name and suited the gown perfectly. The play of dark and light reminded me of midnight and moonlight, and I loved the way the colors bled together.

Alice stepped back in and helped me step into a crinoline slip that poofed out the dress even more, but was still light enough to twirl and sway gently when I moved. "Yes. I love it. What do you think, Gina?"

"Agreed. It's perfect for this occasion. Beautiful and graceful, but not over the top. What do you recommend for shoes?"

Alice stepped closer to the wall, eying the lower shelves of heels and flats. "Is there going to be dancing?"

"I don't believe so, but there's a formal procession, so she'll be on her feet for a while."

"How well do you walk in heels?"

I grimaced. "I can do short distances, but I've never worn them much."

"Then I recommend something like these." She offered a

pair of purple flats that truly looked like ballet slippers, complete with purple ribbons that would wrap around my ankles. "These are incredibly comfortable, and the unique style and color is sure to draw interest."

I tried them on, and had to agree. The ties around my ankles were super cute, and the color matched the middle shade of purple perfectly.

Gina stepped back in with the red velvet case. "Now let's add the jewels and you can twirl for the guys."

When she popped it open, I gasped. I couldn't help it. I'd never seen so many jewels in one place in my entire life. I didn't even know what kind of stones they were. Dark purple, almost as dark as the bodice of the gown, several of them so large they didn't even look real. Diamonds interlaced throughout the stones, adding to the sparkle.

I wasn't the only one impressed. Alice's eyes were as stunned as mine. She looked at the jewels and then me, a speculative look flickering across her face. She was wondering if I was famous. An actress, maybe, or some minor royal. I hoped we could trust her. Just because she designed fantastic gowns didn't mean she wouldn't secretly take a few pictures of me and sell them to a tabloid. If the Triune came asking for information....

"These have been in the Isador legacy for centuries." Gina lifted the necklace from the case. "Just waiting for you to pick out a purple dress."

The necklace was heavy and cold around my neck. Oh. My. Vanity. The jewels looked incredible. Maybe it was my imagination, but the stones seemed to catch the light and spin purple rays into the air around me. The diamonds glittered even more, sparkling like crazy. Attuned to my body, they seemed to glow with my magic simply because they touched my skin.

"Earrings," Gina lifted them out. "Clip-on, since they're so heavy."

Wow, yeah, super heavy. They caught fire and glowed like

purple stars beneath my hair. I tucked the long strands back to admire the earrings more.

"That'll be next," Gina said mysteriously. "Let's go see what your men say."

They already knew what I looked like in the dress. They liked it, a lot, if the bubbling volcano in our bonds was any indication.

Taking a deep breath, I stepped out from the behind the curtain.

Gathered in a ring before me, my Blood went down to their knees as one. "Your Majesty, Shara Isador. Long live our queen."

RIK

I KNEW my queen was powerful, beautiful, sexy, confident, gracious, and kind to a fault—as long as you didn't threaten someone she cared about.

But seeing evidence of her royalty...

It felt like Guillaume's hell horse had kicked me in the chest with both rear hooves, while Daire had jerked the rug out from under me.

On my knees, I could only stare up at her, and praise every goddess who'd had a hand in creating her in this world, and allowing me to serve at her side.

Gina motioned to someone behind us—another sign of how shell shocked we were by our queen's magnificence, that another approached without our knowledge. Luckily, it was several women who then swarmed upon Shara with brushes and clips and cosmetics.

"Not too much makeup," Gina warned. "Emphasize her eyes and lips, but her face should look natural and flawless."

"Her skin already glows," one of the women said. "I've never seen anything quite like it."

155

Because she had never seen a born Aima queen full
of power.

They twisted and tucked Shara's long hair into a loose pile
of curls on top of her head that managed to look messy and
completely natural, while baring her throat and letting the
jewels sparkle.

"Now, the crown," Gina said.

Shara's head whipped around. "What *crown?*"

"You're the queen of Isador. Of course there's a crown.
Several, in fact. But since you're the last Isador queen, you're
entitled to wear Isis's crown."

Turning a large square case away from her, Angela opened it
and Gina reached inside, pulling out a heavy golden crown with
sweeping horns holding a red disk in the center.

"I saw Her wearing that," Shara whispered. "I can't… I
mean, it's…" She swallowed, her eyes gleaming with unshed
tears. "It's Hers. I'm not…"

"She gave this to Her line," Gina insisted, holding the crown
reverently. "I brought the other crown She also wore, if you'd
rather see it. It looks more like a throne. This one…" She hesitated, her eyes hardening, her mouth firming to a hard slant. "I
know the red may clash, but it's the sun. After *his* attack on you,
I thought you'd want to wear the crown that shows the sun is
Her glory. Not his."

Ah, Shara liked that thought. Her chin tipped up and she
nodded. Gina stepped behind her and carefully set the crown on
her head, adjusting her hair so that the heavy gold was cush-
ioned and balanced on her head.

She already glowed with power and beauty, a goddess
incarnate.

But with that crown on her head…

I, Isis, am all that has been and is and shall be.

If I'd still been standing, I would have fallen to my knees.
How could any man stand before such power? Daire took it one
step more and stretched out on his stomach, neck straining to

keep his eyes on her. Guillaume followed suit, and I remembered how he'd lain face down on the floor when he first saw her. Nevarre and Xin went next, easily, but Mehen and Ezra stared at each other a moment, daring the other to go first, and then both lowered to their stomachs at the same time, smoothly, as one.

She looked at me, her eyes wide, her mouth opening to tell me no, it wasn't necessary to show such submission before her glory. Holding her gaze, I leaned forward, palms on the ground, and lowered myself slowly to the ground.

Her lips quivered. Shaken, as if she'd never really understood her power over us until this very moment, she lifted her arm and tore her wrist open.

Gina gasped. "Don't get blood on the dress!"

Actually, I thought the dress would look better with her blood splashed down its front. I could see it perfectly: a sleek white gown that hugged her shape, with red dribbled and splashed down the bodice and skirt with our queen's blood.

Our goddess's blood.

She came to me first and offered her wrist. I rose enough to cradle her hand to my mouth, licking the blood from her skin.

A few drops hit the marble tile, and Daire scooted closer to lick the floor clean. At her shocked dismay, he started purring. *:We can't leave your blood in public like this. Thralls will tear down the walls of this building to taste even a drop. I certainly don't mind. I'll walk behind you and lick up every drop that hits the floor if you'd allow me:*

I called Guillaume to her next, and the rest of her Blood one by one in the order they'd dropped to their bellies for her. Mehen and Ezra were last, and I was tempted to make them share her blood at the same time to teach them to get along.

Mehen managed to surprise me. He jerked his head at Ezra. "You go first."

The big man didn't wait for him to change his mind and dove in to lock his lips to our queen's wrist.

Mehen noticed my arched brow and laughed a little sheepishly. "If I go last, I get to lick the wound shut. That's worth letting the bear go next."

:*Fuck me,:* Ezra muttered. *:I never thought of that.:*

"Um…" Alice swayed slightly, her face pale.

Shara looked at me, her eyes flaring. *:I forgot humans were watching.:*

"It's a very old blood oath ceremony, where knights of old swore fealty to their queen," Gina said briskly. "Could we see the rest of the wardrobe you've selected for her?"

The promise of more sales seemed to shake the woman out of her stupor. She turned to her associates and they scurried around to haul in several racks of clothes Shara offered her wrist to Mehen and he took several swallows before sealing the wound with a firm swipe of his tongue.

I pushed to my feet, but hesitated to touch her. A glowing aura of power hung around her, light spinning from the jewels and the crown, but especially her eyes. Adding her blood had only enhanced her otherworldly appearance. No mortal man lifted Isis's veil or would dare to touch Her. I wasn't human, but I wasn't immortal either. Right now, she carried the kind of goddess-level power that would blast a man to kingdom come for even thinking about laying a finger on her magnificence.

Shara laid her hand on my forearm. Her fingers trembled, her bond achingly fragile. Not scared exactly, but overwhelmed by everything happening to her. She needed her rock. She needed me. So I closed my other hand over hers and stepped closer, offering my heat, strength, and protection. Always. And, most especially, my heart.

19

SHARA

The rest of the trip to Mexico City passed too quickly for my nerves. It seemed like I blinked and we were all dressed in our new gorgeous clothes and back on the plane. Another blink, and we were in Mexico and changing to another car, this one a long black Hummer, thankfully air conditioned. I didn't want the makeup sweating off of me before I even met Mayte.

I was going to meet another queen. My nerves were so jittery, I kept accidentally kicking Rik or Daire on either side of me. Even his non-stop purring against my side didn't help.

"What if I screw this up?" I whispered to no one in particular. "If I forget her name? Or how to greet her? What am I supposed to say again?"

Gina reached across Daire and gave my knee a firm squeeze. "Honestly, it doesn't matter. Be gracious and polite. She's performing for you. She wants *your* aid."

"But we don't know that for sure."

"We do," Gina said firmly. "There's no other reason for her to offer her nest to you. She wants your help. Desperately."

"But what if I insult her accidentally?"

"As long as you don't feed on one of her Blood without her permission, you won't insult her."

That made me shudder and press harder against Rik. He had his arm around my shoulders, so he pulled me in closer so I was practically on his lap, with Daire draped mostly on top of me. "I don't want to feed on any of her people. That won't be a problem." Guillaume made a low noise, drawing my attention to him. "What?"

"Not to confuse the matter, or worsen your anxiety, but she may very well offer one of her court to you as a sign of good faith. If she offers one of her Blood, or one of her direct family, it would be an insult to refuse."

My mouth hung open for a moment. "I'm not feeding on anyone but my Blood. Period."

"But if she wants to swear to you, and you accept, you must taste her blood. She'll offer formal throat to you."

I swallowed hard, trying to settle my stomach. It felt like Nevarre's raven crashed around deep in my stomach with all his friends. Deep down, I knew that I'd have to feed on her. I just hadn't pictured exactly how that would work in my head. I had a feeling it wouldn't be a few swallows, like when I'd given Gina some of my blood to bind her to me as my human servant.

"Before her entire court," Mehen added, not so helpfully, because I groaned and buried my face in my hands. Rik growled at him. "What? It's an honor that her court must witness. They need to see their queen on her knees before you. Her throat bared to you. How you take her will determine how they view you going forward. If you're timid, they'll assume you're weak. If you treat her badly or roughly, they may be angry, but many of them will be afraid to cross you for fear of what you'd do to them. It's a chance for you to teach them a lesson, without touching anyone but their queen."

Guillaume grunted. "We Aima like to read significance into every little touch or gesture."

"Which is why I'm so fucking scared I'm going to make a mistake."

"You're incapable of making a mistake," Rik said firmly, giving my shoulders a good squeeze. He gave each Blood a firm glare for good measure. "Stay true to yourself and act as your heart directs you, and all will be well. Your goddess walks in you. She won't allow you to make any mistakes."

We rode in silence for a few minutes and suddenly, I felt my first queen's nearness. Or rather, her nest.

The air resonated, humming with energy. As we drove closer, the ringing echoed in my ears, making my fangs ache. It wasn't unpleasant—but I had the sense that she could make it hurt very much if she wanted to. The car slowed and finally stopped. The air quivered with so much energy I knew exactly where the blood circle lay.

"We must walk into the nest," Gina said. "Let's see who she sent to greet us and bring us through. That'll tell us a lot about how this meeting will go."

With the car still running, someone approached and opened the car door on my right. Rik sent quick orders through the bond. :*Mehen, then Guillaume, Nevarre, Daire, Ezra, Xin, stay visible. Don't give them a reason to doubt our intentions. Form lines on either side of the road. We'll walk to the boundary with our queen inside.*:

Mehen met my gaze, his emerald eyes flashing with excitement. "Will you free my beast? In case I need to fly you out?"

:*He makes a good point,*: Rik admitted. :*If you're under attack, I'd rather you not have to stop and worry about freeing his dragon. I want him to shift and get you out as quickly as possible.*:

I pulled back the shining leash of magic from Leviathan's neck and Mehen shivered, his dragon bulging outward a moment with a shadow of wings and gleaming claws, before settling down into his body. "Don't kill anyone. Unless, you know, we have to."

He inclined his head with a sardonic wink as he climbed out

of the car. "I'll do my best. But no promises if the bear pisses me off."

One by one, the rest of my Blood stepped out of the car. Gina gave my hand one last squeeze. "It's going to be fine. We're with you every step of the way."

Then it was just Rik and me left in the car. He lifted my hand to his mouth and kissed my knuckles. "I'll never allow anyone to harm you."

"I know." I took a deep breath, held it for a few seconds, and then slowly released it. "I'm not worried about me. I'm afraid I'll offend someone, and we'll be trapped inside."

He turned my hand over, his thumb rubbing gentle circles against my palm, where he pressed a kiss and closed my fingers over it. "Offend them. It won't matter. You're the fucking queen of Isador, and they won't lay a finger on you. But I know you too well to fear that you'll offend anyone, my queen. All will be well."

"Promise?"

He winked at me and slid out of the seat toward the door. "You know it. Wait for me to offer you my hand before you get out."

I pictured him being all mean, bad alpha, glaring at all the people who might be standing around waiting for me to get out of the car. It made my mouth quirk and my nerves settled a little. His hand came down outside the door, and I slipped my fingers into his, sliding toward the door.

Warm air wafted over my face as I stood. I glanced up at the sky first, afraid to see how many people were watching. It wasn't dark yet, but the sun was slipping below the horizon with a glorious explosion of color. I didn't see the moon, but one large, bright star winked at me in the sky.

Rik tucked my hand beneath his arm, his fingers firm and confident on mine. His biceps bulged beneath my hand, his rock troll hovering beneath his skin. Ready to defend me at a moment's notice. Gina gave me an encouraging smile and then turned, leading us down a white-graveled driveway. Stone pillars framed a wide iron gate that opened into the property. As we neared the blood circle, my scalp crawled, my nerves humming with tension. I couldn't see the boundary with my eyes, but fine hairs rose on my arms, quivering like an electric fence was powering up, ready to zap me.

Mehen and Guillaume stood on either side of the pillar, just inside the low stone wall. That must be the very edge. On the other side of the gate, a small group of people waited for us, but I could sense many more on either side, deeper into the property. My heart pounded as Gina paused in front of the gate. She fucking curtsied, and a sudden surge of panic rolled through me. We didn't cover curtsies or bows or—

:Because my queen fucking bows to no one.: Rik growled. *:Not even the Triune.:*

"Welcome, House Isador," a woman said, her low, sweet voice carrying through the night. She was shorter than me with bombshell curves, dressed in a sparkly pink gown that hugged her body. Another woman stood beside her, tall and slender in a white gown. "I'm Mayte Zaniyah, and I welcome you to my nest. Please, be at rest in Valle de Zaniyah."

The queen herself, welcoming us? That seemed unlikely to me, especially for older Aima well used to playing court politics. I glanced at Gina, and her eyes flashed wide with surprise too, her bond shimmering with excitement. She took it as an extreme honor. "Thank you, Your Majesty. We were honored to receive your invitation. I'm consiliarius, Gina Isador."

Mayte inclined her head slightly, a smile curving her lips. "Please, no formality among friends. This is my consiliarius, Bianca."

"Mayte. Bianca." Gina inclined her head to both of them, and then turned to me, inclining her head even more. "May I introduce my queen, Shara Isador."

Mayte's gaze locked on me, and though she smiled and inclined her head, her luminous eyes tugged on me. Frantic, almost. Scared. Worried. Not because of *me*, though, and it finally dawned on me. She was just as terrified of making a mistake as I was.

Relief washed over me and tension melted away. I smiled and mirrored her movements as closely as possible to convey equal respect. "It's an honor to meet you."

Holding my gaze, she offered her hand, and though I couldn't see it, I knew her hand must have slid through the invisible barrier.

I started to let go of Rik's arm to take her hand, but he clutched me hard. "Not until your Blood are through."

Mayte didn't withdraw her hand, and again, I felt an overwhelming sense of urgency from her. Like she was afraid if she didn't get me inside, it might be too late. I listened with all my senses, trying to find anything amiss. Hopefully my magic would warn me if there was a trap of some kind awaiting us.

"Of course, please allow me to introduce you to my Blood," Mayte said. "My alpha, Eztli, along with Diego, Luis, and Maxtla."

The four men stepped forward, and though Rik didn't move a muscle, his bond vibrated with intensity as he scanned each man and found them worthy adversaries. Eztli was the biggest man, though nearly a foot shorter than Rik and nowhere near as massive. All four men moved with lithe grace, lean muscles flowing under their skin with an ease that made me think of jaguars prowling silently through the jungle.

:*They are cats of some kind.*: Daire's warcat rumbled a warning. :*Most likely jaguars as you guessed, but I won't know for sure until they shift.*:

:*She only has four Blood?*: I asked Rik. :*Do you sense any others?*:

:*Not through the blood circle. It's a barrier that our senses have a difficult time penetrating. Once we're through, I'll know better if she has other Blood that haven't been introduced. That would be something to be suspicious of.*:

He moved so he stood behind me, my rock, always at my

back. Then he gave a nod to the other Blood. One of Mayte's Blood offered his hand and Mehen took it. For a moment, they stood there, squeezing each other's hands and staring into each other's eyes. Mehen didn't move a muscle or say a word, but the other man's eyes tightened and he grew pale around the mouth. When Mehen stepped through the circle and then released him, the man opened and closed his fingers several times.

Guillaume went next. He stood at the edge a moment, waiting for one of her Blood to offer his hand. They whispered among themselves a moment, recognizing the Templar knight famous for taking alphas' heads. So I was impressed when Eztli offered his hand rather than making one of his underlings bring my knight through. Guillaume didn't play any games like Mehen, though he did meet and hold the alpha's gaze without straining in the slightest and stepped through. One by one, the rest of my Blood followed them, until it was only me, Rik, and Gina.

Bianca offered her hand and Gina stepped through the circle.

The whole time, Mayte offered her hand to me silently.

:Go now,: Rik told me. *:I have your back until you're through.:*

Taking a deep breath, I slipped my hand into Mayte's. Her fingers closed around me, trembling slightly, though that could have been nerves. Something sparked between our palms, quickly growing warm. She clutched me harder, her eyes shining, and started to pull me through. I could see the blood circle now, a shimmering wall of energy that licked up my fingers, wrist, and forearm. My palm burned hotter. My instinct was to let go, to avoid the pain of a serious burn. A mind trick? Or a warning from my goddess?

The fire burned hotter on my skin. My entire hand felt like I'd fallen into a fire or stuck my hand on a stove. Fire was my gift, but it'd never hurt me before.

"Please don't let go," Mayte whispered urgently, her shining eyes locked on me. Her eyes glowed like moonlight on a crystal clear lake. "I mean no harm to you and yours. I swear it."

"Stop," Rik barked, lunging toward me. He touched my back and I screamed as a thousand-watt bolt of lightning tore through me. I knocked him reeling backward, my entire system powering up in a heartbeat. Pressure built inside me, my magic surging to red-line levels. I didn't know what was happening, but if I didn't release it, my own magic would tear me to pieces.

I tore my lip open with my fangs and power exploded out of me. Ice burned up my spine, meeting the fire in my hand.

Something did not want me in that nest. Wind and lightning tore at me, whipping my hair, tearing at my dress. A frantic howling wind swirled around me, black thick air trying to suffocate me. But I could still see Mayte's eyes, shining like lanterns against the darkness. She'd begged me to not let go of her hand. She'd sworn she meant no harm to any of us. So then who didn't want me crossing Mayte's own blood circle?

Frankly, it pissed me the hell off. I'd been so scared of making a political mistake that it'd never dawned on me that I'd encounter trouble trying to cross into the nest despite Mayte's own blessing. I pulled harder on my magic, pushing back against the storm. But force wasn't helping. As when Ra attacked us, the harder I tried to push the wind away, the more it roared, using my own power against me.

I drew my power back, conserving my energy while I looked for the source of the storm. I let the storm batter me, sinking deeper into the darkness. High-pitched shrieks of vicious glee swirled around me like a hurricane, but I ignored it, even when it felt like something nibbled at me, taking bites of my flesh. The gale sucked the air out of my lungs and I couldn't breathe. I had to be in the tail of the storm, almost at the source. I couldn't see anything in the blackness. My body was quickly slipping into panicked flight mode, but I held on, gritting my teeth.

There. I could feel something pulsing beneath me, spewing up the storm around it. It crouched on top of Mayte's blood circle like a huge venomous spider, claiming her boundary as its own.

My chest ached like my lungs had caved in, but I honed my magic into a fireball, spinning with energy, red and dark with my fury. I willed my fire to explode on that nasty spider. I heard its legs cracking. Hairs catching fire, exploding with pops. A vicious screech. It tried to flee, legs cracking and breaking off, charred in the heat of my rage. Hotter. I felt the sear on my face, sheets of fire rippling up my body like it was going to tear skin from my bones, until finally the spider exploded.

The winds ceased so suddenly I stumbled. Hands closed on me that my body knew even if I couldn't see them. Mehen. Daire. My Blood. Yet I still fell into darkness. Rik roared, the ground shaking and bucking with his fury. Then he was gone. They were all gone. The last thing I saw was Mayte's eyes, still shining as she pulled me through.

20

RIK

What the fuck had we been thinking? Letting our queen enter another queen's nest? My queen was gone.

Fucking gone.

I couldn't feel her bond at all.

I pounded massive boulder fists on the ground and against the invisible barrier, bellowing at one of them to bring me through. I couldn't feel her. It was like she was dead. Again. And I couldn't bear it.

The rest of her Blood surrounded her. Mehen dragged her up into his arms, and the queen who'd fucking betrayed her still clutched her hand. On her knees beside them, but still touching her. Tears ran down her face but I couldn't make sense of what anyone was saying. Probably because I was roaring like a mad man.

"Calm the fuck down, man." The other queen's alpha came to stand in front of me. Safe on the other side, fucking pussy. "Your queen is unharmed."

"The fuck she's unharmed! Bring me through, mother-fucker, before I tear this whole place down brick by brick!"

The other man's eyes narrowed, his fists clenched at his sides. He glared at me through the barrier and I fucking glared back. If I had him on this side of the barrier, we both knew who'd be standing with his boot on the other man's face, and it sure the fuck wasn't me tasting his boot leather.

"I'll bring you through, but don't hurt anybody. What's happened—"

I jammed my hand up to the barrier, ignoring the fierce cramp that rocked up my arm. If I didn't move soon enough, the cramps would eventually knock me out. "Bring me through!"

The man sighed and wrapped his hand around my wrist. Immediately, I surged through the blood circle, shoved him flying out of my way, and grabbed Shara from Mehen. Panting, I clutched her, eyes closed, feeling along her bond gingerly, looking for any injury. At least I could feel her again, her bond whole and gleaming in my mind. I slowed my breathing, but didn't ease my fierce hold on her. She still wasn't moving and I didn't feel her mind stirring at all. It was like she'd gone blank, though her body was still warm. She hadn't died this time. But she was knocked out cold.

The crown had slid down, tangled up in her hair. Gina carefully loosened the tangled strands and took the crown off her head. Her hands were shaking as badly as mine. "What happened? Crossing a nest isn't supposed to be dangerous with the host queen's invitation. I told her there was nothing to fear."

"There shouldn't have been," I gritted out, giving another glare at everyone. Especially the queen, Mayte. "You caused my queen pain."

She drew herself up proudly, though she nodded in agreement. "I'm sorry, but there was no other way. I hoped she was strong enough, and she is. She's wondrous."

"She's unconscious and suffered pain at your hand. I'll not soon forget it."

Mayte inclined her head. "I wouldn't expect you to, alpha,

though I hope to earn your forgiveness. Please, let's go inside and get her comfortable. I'll explain everything once she wakes."

I paid little attention to our surroundings as we walked up to the main house. I was still too shaken at that horrible emptiness I'd felt in her bond. *:G, take over.:*

:Understood, alpha.: Immediately, Guillaume sent the other Blood into a guarding formation, two behind and three ahead, as we walked down a long graveled driveway. People lined the road, whispering as we passed. Isador. Queen. Everyone seemed hopeful and excited, but it only pissed me off.

Her first political meeting, that she'd been so worried about, should have gone off without a hitch, a purely entertaining and light arrangement with a fellow queen. Instead, it'd been a fucking disaster, and she wasn't even awake to realize it. Let alone worry about making another mistake. I half hoped that when she woke that she'd want this entire nest razed to the ground.

Zaniyah led us inside a two-story Colonial style house and into a dark, quiet room with several long couches. "Here, please, sit. Rest."

Biting back a growl, I sat down on the nearest couch, with Gina on one side of me and Daire on the other. The rest of her Blood spread out about the room, grim and cold, ready to kill anyone who looked at us sideways. Mayte had her four Blood and Bianca shut the door behind us, closing out the curious.

"Well?" I demanded, smoothing Shara's hair back off her face.

"Wait until she wakes, so we only tell this story once."

"*If* she wakes," I muttered darkly. Though I already felt a faint stirring in her bond. When she opened her eyes, we all breathed a heavy sigh of relief.

"What happened?" She tried to sit up, her eyes flying wide as she noted everybody staring at her. She looked around, not recognizing the surroundings. "Did I faint? Where are we?"

Mayte came closer. Bristling, I kept a wary eye on her as she knelt before my queen. "Your Majesty, do you remember me?"

"Mayte," Shara whispered. "I took your hand. There was something warm between our palms, like a… a… stone. Then it caught fire, and a hurricane tried to kill me. I couldn't breathe. The harder I pushed on the storm, the stronger it became. I finally found a thing like a spider on your blood circle. When I killed it, the storm died."

"Let me tell you a story about the last time a queen came to visit me," Mayte said softly, looking up at my queen earnestly, her eyes begging for understanding. "Forty-nine years ago, Keisha Skye came here uninvited and asked to parley with House Zaniyah. I knew what she wanted, and I refused to invite her into my nest. She spent the next few years attacking us. She sent humans to infiltrate my court. She had sibs of her own stationed nearby, ready to attack if anyone ventured out alone. She nearly succeeded with her ants, but I don't think she counted on our voracious fire ants being willing to help defend the nest. When all her attacks failed, she made one last trip here to contaminate my own blood circle."

Mayte reached out to take Shara's hand. She flinched, her skin still tender from her ordeal. "She laid a geas upon my own nest, so that no other queen could pass until I allowed her to enter. She couldn't break my circle—but she dropped enough of her blood on top of it to spoil our haven into a prison. I couldn't invite any queens to ally with me, unless I thought she'd be strong enough to break through Skye's geas. You broke that geas, Shara. You were able to cross and reach us."

Fuck. No wonder crossing the circle had hurt her so much. Rage bubbled like acid in my veins. "And you never thought to prepare her for such a trial? To warn her of the danger?"

Mayte bowed her head, pressing Shara's hand to her forehead. "I couldn't. All I could do was hope that if you came, you'd be strong enough to break her hold on us. And you were.

You are. You broke a geas laid by Keisha Skye like it was nothing."

Nothing. Never mind that she'd been knocked out cold for longer than I cared to remember.

Shara lifted her other hand to her temple, her fingers trembling. "I still feel... fragile. Like my head will explode if I move too quickly." She leaned forward a bit to sit up, but slumped back against me.

I tucked her head up beneath my chin and wrapped my arms around her, giving her my body heat and strength.

Guillaume stepped close, knife in hand. "May I feed you, my queen?"

"I will," Mayte cut in hurriedly. "Gladly. It's the least I can do. Zaniyah is ready and willing to swear to House Isador immediately."

Shara looked at her a moment and shook her head. "No. Not yet. I don't know how I feel about that, especially..." She didn't finish the sentence, but her meaning was clear.

Mayte looked at her consiliarius, desperation sharp between them, and yeah. I was fucking glad. They needed to squirm a bit after what they'd done to my queen. Let them worry about facing Skye's rage alone, now that her geas had been broken. Even hundreds of miles away, Skye would have felt that snap in her magic. I could only hope it'd laid her out cold too.

"I want to taste Rik first," Shara said softly.

I raised my wrist and Guillaume made a neat cut for her, mindful of her dress. I pressed my forearm to her mouth and glared at Mayte and her Blood. Especially her alpha. If Shara decided to take Mayte as a sib, I didn't want those Blood anywhere near her. They didn't deserve a single drop of her blood. Not after silently letting her step into a trap of Skye's making.

"Why doesn't she bite to feed herself?" One of the other queen's Blood whispered to his friend, a little too loudly.

"Because she doesn't want him to come until he's inside

her," Daire said on a rumbling laugh. "Our queen doesn't like to waste a single drop."

She fed a long time, enough that I started to feel a pleasant lassitude flow over me. But I didn't stop her. I wouldn't, not in front of these strangers who'd already allowed her to be harmed. Finally she licked the small slit and lifted her mouth, but she wasn't done yet. In fact, her hunger had grown as she felt incrementally better. Guillaume made a cut on his wrist and offered his blood without a word. She fed from him almost as long again, making Zaniyah's court uneasy. They whispered among themselves, watching as she went through us one by one, feeding deep and long from each of us.

Her message was crystal clear, whether she intended to make the point or not. She was powerful enough to feast on seven powerful Blood and bring us to our knees.

And still need more.

That was simply how great her need—and her power—was.

Each swallow of our blood strengthened her, yes, but it also increased her confidence and her stature among these new Aima. It wasn't common for a queen to feed from so many at once, let alone so deeply. She made them all wait while she saw to her need too, as her right as the highest, most powerful queen. When she was done, she didn't apologize for the delay or ask for dinner to be rescheduled or moved. She simply turned to Gina and held out her hand.

For her crown.

She placed it carefully on her head and accepted both Guillaume's and Mehen's offered hands to stand. She waited a moment, making sure she was steady. Then every inch the proud, regal queen, she looked at Mayte. "My Blood need to eat now."

"Of course, of course." Mayte nodded to Bianca, who hurried out the door clapping her hands and calling out in Spanish. "This way, Your Majesty. Dinner is ready."

Shara turned to me and held out her hand. I wrapped her

hand around my arm, folding her close to my side, and led my queen to dinner.

Head held high. No more nerves. Shara Isador owned this fucking nest now, and by the goddess, she knew it.

21

GUILLAUME

I t'd been decades since I'd ridden into a queen's nest and laid sword to her Blood. But for the first time since being freed of Desideria's yoke, I burned to kill every single Zaniyah Blood in this nest of my own free will. For once, I relished my reputation. I kept my eyes locked on the queen's alpha. His head would be mine. Rik wouldn't mind. He'd told me to take over. And no wonder. I couldn't imagine what it'd felt like to be trapped on the outside of the nest while our queen succumbed to such a trap.

We paused at an arched doorway leading out to a cobbled plaza. Tables had been set up with colorful lights and lanterns strung between the walls. The low roar of people talking suddenly silenced when they realized their queen had joined them.

Bianca called out in a loud voice, "Our queen, Mayte Zaniyah, and her alpha, Eztli Zaniyah."

All the people pushed up to their feet and bowed as their queen walked past to take her seat at the ceremonial table against the opposite wall. She stepped up onto the platform and

175

moved behind one of the grand wooden chairs waiting, but didn't sit.

Bianca looked at me and then Rik, wondering which of us was going to determine the procession. I didn't wait for Rik to say one way or the other. He'd take control back when he was good and ready. Besides, Rik was young enough he probably hadn't even seen a formal procession. Me, I'd survived several. "Daire Devana Isador."

Daire immediately stepped up beside the other queen's waiting Blood.

Her eyes widened slightly at his entire family name, but she announced his name in full as I'd given it. "Luis Zaniyah and Daire Devana Isador."

"Nevarre Morrigan Isador."

He stepped forward and she called out his name along with Diego Zaniyah.

"Ezra Ursula Isador."

The big man stepped forward, winking at Shara when he caught her staring. He'd trimmed his beard and slicked his hair back in a bun. With the formal suit, he looked nothing like the wild grizzly we knew. "I clean up good, huh?" He whispered, way too loudly, and guests at the nearest table snickered.

Bianca announced him with Maxtla Zaniyah. Like our queen, Mayte's alpha was actually fairly young. Maxtla was her oldest and strongest Blood, even showing some graying at his temples. Ezra would either piss him off with his blunt remarks, or they'd end up grand friends over a few mugs of ale. I wasn't sure which way it'd end up yet, but if I were a betting man, I'd place my money on the latter.

I gave Xin's formal name next. "Wu Tien Xin Isador."

Since Zaniyah didn't have any other Blood, a few sibs from her court stood ready to walk in with us. The whispers were louder in the plaza as the guests waited eagerly for each introduction. It was apparent now that we were coming in from youngest to eldest, and yes, the more famous. Even a relatively small nest in Mexico would recognize some of the rest of us. Bianca announced Xin with Armando Zaniyah, a handsome young man with a winning smile, who beamed up at Xin like he was already smitten.

Two more of Zaniyah's court came forward, moving as one with an eerie silent coordination that spoke of twins. They looked at each other a moment in silent communication, and then they turned toward Shara and took another step closer to her.

Rik and Mehen both growled at them, stalling their approach. But it made me look at the two men a little closer. None of Mayte's other Blood or sibs had thought to approach our queen. These two were older than Nevarre, I thought, and maybe as old as me. Definitely older than the young sib they'd sent out. These two carried a sense of ageless power that made them harder to age correctly.

Which told me they might be very old indeed, and if so, fairly powerful. Then why weren't they Mayte's Blood?

"I'll take over now," Rik told me.

I stepped up to Bianca, side by side with the twins. Neither of them spared a glance for me, which would have pricked my ego, if that sort of thing bothered me.

Bianca announced us. "Itztli Zaniyah and Guillaume de Payne Isador."

I felt the surge of appreciation in Shara's bond, and I was glad I'd given her house name. Most Blood took their queen's name, but I never had, until Shara claimed me as her own.

"You're old," Itztli muttered beneath his breath as we walked toward the main table. "But you're not alpha."

Centuries of marching to someone else's command kept my step steady despite his bluntness. "My queen has her alpha. I don't need to be alpha to serve."

"He's big," the man admitted as we turned to face the room. "But I think I could take him with my brother's help."

A laugh spluttered out of me before I could contain it. "Good luck with that."

Rik caught a sense of where the man's thoughts were headed through my bond and narrowed a hard look on the waiting brother.

Mehen's lips pulled back in a fierce, hard smile as he gave his name to Bianca.

Her eyes widened and she gulped, but announced him. "Tlacel Zaniyah and Leviathan Gorgon Isador."

The man standing beside me humphed beneath his breath. "Leviathan? As in king of the depths?"

Figured. The bastard didn't give his real name. Not that I could blame him when Leviathan carried so much promise of destruction and mayhem. "Yep."

"And he didn't take your alpha?"

I laughed again. I couldn't help it. "He was too busy being fucked senseless by our alpha and queen to worry about taking anyone's position."

Rik looked at me, waiting for an explanation.

:He thinks he and his twin could take you. I'm guessing they have designs on becoming Blood.:

Rik's shoulders and biceps seemed to swell, making him bigger, broader, and meaner than ever. Our queen looked like a child standing beside him, or better yet, our beauty to the massive hulking beast.

"Her Majesty, Shara Isador, and her alpha, Alrik Hyrrokkin Isador."

"Hyrrokkin," the man grunted beside me. "That explains much. Does he shift into a wolf too?"

I knew the reference he was thinking of—a giantess riding a wolf into battle. But the hell if I'd make things easy for him to figure out. "Nope."

Whispering among themselves, the crowd turned uneasy as my queen entered the plaza. Now that she'd broken the geas, they had reason to fear her. They knew how powerful she was.

They knew why Mayte had invited her. So the guesses about how exactly Zaniyah would be absorbed into Isador had begun. The higher queen would decide all their fates, even down to whether this nest would still stand when Shara was done.

Positioned on either side of the procession aisle, the twins' attention locked on my queen. Shara came toward us, her head high, her step slow and measured. No one watching would suspect it was because she still felt weak from breaking Skye's geas on the nest. But we knew. Her cheeks were paler than normal, her eyes burning too brightly with hunger, a hint of fang still showing as she walked past. Even after feeding deeply on all of us, she still hungered.

Her step faltered ever so slightly as she passed between the twins.

:I know,: Rik growled in our bond before I could say anything. *:She feels them. We'll see if they're called or not. I don't care to have any of Zaniyah in our ranks. Not after what they allowed her to face without a single warning.:*

The bullshit geas was just that. Complete and utter bullshit. I could not fathom how men who wanted to serve as Blood to a queen would stand silent and watch her walk into a trap without saying a word. Maybe I'd start with beheading these two before I took out Zaniyah's alpha. All three heads lined up as tribute to our queen would still not be enough to make me, or any of us, but especially Rik, forgive their silence.

Not fucking close.

SHARA

AFTER SPRINGING SKYE'S TRAP, worrying about political etiquette seemed ridiculous. I didn't care what Mayte thought of me now. I'd already achieved something no one else had been able to do. She owed me. She needed me, just as Gina and my Blood had said. I could relax and enjoy the food and conversation, at least as much as I could with this hunger still gnawing at me.

I needed a nice long session with a couple of my Blood. No, fuck that. All of them. I wanted their muscles against me. Rik's massive arms. Daire's purr. Nevarre's hair.

Fuck. I had to distract myself before I simply got up and dragged my Blood off to find a bed somewhere.

Rik stood behind me, one hand on my shoulder. Gina sat on my right, and Mayte on my left. Her alpha stood too, but not shoulder to shoulder with Rik. I don't think her alpha dared stand that close to my Blood for fear that he'd crush his head like a melon.

The rest of my Blood were seated in front of us, facing the rest of the tables, alternating with Zaniyah's Blood. Servers moved through the room with pitchers and bottles of wine. The smells wafting from somewhere behind us made my stomach growl. Loudly enough that all my Blood turned to look at me and then gave a pointed look at the queen sitting beside me. At least my Blood were going to eat, though I worried about Rik if he was going to stand through dinner. I'd tapped him pretty hard.

"Some wine, Your Majesties?" A server offered a bottle, label up. I glanced at it and nodded, though I had no idea what kind it was.

He poured some for both of us, a fine tremble in his hand that almost splashed some red wine on the table. "Thank you."

"Tell Sarah to start serving the first course."

The young man nodded and backed away.

Mayte offered a basket, lifting back a gingham napkin to reveal warm, soft tortillas. "Hot and fresh from the kitchen. Sarah bakes them in an cast iron skillet over a fire."

I took one and tore off a piece, surprised at how thick the tortilla was. Nothing like what I'd had back home, and thank the goddess. These were fantastic and I told her as much.

"I hope you enjoy the rest of the meal as well. We decided to keep everything pretty traditional, though Sarah always likes to throw in a few surprises."

"If everything's as good as this tortilla, then I can't wait." I wasn't very good at small talk. Or rather, I'd never really had the opportunity to practice carrying a conversation. "Have you lived here your entire life?"

"Oh yes. My grandmother founded this nest when Mexico City was still Tenochtitlan. She's still alive, though prefers a quiet life now and passed the nest to me. My mother died over five hundred years ago when the Spanish came through." She took a sip of her wine, and so I did too, though gingerly. I didn't want to risk intoxication until I got more than a tortilla on my stomach. "They say you weren't raised in a nest."

"No, I wasn't." I hesitated a moment, trying to decide what story to share. The commonly-known one that was a lie? Or the truth?

I touched Rik's and Gina's bonds. *:Should I let her believe I'm half human? Or tell her the truth? Would she even believe it?:*

Gina leaned forward and turned slightly so she could join the conversation. "Shara had an unusual upbringing. So unusual that we haven't divulged any details to the Triune."

"I see." Mayte was silent a moment, though I wasn't sure if she was communicating with other people through her bonds or just thinking. She tipped her head toward me. "I have secrets I don't divulge to the Triune as well."

Bianca scooted her chair closer to her queen and kept her voice low so that I strained to hear. "There's more than one reason that we like to keep to ourselves. In some ways, Skye's geas helped keep us isolated. That's not always a bad thing."

"If she couldn't have me, no one could," Mayte said bitterly. "All my efforts..." She blew out a sigh. "I'd honestly given up hope, until I had an unexpected, but most welcome, phone call from the Isador consiliarius that you were coming to my area. A new queen. Even better, an Isador queen. That name alone breeds fear and respect, even among the Triune. I could only hope you would consider my invitation. I refused to even let myself hope…"

The servers returned and set stoneware bowls of soup in front of us. It smelled so good I started salivating.

"If you'd like a vegetarian posole, Sarah always makes an extra pot."

"No, thank you, this is perfect. I'm not a big meat eater usually, but this smells incredible."

It tasted even better. The pork was so tender it fell apart. I ate a few bites, enough to settle my stomach, but I couldn't stuff my face while my alpha stood at my back unfed. Especially after he'd let me feed for so long earlier.

:I'm fine, my queen.:

I rolled my eyes and sat back in my chair, tipping my head up in his direction. "Would it shame you to come down here beside me so I can share a few bites?"

He dropped down to one knee between me and the other alpha, using his massive shoulders to block out the other man. "You could never shame me, my queen. But there's no need—"

I lifted the spoon toward his mouth. :Please. Let me do this for you.:

Eyes smoldering, he opened his mouth and let me feed him a bite. I scooped another bite onto the spoon, knowing full well he'd eat better with less argument if I ate some at the same time. So I alternated bites until the soup was gone. Then I gave him a drink of my wine, carefully turning the rim so that I could press my lips to the glass where his had been.

:My queen. You undo me.:

My lips quirked in a smug little grin. :That was my plan all along. Can't you guard me as well down here as you can standing at my back with a wall behind you?:

The servers removed the soup bowls and placed small colorful plates of salad before us.

He shifted closer, sliding his arm behind my back so I was

cradled into the crook of his shoulder. *:I'll stay here on one condition.:*

:Yes?

:You let me feed you again.:

I stole a quick glance at Mayte beside me to see what she thought of my alpha breaking the formal dining rules. She met my gaze, her lips curving in a laughing smile. "If he can do it, you can too, Eztli. I insist."

:Isn't it rude to feed like that during a formal dinner?: I asked Rik.

:No more rude than an alpha going down to his knee beside his queen.:

Grumbling beneath his breath, the other alpha went to his knee beside his queen, positioning himself to protect her from Rik if need be. "There's no precedent for this."

Mayte shrugged and pushed her salad plate toward him. "We don't live by precedent here anyway. I don't know why we even tried to be so stiff and formal. It's not us."

She looked up at me, her eyes softening, gleaming in the soft lights hanging above. I was struck again by how beautiful her eyes were, even though I couldn't pinpoint what color they were, exactly. They reminded me of crystals or prisms, faceting light back in all the colors of the rainbow, luminous and unshadowed. Could a queen lie and cheat and plot devastation while having such crystalline eyes? I didn't want to doubt her. I didn't want to spoil the vision of her shining eyes pulling me through Skye's hurricane.

"Would it offend you or your court if my alpha fed me again?"

Her eyes flared wide, and guilt slipped across her face, tamping down some of their brightness. "Of course not. We're in your debt. If you're still feeling the aftereffects of breaking the geas, then you must feed. I insist."

:G.:

My knight stood and came to lean across the table, knife in hand.

"Why does he cut for you, Your Majesty?" The other alpha asked.

Mayte squeezed his arm. "I'm sorry my Blood are so curious. It's none of our business."

"When Rik and Daire first found me, I didn't even know what we were. I didn't have fangs for several days, and when they finally came in…" I gave her a rueful shrug. "Let's just say that my bite is great for sexy times but not so great outside the bedroom, if you know what I mean."

"Oh. *Oh.*" Mayte arched a brow, staring at me with a speculative look on her face that made my cheeks warm.

Then she dropped her gaze to my mouth, and I would have fallen out of my chair without Rik there to steady me.

"Does this magical bite work on women?"

I opened my mouth. Closed it. Shrugged wordlessly. I had no idea. They'd told me that Mayte would want to offer her throat to me…

But it'd never dawned on me what that would mean. Especially for an orgasmic bite like mine.

"Could be interesting to find out," Mayte said softly, turning back to the salad she shared with her alpha. As she ate several bites, she turned her head away slightly.

Flashing her throat at me.

I wasn't familiar with the ways an Aima queen might flirt with another queen… but that seemed pretty blatant to me.

I met Guillaume's gaze and he made the quick cut on Rik's throat for me. *:Thank you.:*

:My pleasure, my queen. If you need other assistance…: He arched a brow at me, a twinkle in his eye that made my cheeks color more. *:I'm ready to serve in any way you desire.:*

Daire's warcat rumbled in my head. *:I could slip beneath your dress under the table.:* I felt the distinct swipe of his big tongue firmly stroking over my skin, even though he didn't physically touch me. *:Nobody would know.:*

My eyes about bugged out of my head. I quickly turned my

attention to Rik, licked the blood from his throat, and sealed my mouth over the small cut. *:I don't want to turn my first formal dinner into an orgy.:*

Daire pouted and his warcat bumped me playfully in the bond. *:In my opinion, that's the only way to turn a boring political dinner into something much more memorable. I'm sure Mayte wouldn't mind. Especially if you bite her. She'll love it.:*

:I'm not biting anyone, especially at another queen's dinner table in front of her entire court.:

I tried to wrap my mind around Mayte and what our possible alliance would mean. I'd assumed it'd be political only. But even with my mouth locked to my alpha's throat, I could still see her shining eyes. The way she'd looked at my lips, offered me her throat. So feminine and pretty and—

Not Blood.

Certainly not *my* Blood. I couldn't see them in the same picture frame as her. I didn't want my Blood touching anyone but me. The thought of Daire or Nevarre stroking a hand through her hair or caressing her back made me want to rip her eyes out and send Leviathan to blast this whole nest to the ground.

:I'm game,: Mehen immediately said in our bond, giving me an image of dragon fire bathing the court, people running from the plaza screaming.

I didn't want that. Not really.

But I didn't want Mayte touching *my* Blood.

I tried to picture her alpha touching me and my mind flinched away from that too. Not because Rik would be glaring at the other man, still remembering how they'd let me walk right into Skye's trap. He'd glared at Mehen after he broke my arm and that had been smoking hot. Because they were both *mine*.

This Eztli guy was hers. I felt nothing when I looked at him, even though I recognized that he was a damned fine dark-skinned man with broad shoulders, trim waist, and lithe, powerful movements. He wasn't mine. He'd never be mine. I didn't *want* him to be mine, because he was already *hers*.

Rik pushed the empty salad plate away and started shoveling into the next course. Roasted or grilled meat of some kind. He knew I wouldn't want to eat much of that and so didn't feel like he was depriving me by eating it. His throat worked beneath my mouth as he swallowed. We were both eating, feeding, though in different ways, and it satisfied something primal inside me to know that he ate food to make sure he had the strength and energy to feed *me*. *:I'd rather have your blood any day.:*

:I know.: I sensed hesitation in his bond, a question. Or maybe he wanted to suggest something but feared my reaction.

How he could think that, while letting me take his blood in front of over a hundred people, I had no idea. I nestled my face against his bare throat and lightly scratched his skin with my fangs, making him shudder.

:We can arrange things however you like.:

:I know.: I did, really. He'd never been unwilling to do whatever I asked. But I didn't know what I wanted in the first place. Not exactly.

:You don't want us touching her. You don't want to touch her Blood. So what's left?:

Me. Touching her.

Rik at my back. Inside me. And those shining eyes staring into mine.

22

SHARA

I made it through the incredibly long dinner without fucking anyone, much to my Bloods' disappointment. My fangs throbbed in time with my heart. Not to feed, exactly, because Rik had already slaked my thirst. I wanted to sink fangs into him just for the pleasure of it. To be inside him, and feel his pleasure roaring through our bond. As the festivities continued with a band setting up in the corner, and a crew removing the tables, I didn't know how much longer I could last.

So, of course, my Blood found reasons to come closer and tempt me.

Nevarre bent down close so his hair slid over my bare shoulder and asked if he could fetch me anything. Guillaume kept playing with his knives, popping a blade up from thin air and twirling it, the flash catching my attention. He thought about deliberately nicking himself.

:Don't even think about it.: I warned him. *:I know you're too skilled to ever cut yourself accidentally.:*

Ezra and the older Blood he'd been paired with were getting along famously after a few gigantic mugs of beer. I thought he was fairly well distracted, until he offered to sing me a dirty limerick.

Even Xin joined the games, startling me when he seemed to materialize between me and Gina. :*I thought I'd use my gift later and search the nest. See if she's got anything to hide.*:

Squatted down beside me, he braced his arm on the table and leaned in close. I loved every part of a man's body, especially my Blood's, but I'm pretty sure people must have written poems dedicated to Xin's forearms. His muscles didn't bulge like Rik's, but veins and ligaments roped beneath his skin. My eyelids fluttered a moment, remembering when I'd taken him alone. The way his powerful, lean body had worked so hard to please me, even when he feared he was breaking into a thousand pieces and would never be able to serve me again.

:*That's a great idea.*: Even in our bond, Rik's words rumbled with deep, low bass. His rock troll wanted to come out and play too. :*I can't believe she's only got four Blood and has still been able to defend herself from Skye all these years.*:

Daire leaned across the table and propped his chin on his hands, braced on his elbows. "Maybe you'd like to dance, my queen?"

He didn't even purr, and I still shuddered at the thought. Swaying to music, him draped around me. I'd never be able to keep my fangs out of him.

Mehen slammed his palms down on the table on either side of Daire and leaned in with an aggressive shove against his back. His eyes glittering with emerald fire. "I'm eager to punish him for you, my queen."

Mayte watched all this with a mixture of amusement and, dare I say, arousal on her face. "Punish him for what?"

Arching his back so he could rub against the other man, Daire batted his eyes at her. "Everything."

I had my hand fisted in his hair, jerking his face around to mine, before I even realized I'd moved. "Don't give her your kitty-cat eyes."

"These eyes..." He gave me a long, slow, sensual blink, his eyes blazing with heat. A deep purr rattled the table enough my wine glass tinged softly against my plate. "Are only for you, my queen."

Mehen's bond rumbled like a distant thunderstorm. *:Please, Shara, my queen. I've been good. For me, at least. I even let the bear go first.:*

I didn't have to ask Daire what he thought about the other Blood's plea. *:The big mean dragon should definitely punish me for you. We'll provide a loud distraction so Xin can more easily slip away undetected.:*

Daire knew full well that Xin didn't need any help, not when he would vanish without a trace.

"You allow them to..." Mayte didn't finish the sentence. "Sorry, that's none of my business."

I looked at her, the blush spreading across her cheeks, her lush lips softly parted, her tongue darting out to moisten them. Her alpha and the other three pressed close, drawn to her need. Just as my Blood were drawn to mine. She wanted very much to be a part of my *business*.

The two other men standing expectantly in front of the table had no reason to look at me. Especially not with that dark, sensual look.

Mayte saw me take note of them. "My older twin brothers, Itztli and Tlacel. Everyone in my nest is at your disposal. If there's anything you need... Or want..."

"We ask that you accept us as Blood," one of the men said.

At first glance, I couldn't tell them apart. Bronzed, lean, lithe, tremendous warriors by the way they stood and held themselves. They were attractive, yes. I could be interested in them.

Could be.

I narrowed a hard look on them, which seemed to surprise them. That only infuriated me more. They actually thought I'd fall over myself accepting them? When I had seven Blood I loved more than life itself?

"I don't take Blood for strength or numbers or political gain. Being my Blood comes with certain…"

"Requirements," Rik bit off the word, his voice graveled.

"Risks," Mehen snarled, and even Daire shot them a dark look as he stood, though he didn't draw away from my other Blood. "Service without reservations."

Guillaume flicked the knife to his other hand without even looking at it. "Honors that you can't possibly fathom."

The two men glanced at each other and then shrugged. "Like what?"

I laughed. I couldn't help it. "Do you honestly think I'd take two men as Blood who stood by and watched me step into a trap that nearly killed me?"

A small, strangled sound escaped Mayte's throat. Her brothers whirled on her. "*What?*"

"I'm sorry," she whispered.

"You didn't warn her about Skye's geas?"

"How could I?" She shot an imploring look at me and back to her brothers. "I was afraid if she knew, that she wouldn't even try, and I had to protect… us."

That small hesitation sent alarm bells going off in my head. She was hiding something. Attractive or not, powerful or not, smart politically or not… Even if I disregarded exposing me to such risk by not telling me of the geas, there was no way in hell I'd sign on blindly to become her ally when she kept secrets from me. Let alone take her brothers into my Blood.

Studying them both, I started to see small differences between them. They both had shoulder-length dark hair, but one wore his hair in a high pony tail, and the other had his swept up in tight braids on each side into a ridge that fell down the top of his head like a mane. They both had tattoos on their cheeks, but one was a black sun and the other a red spiral. They wore black suits like my Blood, but with dark red shirts underneath and no tie, leaving the neck of their dress shirts opened.

A glint of gold and green flashed at the black sun brother's throat. Some kind of jewelry, I guessed. He looked at me and for the first time, I felt a twinge of pity for him. The abject longing on his face was like a knife to my heart. Not for me exactly, since he didn't have any idea who I was. Not really. No, he longed for what I represented: power, honor as my Blood, and stature among his people. "You know how long we've waited for a queen of our own."

"I know, I'm sorry," Mayte repeated, swiping at her eyes. "I'll fix this." Squaring her shoulders, she met my gaze. "Your Majesty, name your price for full restitution, so that you may freely consider my brothers as Blood. Whatever it is, I'll pay it, unless it harms any in this nest other than myself."

"It's not that easy." She flinched, and I hurried quickly to explain. "I made an oath that I would never take a Blood that I didn't love."

"You…" the other brother drew my attention, his voice rippling with melodic undertones that still managed to rumble. "You love them? All of them?"

"Yes."

He started to step closer, but Guillaume and Xin slid in front of him, blocking his path to me. "Will you not even give us a chance to earn your love?"

Gina leaned close and whispered, "It would be a smart political move."

I nodded slightly, keeping an eye on them. "But can I trust them? Or her? After what they've done?"

She shook her head slightly. "No way to know unless——"

I blew out a sigh. Unless I tasted their blood. And then it would be too late.

Rik stood slowly, drawing the twins' gazes to him as he unfolded his impressive body to his full commanding height at my side. :*You don't have to decide anything tonight. They might need some convincing about who's alpha, and I'd rather not subject you to any further strain tonight.*:

That sealed it for me. If they wanted Rik to bash their heads in, they could wait another night. I had more important things on my mind. I stood too. "I will consider your request and give you a chance to convince me and my alpha that you belong with us. But not tonight. After what happened earlier, I need to rest first."

Resigned but with her mouth a firm slash of determination, Mayte stood. "Of course, Your Majesty. Let us show you to your rooms."

23

MEHEN

Rather than fire, my dragon blasted me with lust.

I burned with need. All the feeding and touching and sleeping in a big sweaty hot pile was well and good...

But Shara had only fucked me that one time.

One. Fucking. Time.

It was all I could do not to scream *:fuck me, fuck me, fuck me!:* every time I touched her bond. I was going to lose my mind if she didn't take me again. Or at least allow me to take someone.

I really wanted to fuck Daire senseless and see how good that purr felt with my dick inside him. But I wasn't picky. I'd fuck any of her Blood. Hell, I'd even beg hung-like-a-horse Guillaume to fuck me. Or the bear. Ezra hated me. I didn't fucking care.

As Blood, the utmost peak of pleasure would always be found with our queen, so the last thing any of us wanted was two more Blood. We'd have even less time with her. Though these two clowns might be entertaining. They kept eying Rik's broad back like they had a snowball's chance in hell of taking our alpha. When I, Leviathan, king of the depths, had surrendered.

Utter nonsense. But it would be fucking hilarious to watch Rik snap them both like twigs.

The Zaniyah queen led us up a grand staircase. Pausing at the top, she gestured to a pair of double doors to her left. "My main quarters." Then a matching pair of doors on our right. "The guest quarters." She nodded to the two wannabes who'd followed us, and they pushed the doors to the guest rooms open. "I hope you find everything satisfactory."

"I'm sure we'll be quite comfortable," Shara replied. "Thank you. Dinner was wonderful."

Mayte smiled but clutched her hands together before her. "Our pleasure. Please let us know if you need anything."

"I will. Good night." Shara started toward to the French doors, where the two men silently watched with a tight, resigned look on their grim faces. Hoping she might change her mind at the last minute…

Snickering beneath my breath, I watched as Daire and Xin slid in tight on either side of her. Naturally, Rik had her back. Guillaume paused before her, blocking the way, and yeah, the hard-ass motherfucker stopped her within arm's reach of them on purpose to torment them. "Allow Nevarre and Leviathan to scan the room first to be safe, my queen."

She nodded and I stepped around them with Nevarre. The guest suite was nice enough and our bags had already been delivered. A private sitting room with comfortable-looking leather couches and chairs. A small bedroom for the consiliarius, a decent sized full bath, and a large bedroom.

With a sadly lacking bed. If it was even king sized, I'd eat Rik's ass while Guillaume fucked me.

A double set of French doors led out to a balcony that overlooked the plaza, still lit with the colorful party lights. Music filled the night, but since the queens had retired, the musicians played soft ballads and folk tunes rather than dancing music. I opened my senses fully, letting my dragon perk his head enough to seek anything amiss.

:Outside access to the plaza,: I told Rik and Guillaume in the bond. *:The room is empty.:*

"All clear, my queen," Guillaume said aloud, dropping his arm and stepping aside.

She swept into the room without a second glance at the men asking to join her Blood. Even though one of them inhaled loudly as she passed and groaned beneath his breath.

"I'd best not find you lingering out here." Guillaume produced a foot-long knife from somewhere on his person. He tested the edge with his thumb. "Or I may see if I still have the right touch." He looked up at the nearest man and smiled. "It takes a smooth, yet powerful, stroke to behead a man with one swipe of even the sharpest blade."

The twins bowed deeply. "We hear and obey."

I snorted. "Sure. Sure." And I fucking slammed the door in their faces.

Gina's phone rang. "Excuse me, Shara. I'll be in my room if you need anything."

I muttered, "I hope that room is soundproofed."

"Doubtful," she laughed, shaking her head. "But not to worry. I brought headphones, and I have several calls I need to make to London. Good night."

"Good night, Gina."

With the doors closed and the strangers gone, Shara let down the facade she'd held all evening. Weariness weighed heavily in our bond. And yes, oh, yes, need. She burned almost as badly as I did.

As we all did.

She took the crown off and handed it to Nevarre. Her hair was falling down from the complicated twists and knots the hairdressers had done in Dallas. She tried to comb her fingers through it, but the heavy strands were too tangled.

Rik rummaged in his bag and pulled out a hairbrush. "Allow me, my queen."

Tiredly, she nodded, reaching behind her to tug at the zipper of her gown. Daire closed his fingers over hers, kissed her fingertips, and took over for her. The gown slipped to the floor and she leaned back against him with a sigh.

Of course the little fucker started up that damnable purr that she loved so much.

"Change, please, everyone. Get comfortable."

Daire voiced what we all wished to say. "Or strip?"

She smiled and moved toward the bed. "If that's your wish."

Rik shrugged out of his coat and hung it in the wardrobe. "Xin, make your rounds and see what you can find. Guillaume, Ezra, Nevarre, you're on first watch. Keep a close eye on the twins. When our queen's desire and blood are in the air, they may not be able to resist."

"Then they'll be dead," Guillaume said coolly. "Nevarre, you take the balcony. The bear and I will take the front room. Your raven has better sight and will see anything trying to approach from a distance."

Nevarre tossed his coat to Rik, yanked his shirt off over his head, and unbuckled the leather belt that snugged the heavy cloth of his kilt about his hips. In seconds, he was naked and dropped the folded kilt on top of his bag. Feathers sprouted down his back as he strode to the balcony door.

Rik hung up Nevarre's coat and his pants, and then moved to join Shara on the bed. Leaning back against the headboard, he opened his thighs wide and she settled against him, wrapped in his heat. He fucking took up the entire width of the bed.

Shara laughed softly as he carefully brushed out her hair. "I guess she wasn't expecting a visiting queen to take more than one Blood to bed at a time."

"They're in for a shock then," Rik replied. "You know they're going to hear everything we do."

"She wanted to join us."

"Yes, she did."

Shara was quiet a few moments and then laughed again. "If I decide to take her, I hope to Isis that her bed is bigger than this one."

I stripped off the tailed coat and hung it beside Rik's. Daire threw his pants at me, slapping me in the face with material that smelled like him.

Sassy, purring cat.

I gritted my teeth and hung his suit up too. Very deliberately refusing to look at him. Not until she said whether or not I could have him.

"What do you want tonight, my queen?" Rik's low rock troll voice rattled the floor boards.

"Can you fuck me while I watch Daire torment Mehen?"

"Finally," Daire growled, trying to sound put out but we all heard the tease in his voice. "I thought I'd have to steal his dragon hoard to get his attention."

Rik chuckled. "Your wish is our command."

I closed my eyes a moment, breathing deeply to settle my control. Yes. Thank the goddess. "There's no hoard of gold, D." I slammed the wardrobe door shut and dared to look at him. "Only teeth and claws."

He stood beside the bed, his back to me, his fine, rounded ass a blatant invitation. He winked at me over his shoulder. "Promises, promises."

My fingertips burned, dragon talons threatening to burst free. I made myself breathe deep and held it for a count of five. Controlling the beast wasn't something I had much experience with. Not after living as Leviathan for centuries. I hoped the little fucker was up to the challenge of wrestling with my dragon.

Daire's bond rumbled inside me, winding inside me like a cat twining around my ankles. *:I've got teeth and claws too, my friend, and I've had years of playing with our alpha. I hope you're up to my challenge.:*

197

I shuddered. Goddess. That incessant purring was going to be the death of me.

SHARA

I was tempted to borrow one of Guillaume's knives to cut the sexual tension hanging thick and raw between my two Blood. It was crazy to think that Leviathan—or rather, Mehen—hadn't been with us very long at all. Days. Not quite a week.

And while I tried to see to everyone's needs...

I couldn't fuck them all every single day.

Multiples at a time helped, but with all the planning for this trip and growing the grove and repelling Skye's ant attack, I'd been too tired to take too many to bed at once. And yeah, dealing with Mehen could be... exhausting. He was so demanding, so strong, so out of control. I was tempted to throw a noose around his dragon's neck in our bond, but I didn't want to make him think I didn't trust him.

I focused a very light touch on only Daire's bond. *:Are you okay with this? Even if he gets rough?:*

He rumbled louder and started toward me. If he'd been shifted to his warcat, he would have flipped his tail from side to side. *:No worries, my queen. I'll love it. He won't find me as easy as he expects.:*

I'm glad he warned me, because as soon as Mehen laid a hand on his shoulder, Daire snarled and whirled, dropping into a crouch as he made a swipe across the man's chest. Those weren't fingernails that left bleeding scratches in Mehen's skin, either.

With a roar, Mehen lunged for him on the floor. Daire crashed up into him, clawing and biting.

My heart pounded. I watched as they wrestled and tumbled across the floor. Someone slammed into the foot of the bed with a grunt. Now I couldn't see them, but I could hear their labored breathing. The bed thumped. Again. Hard.

Nuzzling my neck, Rik closed his hands around my waist and lifted me up into his lap. Hard dick beneath me, the sound of a struggle nearby. Goddess. I was so wet as he slid back and forth, tormenting me. Tormenting us both. His breath caught against my ear as he slowly eased just the tip of his dick into me.

It was so strange to not be able to see him. With me facing away from him, the angle was weird, yet oddly exciting. He closed his thighs, giving me something to brace against as he filled me. With agonizing slowness, he finally settled me back against his groin, fully inside me.

"How does that feel?"

I groaned, tightening my muscles on him. "Incredible."

Shifting my weight forward a bit, I braced my hands on his thighs. He smoothed his hands down my back, his fingers and thumbs kneading my muscles. Goddess, I loved his hands, the slow, steady, firm stroke of his fingers. He knew exactly how to touch me. Hard, firm, but then gentle and slow. The punishing strength of a giant. My alpha, with enough power in his big body to hold down a dragon so I could fuck him.

Yet so incredibly tender when he touched me.

"Motherfucker," Mehen growled, his breathing loud. It sounded like they were almost underneath the bed.

"Cocksucker," Daire snarled back.

"No, that's going to be you, you little fuck. You're denying our queen her viewing pleasure."

With a loud heave, Mehen surged up back into my line of vision and slammed Daire onto his stomach on the edge of the bed. Mehen gripped a handful of Daire's hair and had his other arm locked around his waist, using his weight to hold him down.

"There's not enough room for you two up here," Rik said in a mild rumble. "Especially if you're going to wrestle."

Both of them were bleeding, and ironically, it looked as though Mehen had taken the most damage. He had wide swaths

of claw marks on his shoulders and chest, and a nasty-looking
bite on his right forearm that wasn't entirely human looking and
certainly not two neat Aima punctures.

"I don't need a lot of room," Mehen growled, bearing down
harder on the other man.

Daire writhed beneath him like a slippery eel and managed
to break Mehen's grip on his waist. Claws unsheathed with a
fierce growl rattling in his throat, Daire slashed at the other
man's face.

I gasped. I couldn't help it. I could all too easily envision
torn flesh, skin sagging down in strips. I'd seen what kind of
damage Daire was capable of. For all his purring and playful cat
personality, he'd not hesitated one second when Ra's skeletons
had attacked us. He'd charged in and ripped the lead skeleton's
arm completely off. Even when he took a sword through the
chest to protect me.

Mehen twisted his face aside at the last minute. "Good. You
turned around for me."

He wrapped his hand deeper into Daire's hair and jerked his
head sharply to the side, throwing him off balance. Which made
it easier for him to pin Daire between the aggressive weight of
his body and the mattress behind him. He stood over Daire, his
thighs locked on either side of his body, squeezing the life out of
him until Daire finally ceased struggling, though his body still
vibrated with tension.

"Open your fucking mouth," Mehen growled, giving his
head another jerk.

Daire stuck his tongue out and then clamped his lips shut
firmly. *:Make me.:*

Mehen punched him in the side hard enough that Daire's
breath whistled out on a groan.

I stiffened, afraid this struggle was getting out of hand. But
Rik soothed me with his hands, settling me back against him.
:They're fine.:
:But his ribs...:

:He's fine.:

And Daire was. I felt his rising lust in the bond. The meaner Mehen got, and the harder he hit him, pinned him, the more Daire struggled. That was his favorite part.

I remembered our first night with all three of us together. How Rik had pinned Daire's arms for me so I could torment him while Rik fucked him. The harder he struggled, the harder Rik had squeezed him. Daire had blooded him too, but Rik had only laughed.

Mehen wasn't laughing. But his bond raged with emotion. Lust I expected. The mighty dragon had made it clear he'd fuck anyone, or let any of us fuck him. Hundreds of years trapped in a dragon prison would do that to a person. His desire sharpened with a rabid hunger that made him borderline dangerous.

Which Daire fucking loved too.

Mehen punched him again, making him grunt through tight lips. Again. "Open that fucking mouth, D. So I can stuff it."

Daire glared at him mutinously. So Mehen smacked him right in the mouth. Drawing blood.

I quivered and started to fight free of Rik's arms myself, but he held me firmly, murmuring softly in my ear. "Look at him, Shara. Really look at him."

Panting, I watched as Mehen bent and licked the splatter of blood from Daire's shoulder. His tongue swiped over Daire's chin. The corner of his mouth. Across his lips. Licking, rumbling, Mehen coaxed his lips into softening enough for him to sink his tongue deep into the other man's mouth.

Oh. My. Smoking. Hot. Fuck. Alert.

Mehen pinned Daire's head back at a painful angle, using his whole body to crush Daire against the mattress. He shoved his tongue deep into Daire's mouth. Tongue fucking him. And Daire melted against him like a cat settling in to lick up a bowl of cream.

Lifting his head, Mehen looked up at me, his eyes glittering emeralds. "There, my queen. Now the real show begins."

24

DAIRE

There was an invisible button inside me. Sometimes a partner had to work extremely hard to find it, but once that button was pushed, my brain shut off. I was all body. All sensation. Nothing else mattered but existing in that slow, dreamy space for as long as possible.

Sometimes it was high, up in the clouds, soaring.

Sometimes it was dark and silent, sinking into a forgotten cellar or cave deep in the earth.

I needed them both. I needed to soar, and I needed to sink.

Mehen was definitely of the deep sinking stone sliding into the bottomless ocean variety. I could taste my blood on his tongue, and I wanted more. I wanted to go deeper still.

With his right hand fisted in my hair, he eased back off me and let me settle on my knees with my upper back braced on the mattress. "Open your mouth now, D."

Staring up at him, I gripped his hips and opened my mouth so wide my jaws ached, waiting to see how he'd use me. It'd tell me a lot about what kind of man he was deep down where he didn't like to look very often. Ezra was all growl and no bite. Rik was growl *and* bite, but he was alpha. I expected him to break me open and look inside at his leisure. It was his right as my alpha, and I expected nothing less than he use me as he wanted, when he wanted.

Though now that we had Shara, he hadn't needed to break me open, shatter me, and put me back together again.

Even though *I* needed it.

I loved Shara with every non-aggressive, non-dominant bone in my body. I loved it when she took me. I loved it when she let Rik take control, too. I didn't need an aggressive, dominant queen ruling over me all the time. I loved to be able to cuddle with her and tease her and make her smile. With all the blood and danger and power in her life, she needed my lightness.

She needed me.

I loved to be needed.

But I needed this, too. I needed to be broken. Tamed. Forced. To have my body owned and used and treasured, despite being broken.

Mehen twisted his hand deeper in my hair, forcing my neck in a painful arc. Perfect. Then he shoved his dick in my mouth.

No *"here's a little taste, so you can feel how thick and wide my meat is."* That wasn't Mehen's style. He rammed balls deep with a *"swallow my dick down your throat until you're raw and maybe when I'm done I'll let you breathe."*

Exactly the way I liked it.

He wasn't the biggest man I'd given head to, but he was definitely the roughest. I couldn't put my hands to good use teasing his balls or playing with his ass. I was too fucking busy holding on to his hips for dear life. He slammed deep again and again, grinding down my throat, and likely rubbing himself sore too. I wasn't trying to scrape him with my fangs, but when a man fucked an Aima's mouth that hard, accidents happened, though he didn't seem to mind.

Face tight and grim, he stared down at me, his eyes blazing like Shara had loosed green fire inside him. My jaws ached, my neck muscles screaming from the unnatural angle. His scent burned in my nose, part dragon fire and part serpent. That inherent dangerous scent that our queen's cobra carried. It made the tiny hairs on my nape quiver with alarm, bringing the thrill of being used by him to an all new level.

All too quickly, he jammed deep on a guttural growl and emptied his load down my throat so deep I didn't have to swallow.

I sucked in a frantic gulp of air when he gave me a quick breather.

Panting, he bent down and glared into my eyes. "You didn't fucking purr." Stepping back, he hauled me up by my hair, twisted me around, and threw me up on the bed. "When I fuck you, you'll purr. Loudly. I want you to vibrate my balls. Now make yourself useful and eat our queen's pussy while our alpha fucks her, and I fuck you."

SHARA

DAIRE CRAWLED TOWARD ME, straddling Rik's legs. His hair was a mess, his lips swollen, blood and drool and come dribbling down his chin. He swiped his tongue across his lips, cleaning up before he touched me, though I really think he did it to tease me with that ridiculously talented tongue.

His eyes. Goddess. Dazed out of his mind, high as a kite, and yet completely grounded too. He was fully aware and coherent, yet at the same time, he'd separated his mind from his body. His body wasn't his any longer. It belonged to Mehen. Completely.

Soft, tender lips pressed to mine. I could taste his blood and the bite of Mehen's semen.

A sharp crack made me jerk my head up. Joining us on the bed on his knees, Mehen brought his hand crashing down on

Daire's buttock again. "That isn't where I told you to put your mouth."

Ignoring him, Daire nuzzled my neck, lipping along my jaw and up to my ear.

It wasn't like he could easily get his mouth on my pussy when I was leaning forward like this. Rik was already inside me. It just seemed so… so… raw.

And so fucking hot.

I couldn't get that image out of my mind.

"Don't punish him for something out of his control." I fought to keep my voice even, but the sharp tones made me wince. I wasn't angry, exactly. My emotions were turbulent and jumbled. Aroused. Furious that they'd hurt each other and mad at myself for enjoying it so much. And so damned needy. All of us. A mess. Just like Daire's face and Mehen's bleeding chest and arms.

He'd already used Daire's mouth so hard I was surprised his dick wasn't bleeding too.

Yet I was so fucking wet that I could smell the musk of my own desire. Sitting here with Rik deep inside me, not even thrusting, it was all I could do not to come. Or sink my fangs into Daire and make him come. Or both.

"Why not?" Mehen retorted, his eyes flashing. "He likes it well enough. Why else do you think he's still not doing as he was told?"

Rik flexed his big body beneath me and my eyes rolled back in my head. Everything inside me clamped down. I clutched Daire's head and came so hard I screamed and bit my own lip.

Daire moved to lick the blood from my mouth, but Mehen lunged over the top of him, shoving his shoulders down and forcing his head to stay low. "Oh no you don't. I don't want to wait another minute to fuck you."

As he'd done after smacking Daire in the mouth, Mehen licked my chin and sucked my bottom lip into his mouth. Here, then, was how the ferocious dragon could be tender. Licking blood from a wound.

The first time he'd tasted my blood flashed into my mind. How he'd clutched my hand in his mighty jaws... and yes. It'd hurt like a bitch. He'd broken my arm.

But he'd *licked* my blood from my skin. When he could have ripped my hand off and bathed in royal blood spraying from what was left of the bloody stump.

He groaned deep in his throat and pushed his hips against Daire. The way Daire groaned too told me my blood had made Mehen hard again.

Rik slid his palm around my throat and pulled me back against him. My throat. In his hand. Such a turn on. He pushed up a bit inside me, reminding me of his size. How patiently he waited while I watched my two other Blood, yet with one simple touch, he reminded me of his complete and utter control. He made this possible. My alpha ensured I could safely watch a rabid dragon and a teasing warcat pound the shit out of each other and still enjoy it. Because I trusted him one-hundred percent. If he needed to wade in and thump some sense into one or both of them, he would. Without hesitation. Not because he was jealous or wanted to drive them from me, but because he cared as much as I did that everybody should be safe and loved as much as possible.

Even if that meant he had to sit behind me, mostly forgotten, while two men fucked on top of his legs. Or while one of them dipped low to slide his tongue along my slit and tease the base of his cock.

"That's a good kitty," Mehen growled roughly as he tore his wrist open. "Make our queen come again for our alpha. Make her squeeze his dick in half."

He bled all over Daire, and me, and Rik, carelessly slinging blood on the sheets. The sight of his blood dripping down Daire's back as he bent low between my thighs made me crazy. My fangs descended and I dragged my hands up Daire's back, smearing blood into his skin. He slid his tongue around Rik's cock buried inside me and leisurely made his way back up, sucking on my flesh as he went. When he finally closed his lips around my clit, my back bowed and I clutched his head, because Rik swirled his hips up in a lazy, powerful roll.

My heart fluttered frantically, my thighs quivering. I watched as Mehen worked his fingers into Daire's ass, loosening him up enough to shove deep in one hard thrust that made Daire rumble against me.

Oh goddess. That purr. I couldn't imagine a vibrator with even a fraction of that incredibly powerful rumble. Mehen's head fell back, the tendons in his neck and shoulders standing out in stark relief. Shuddering with bliss, he breathed out, "ahhhhh."

Yeah. Me too. I couldn't sit still. Not with Rik so hard inside me. Daire sucking on me. That purr sliding along my nerves, racing from my clit, to my nipples, and up to my mouth. My fangs throbbed deep into my jaws and down my throat.

Cracking his eyes open, Mehen seized Daire's hips in both hands and ground harder against him. He stared into my eyes while he hauled himself out and slammed back, hard, making Daire's breath sigh out against me. Mehen wasn't even touching me, but I could feel him moving inside Daire by the way his mouth moved on me.

Rik slid his right arm around me, his fingers splayed on my stomach. He stroked over my throat, bringing me back harder against him. Even the weight of his big hand changed the angle slightly, making the head of his cock rub new nerves inside me. I felt like a guitar in his hands, his fingers strumming chords from my throat. He pushed a little harder on my abdomen, giving himself just a little more depth inside me. Impaled and stuffed, I writhed beneath Daire's mouth and the green fire in Mehen's eyes.

I hugged Daire's shoulders with my thighs, my hands in his hair. He sucked harder, groaning and moaning against my flesh with every punishing thrust Mehen gave him. The king gave him no quarter. No tenderness. He pounded him mercilessly, breathing hard, sweat dripping down his forehead. His eyes flashed with power, the scales flickering and gleaming on his shoulders as the dragon slid and writhed beneath his skin.

His lips twisted in a grimace and he dragged his right hand down Daire's back, leaving deep bloody scratches from his talons.

The smell of blood tormented me, but none of them wanted to get close to my fangs. I wouldn't be able to keep from sinking them deep and then this would be over. I didn't blame them. I didn't want this over either. But my hunger ravaged through me like wildfire ripping through a drought-stricken forest.

Three men. So close. Touching. But nothing I could easily bite. It would have made me laugh if my fangs didn't hurt so badly. It was a good hurt, though. The kind of pain that made my pleasure surge even higher.

Tremors rocked Daire's shoulders. He purred louder, more of a growl, a desperate pleading roar, and Mehen's furious rhythm faltered. He plunged deep and gritted his teeth, fighting back his release, but Daire wasn't having any of that. His rumble dropped even lower, hitting a new bass that made my toes curl and I shattered again. Mehen let out a wordless roar and the bed rocked with the fury of his release. He fell across Daire and pressed his bleeding wrist to my mouth, which pushed me over the edge.

Naturally, Rik sank his fangs into my shoulder, making sure my climax soared to a whole new stratosphere as he came inside me.

Panting and sweaty, I forced my eyes open. Our bonds shimmered with feel-good endorphins. On his side, Mehen lay against Rik's thigh, hugging Daire's back. I'd probably suffocated him, my thighs locked around his head. I released him but he didn't come up right away. He'd sank his fangs into my thigh and I hadn't even realized it.

Rik reached around me to tap him on the head. "Not too much. You know what she's been through today."

Licking his lips, Daire came up over me, draping himself on top of me. "Just a taste."

I stroked his hair back out of his face. "You okay?"

"Mmmmm. Fabulous."

"I should look at those scratches on both of you and see if they need to be healed."

Mehen grunted, shifted beside Rik, and almost fell off the bed. He grabbed at Daire's hair and Rik's thigh, holding on until he got his balance. "Don't be ridiculous. These scratches aren't worth you wasting a single drop of effort to heal. They'll all be gone in the morning."

My eyes were already heavy. I yawned and Rik immediately said, "Go, find a place to sleep. She needs her rest."

Daire buried his head against me. "No cuddles tonight?"

Even Mehen looked disappointed, though he sat up and smacked Daire's ass lightly. "Come on, D. Let's go see if G's had any problems with those two idiots."

I wished they could stay, but this fucking bed…

Daire kissed me and then padded after Mehen. "I call the couch."

"Fuck that shit. You can sleep on the floor. There's plenty of pillows."

I bit my lip. If they had to sleep on the floor, then I should sleep with them.

Rik shifted me off to the side so he spooned against me. "Fuck that shit. My queen doesn't sleep on the floor."

And I fell asleep before I could argue with him.

25

SHARA

The absence of Rik's heat against me woke me more than the low voices. I sat up and immediately, both Rik and Xin turned away from the French doors leading out to the plaza and came to me.

Rik sat beside me and wrapped his arm around my back, his hand sliding down beneath my opposite thigh, offering his shoulder up as a back rest. "Sorry, my queen. We didn't mean to wake you."

"Did you find something?"

Xin crouched down beside the bed. "Indeed, I did. She's hiding another Blood, my queen. An extremely powerful, old Blood, like Leviathan."

"She has a king?"

Xin shrugged. "Maybe he's a king. Maybe he's something else. I smell her blood in him and he's ancient. At least as old as your king. He couldn't see me, but he knew something was near. I didn't dare push deeper to see what he was guarding."

"When her brothers pressured her about why she hadn't warned me, she said she was protecting 'us', but she hesitated, like there was something else. *Someone* else. Maybe that's who this old Blood is guarding."

"It's concerning that she never mentioned him," Rik added. "All she had to do was say she had another Blood she'd assigned elsewhere and none of us would have taken that amiss. A queen may send her Blood to any task. Why hide that she has a fifth Blood, unless she specifically doesn't want you to know?"

I tried to think through scenarios. She wanted to become my sib. She'd offered before we retired for the night. She'd invited me to her nest, without warning me of the geas that made such a visit extremely dangerous. Each secret alone was enough to make me not trust her. But added together...

"Could this Blood be a member of Skye's court? And that's why she hid him—so you and Daire don't recognize him?"

Rik focused on Xin. "Picture him in your mind. I'm going to try and see him through our bond."

Xin nodded and sat back on his heels, his hands loose on his thighs. "I'm ready, alpha."

I closed my eyes so I could see our bonds more clearly. Rik's bond was always like a volcano with streaks of red, molten rock sliding down his sides, even if his bond was quiet. Xin's bond was more like his wolf. Still, quiet, nearly invisible, a blanket of soft, damp fog. I watched as Rik sent a stream of lava rolling toward Xin's fog. I tensed, afraid it might hurt him, or burn his fog away, and I'm sure Rik could have done either if he'd wanted. I'd felt him send an alpha surge in the bonds before that had affected even Mehen's dragon. Xin's bond vibrated in response, but rather than dissipating, his fog thickened around Rik's bond, drawing him in. I reached for him too and immediately stood with his wolf in a dark hallway. The air felt heavy and smelled slightly of damp, like a basement. I felt the impression of weight and distance above us. Interlocking stones covered the floors, walls, and ceiling. So maybe a man-made tunnel rather than a hallway.

Light flickered at the end of the tunnel and a man stood in

front of a thick wooden door. Arms crossed over his chest, feet planted wide, the man definitely screamed protector, his glare sending a clear message. *Leave this place.*

Rik moved past me, ducking a little to pass beneath one of the lower sections of the ceiling, until he stood in front of the man. It was so strange, because it wasn't real. We weren't really there, even though I could smell the dank, thick odor of dirt and something else. Something feral.

It wasn't this man. It was something behind that door.

Something precious. Something that he would willingly die for.

Then it dawned on me. The man was as big as Rik. Maybe... even slightly bigger.

Rik gave me a look over his shoulder, brow arched. "He's not bigger than my rock troll though."

"Unless he can shift into something bigger than he already is."

Rik snorted with disgust. "Mehen's dragon is bigger than me, but we all remember how that went down."

"It doesn't matter how big he is. I don't feel drawn to him."

Despite his confident words, a crease eased in his forehead. My big, bad alpha liked being my biggest and baddest. *:That will never change.:*

"I don't recognize him and he doesn't smell like Skye. A man this big, this powerful, would have made an impression on her. She would have been damned near giddy to have the opportunity to break him."

"Is he alpha?"

"Yes and no. He's like Mehen, or Guillaume. Old and powerful, yes. He could be alpha if he chose. But he's not. Maybe Zaniyah already had an alpha when she called him."

I opened my eyes and swayed slightly, disoriented. It took a second for my brain to make the adjustment to the guest quarters, rather than the dark tunnel. "At least he's not a plant by

Skye. Other than that, we don't really know what he's protecting or why she lied about him."

"Should I go back and try to learn more, my queen?" Xin asked.

I cupped his cheek and he turned his face into my caress, rubbing deeper against my palm. "No, thank you, Xin. I don't want to risk you being discovered. I'll find out what she's hiding."

"How?"

I yawned, which Rik immediately took to mean I should be picked up, shifted deeper into the bed, and tucked in against his big body. Not that I was complaining. "What time is it?"

"Four in the morning," he replied against my shoulder, his lips a soft caress.

I listened to my bonds a moment, taking a quick inventory. Mehen had switched with Nevarre on the balcony. Daire had taken over for Guillaume at the door, though Ezra was still up and gave no sign of leaving his post now that Daire had joined him. Gina was sleeping. "Xin, could you write a quick note for Gina and ask her to set up a meeting with Mayte first thing this morning? Like eight. Slide it under her door. I'm sure she'll be up long before I will."

Xin nodded and immediately stood to go in search of paper and pen.

Rik rubbed his nose behind my ear, breathing in my scent. "Are you sure you want to be up so early, my queen?"

"Regretfully, yes," I sighed, closing my eyes. "I have a feeling it's going to be a very long day."

26

NEVARRE

My queen was many things. Gorgeous, powerful, sensual, a walking, breathing goddess incarnate.

But she was not a morning person.

Rik held her coffee cup beneath her nose but she still gave him a bleary look of exhaustion. "Whose stupid idea was it to be up so early for a meeting?"

He grinned at her and lifted the cup to her mouth. "Yours."

Gina unzipped the traveling wardrobe that contained our queen's clothing. "What image do you want to portray this morning?"

"That I'm not death warmed over."

"Something business like? Or sultry? Innocent and sweet, or formidable?"

Shara groaned. "I don't really care about fashion much. You pick. I'll wear it."

"Hmmm." Gina surveyed the dresses of various lengths inside. "I take it you found something interesting last night, and you intend to put her feet to the fire."

"You could say that."

"So something formidable and powerful, but not terrifyingly so."

She touched one of the dresses and wings fluttered in my mind. Not my raven's, but my goddess's.

Gina had already moved several dresses down, still looking for the right outfit. I stepped closer and pulled the one Morrigan had liked. At first glance, it was a somber dark green with long sleeves and a high waist that didn't really scream Shara's style, though it was pretty enough. Almost business like with a modest length that would hit below her knees and a full layered skirt that managed to look filmy without looking fragile or risque.

"This?"

I nodded. "Morrigan likes this one very much."

"Then I'll wear it," Shara replied.

"High heels or something more comfortable?" Gina asked.

"Comfortable but formidable."

Gina snorted. "Now that's a tall order. Let's see what we brought from Dallas. There were a few pairs that caught my eye and I'm sure we packed them, though they might still be in the jet."

Shara knocked back half the cup of coffee, even though it was hot. "It's not worth sending Angela up here for shoes. Whatever we have is fine."

Gloriously naked and uncaring that we looked at her, she stood, her body like a Grecian statue. How could we not worship her with our eyes and our bodies and our mouths every chance she gave us? She was fucking gorgeous. A goddess in living breathing flesh. I brought the dress to her, expecting Rik to take over. Or Daire. He made himself useful like that quite often. But she turned around and held her arms up, waiting for me to drop the dress over her head.

I swallowed hard. Dressing my queen was such an intimate thing. Something a human man might do for his wife, a small way to take care of her. Intimate, because I would know what she wore beneath that dress. Or rather, what she didn't. "Do you want a bra?"

Just saying it made my cheeks burn and Daire snickered beneath his breath.

She flashed a smile over her shoulder. "No. It's too hot, and if I have to wear a fucking dress, I'm going to at least be comfortable."

I slipped the gown over her head and helped her with the hook at the base of her neck. From the front, the dress was very conservative, but the back... It made me gulp, afraid she would be offended. Her entire back was bare, dipping deliciously low into a point that directed my gaze straight to the shadowed crevice at the top of her buttocks.

Rik narrowed a hard look on me. "We've already got the twins to deal with, and you select a racy dress like this?"

"It's racy?" Shara peeked at the back in the mirror and her eyes widened. "Wow. Yeah. I can see why Morrigan liked it. It's fine, Rik."

"Are you sure? I don't want those two idiots bothering you needlessly and all that skin..." His voice thickened, his eyes heating as he trailed a smoky look down her spine.

The dress was cut low enough that it was obvious that our queen wore nothing beneath it. No bra. No panties. Just sweet skin begging for a soft caress.

"We didn't bring any green shoes along, but either of these black shoes will work." Gina set two pairs of shoes out. One pair of simple flats with a bit of sparkle on the toes, and the other heels. "You said comfortable, so these heels aren't too high. They shouldn't be too much of a chore to walk in."

Shara slipped her foot into one of each shoe and looked at herself in the mirror. "Yeah, the heels. I think I'll be fine in them."

"Jewelry." Gina set a heavy case on the bed and opened it, both sides sweeping out to reveal a fortune in stones and gold neatly compartmentalized inside. "I'm thinking something unexpected and understated, like the front of the dress."

Shara looked at me, her eyes glowing with soft emotion that made my throat ache. "Let Nevarre pick. What does Morrigan want with this dress?"

I held my hand out over the rings and necklaces and earrings, waiting until something made the fluttering noise inside my head again. I lifted out a heavy silver chain with an intricate twisted black wire tree medallion. Morrigan's Grove. Of course. I slipped the chain around her neck and latched it for her. The tree hung perfectly in the center of her chest. Exactly where the large spiked thorn had punctured her.

Rik handed her the cup and she sat back down on the side of the mattress, both hands wrapped around the cup. "Now it's your turn."

"How dressy do you want us today?" Rik asked as we each headed to our bags.

The only suit jacket I'd brought was the fancy tailed one. I didn't care to wear it again, but I'd do what my queen asked of me.

Mehen opened up the wardrobe. "If you want us to dress in formal wear, we should ask Zaniyah if we can get a few things pressed."

"No formal wear. But I do want you all to look mean and formidable. Something in black. I don't care if it's jeans, but black head to toe." The she looked at me and smiled. "Except you, Nevarre."

"I have pants..."

She shook her head. "You know I love that kilt."

Daire gave me a dark look and tossed his hair back over his shoulder. He'd been pouting about my kilt ever since she called me the night she sealed the nest.

"You don't have the knees for it," I said to him.

He snorted and pulled some black jeans out of his bag. "I don't think it's your knees she's looking at."

I pulled on a plain black T-shirt with the kilt, thick socks, and my heaviest combat boots. The rest of Blood pulled on black jeans and similar shirts. Rik put on a pair of black cargo pants, but Mehen put on leather pants and a silky black shirt unbuttoned midway down. Daire laughed at him.

Until Shara slipped her hand inside Mehen's shirt and stroked the gleam of scales in his skin.

Someone tapped lightly at the door and Guillaume called, "It's a young woman to help with your makeup, my queen."

"Okay, let her in."

The young woman hesitated at the bedroom door, as if shocked to be allowed so deep into the queen's quarters. Her eyes widened as she looked around the room at all of us standing around our queen, still in protect mode even though we were dressing. Then she saw the blood splattered all over the sheets and a pink blush stole across her cheeks.

A minor sib, I decided. She knew what queen's blood meant. Especially on the bed.

"Your Majesty, I'd be honored to help you with hair and makeup, if you'd like."

"Of course, thank you."

Rik pulled a wooden chair out from the small desk in the corner for Shara to sit down in, and the woman set to work.

"A light touch, please. It's too hot for much make up. And something simple with my hair."

"Though it should be up," Gina added. "The back of the dress won't carry the same impact if it's half hidden by your hair."

Sitting there, Shara fidgeted a little as the woman brushed her hair. My queen wasn't used to having people take care of her. She smoothed the skirt and her eyes suddenly lit up. "Pockets! A dress with pockets!"

I shared a confused look with Daire, not sure what the big deal was. He went to a tattered, faded bag that no one had touched yet, and pulled out a small pocket knife that he slipped into his pants. *:I'll carry your knife for you until she's gone:* he whispered to her.

Her eyes welled up with tears. *:Thank you.:*

:Why is she sad?: I asked Daire softly, trying not to let her hear my words.

:She's not sad. She's touched that we still carry her bag for her and that I remembered she likes to have her knife on her. Even if she's wearing a dress.:

I looked at the faded bag, horrified that it was my queen's. It looked like something that'd been tossed in a corral with a flock of sheep for the winter. I'd known she wasn't raised in a nest, but I hadn't realized the extent to which she'd been deprived of a queen's lifestyle.

:With no idea of what she is, she survived alone, on the run, with no legacy or protection, for five years.:

Now it was my turn for my eyes to well up with tears. Two years ago, I'd lost my Brigid. I, too, had been alone and on the run in a way. Though I knew what I was, and had enough power to not starve or fear for my life, it'd still been a miserable existence.

That my queen had suffered so...

:Intolerable.: Rik growled softly in our bond.

And all the other Blood nodded with agreement.

SHARA

WE PAUSED outside a bright sunny room while the young woman who'd done my hair stepped inside and spoke to her queen. "They're here, Your Majesty."

Mayte set a cup of tea down and stood, smiling, though I thought she looked tired. Probably as tired as I looked. I'd slept less in my life many times, but now that I was queen, I was tired all the time. I didn't know if it was the blood loss, or the battles, or everything combined.

:It's exhausting just carrying the amount of power that you have,: Rik said in our bond. *:You don't realize the toll such immense power takes on you, even if you're not immediately using it. Plus, you've been under constant attack in one way or the other since you came into your power.:*

I sighed. Yeah. Constant attacks definitely took their toll. I tipped my chin up a bit and put on a hopefully polite, but coolly reserved, face.

"Good morning, Your Majesty," Mayte said, offering her hand. "I hope everything was to your satisfaction last night."

Her cheeks colored slightly, her eyes bright despite the shadows beneath them. She knew exactly how satisfied I'd been last night. "Thank you, yes, and good morning to you too, Your Majesty." I slipped my hand into hers, and again, felt a heat grow against my palm, like we clasped a warm, flat stone between our palms. "Do you feel that?"

"Yes," she whispered. "I felt it before too, but I thought it was the geas."

Braced for the heat to flare and blaze up my arm, I finally took a deep breath when nothing else happened. "I guess it's a queen touches queen thing."

She guided me to sit beside her so that we both looked out a large bay window, and Gina took a seat to my left. Mountains rose in the distance and horses grazed in the fields. Roses climbed around the windows, yellow, not black-red like the ones in my grove, but I still mentally flinched at the sight. I cast a quick look at her arms, bared by the short-sleeved pink dress she wore, but I didn't see any scars. Had the thorns pierced her like they'd done to me? Or did she just like flowers? I didn't feel like I knew her well enough to ask.

"I've never felt that before," Mayte admitted as she sat down. "Though I can't say that I've touched many queens before, either."

Her hair was pulled to the side and plaited loosely in a fat, thick braid. The pink dress was soft and flowy and frilly, extremely feminine, and not something I could pull off. On her, though, it looked beautiful, highlighting the dusky brown tones in her lovely complexion.

Her alpha had his back to the wall, standing a foot from her chair, his hands casually jammed in his pockets. But he watched carefully as my Blood positioned themselves nearby. Rik on my left, though he stood, too. Guillaume and Mehen stood in the doorway, and the rest of my Blood took up defensive positions down the hall, guarding the other entrances. I didn't see any of her other Blood, or her brothers, thank goddess. Though Rik's bond shimmered with eagerness. He'd love a good fight, a reason to shift into his rock troll and thump some heads.

"Have you met many queens?" I asked as she poured some ice water for me.

"When I was a child, Grandmama had many informal dinners and parties here, though she was careful never to draw the Triune's notice. Keisha Skye even came here once when she was barely more than a fledgling. Many queens we used to know even a hundred years ago are long gone now. Would you like more coffee? And please, help yourself. I wasn't sure what foods you liked. I'm not much of a breakfast eater myself."

"Yes, please." She lifted a carafe and Daire suddenly slipped up beside me to take it from her. He poured fresh cups of coffee for me and Gina, and added cream to my cup while Rik filled a plate for me. Despite it being an informal breakfast, Mayte had selected white china with a frilly silvered edge and soft pink rose border. My water glass was heavy, making me think it was real crystal. The linen table cloth was also a dusky rose pink.

Note to self. Mayte's favorite color was pink.

:*What is your favorite color?*: Rik asked with a rumble.

:*I like all colors.*:

He made a soft sound as he set my plate before me. Mostly fruit, with some kind of tart. I broke off a small piece to taste. Crispy on the outside but soft on the inside and lightly sweet like a bowl of oatmeal cooked into a cake. Delicious.

"So where are your other Blood today?" I asked Mayte, nibbling another piece of the cake.

She laughed softly. "They're occupied with keeping my brothers out of your hair until we can meet this morning. I have to admit, they put up quite a fuss last night."

I widened my eyes and quirked my lips. "It's taking four Blood to keep your brothers in line?"

"No, not four..." She hesitated and flicked a quick glance up at my face. "They've waited a long time for a queen. They don't mean to be rude."

"I find it very rude." I sank my teeth into a huge ripe strawberry, watching her reaction.

"Oh." Mayte wrung her hands in her lap, dropping her gaze to her plate. "I'm terribly sorry."

"For which part?" I kept my voice light as I finished the strawberry. "That your brothers want me only because they've had to wait so very long? Or that you didn't respect me enough to warn me before I tried crossing into your nest at your invitation? Or that you have a fifth Blood you neglected to mention?"

"I already apologized about the geas." Her head jerked up, her voice sharpening. "And I don't--"

"Don't compound the insult by lying to me."

She sucked in a deep breath, her hands clenched tightly in her lap. "So one of your Blood was sniffing around my nest last night."

She managed to sound insulted, despite being caught in a lie. "After the way I was welcomed into a vicious trap, do you honestly think I would sit quietly in my room and not send my Blood out to see if you were hiding anything else?"

Defiant, she stared at me a moment, but then her shoulders slumped. "He said he felt something, but when he investigated, all he found was a faint wolf print at the outside door."

I didn't say anything, choosing instead to continue eating. Sometimes silence was the best way to demand an explanation.

"I've made a mess of this," she finally said with a rueful smile. "All my grand and careful plans thrown to the wayside."

"I haven't done this queen thing very long." I set my napkin aside and took a sip of water before continuing. "But it's common sense that if you're wanting to make someone your ally, it's not going to go well if she's mislead from the very first step."

"I know. I'm sorry. I have a very good excuse, I promise you. The only reason I haven't been completely forthcoming is because of what's at stake. I need your help very much. In fact, after meeting you, I can easily say that no one else will be able to help me like you can. I need your help, Shara. I formally ask for Isador's protection and will offer throat at your convenience."

I hesitated, tipping my head to the side as I studied her. She met my gaze, her eyes resigned, yes, but also fiercely determined. "What's at stake?" I asked softly. "Who are you protecting?"

"Come. I'll show you."

27

RIK

I couldn't be prouder of my queen. She might claim not to understand politics, but she'd handled Mayte perfectly, down to quietly and calmly getting her to admit to everything. However, I did not like the place Zaniyah led my queen. Outside to the rear of the house, to an old cellar door with a massive antique iron lock on it. The thick oak and iron hinges would give even my rock troll a workout if I needed to bust Shara out.

Mayte touched the lock and it opened without a key, so it was coded to her blood only. Her alpha grunted as he lifted up one side of the door and threw it back.

I didn't look at Xin, so that the other queen wouldn't know which of us had penetrated her safeguards, but I gave him a salute in the bond. *:How did you get inside?:*

:I have my ways.:

:Impressive,: Shara said, her bond gleaming pearly rainbows. She was pleased with how things had gone so far, understandably, and she was eager to see what Mayte was hiding, until she saw the dark hole she had to enter.

Mayte went first. "Let me get a light." She disappeared from view a moment, and then light bloomed from a large flashlight.

Shara quirked her lips. She'd expected some kind of magical shit. We still didn't have any idea of the kind of powers Mayte had. Maybe she couldn't manage a light or a fireball. *:Before you decide whether or not to accept her, you should ask her to display her power.:*

:Good idea. Is this tunnel safe?:

:It will be.: I turned to Guillaume, Ezra, and Xin. *:Guard the door and our queen's way out.:*

They nodded.

I looked at Mehen, Daire, and Nevarre. *:If anything happens, your primary objective is to get her out. Out of this hole, out of the fucking nest. Whatever it takes.:*

:Understood.:

I gave a hard look at Eztli. "One of us goes first."

The man gave a sardonic bow of his head. "Be my guest."

I jerked my head at Nevarre and he went down the stairs and past Mayte, deeper into the tunnel. Eztli went next, then Mayte, Gina, and Shara, with me and her other two Blood close behind. My fingers itched to touch her, to keep a hand on her, but the tunnel was too narrow. I didn't like that I couldn't keep a hand on her. That would delay me one more second from getting her to safety.

:Don't worry so much,: she whispered soothingly, giving me a squeeze in the bond. *:I'm not completely powerless, you know.:*

:But I'd rather you not have to bleed today, unless you're choosing to feed us, not to save us.:

"Just a little further," Mayte said after a few moments.

Nevarre sent back a quick image of the tunnel ahead. A very large man waited, arms crossed and scowling just as Xin had showed us last night. As we neared, I could feel his power rolling off him in waves.

Fuck. This man wasn't an alpha. He was something else entirely. Something more.

I shook my head, trying to understand why Mayte had kept

her most powerful Blood hidden away. Why did she fear Skye, when she had this kind of Blood at her side? Fuck, why was Eztli alpha at all?

"Your Majesty, may I introduce you to Tepeyollotl. My heart, this is Shara Isador, descended from Isis. She came, exactly as you said."

The man looked at each of us, his golden eyes flashing, even though the flashlight wasn't shining in his face. Predator eyes that mostly hunted at night. A black stripe crossed his nose and across each cheek. He wore jeans, but his upper body was bare, covered with tattoos and symbols.

Focusing on Shara, he bowed at the waist, his fist over his heart. "Your Majesty. My queen has put all her hopes in you."

"Me? Why?"

He looked at Mayte. "It's time to reveal all to her."

"Yes," she replied steadily. "We can go no further until she knows the truth."

Mayte laid a hand on the lock, same as before, and it opened. Even the big man had to exert force to get the door moving. It slid open with a grinding creak.

I'd been expecting some kind of root cellar or unsavory prison cell, but the walls were stacked stone, and the ground was covered with flagstones. Eztli and Nevarre stepped through the door, followed by the queens. I hesitated, eying the heavy oaken door with wide planks that had probably come from a several-hundred-year-old tree. If this big man shut the door behind us...

Even my rock troll would have a difficult time tearing through.

:I came in from above,: Xin said in my mind. *:If he blocks the way, I can still get her out.:*

More at ease, I gave the man a nod and stepped through, with Daire and Mehen on my heels.

"This area used to serve as a wine cellar and overflow storage for the kitchen," Mayte said as they approached another door. At least this one wasn't locked and didn't look like it weighed a ton. "The original entrance was blocked off decades ago to create a more secure area. With Tepeyollotl outside, this is the safest place I could find."

She tapped lightly on the door. "Grandmama, it's me. I have visitors."

"Come in," a woman called softly from the other side. "But quietly."

Mayte pushed open the door and stepped inside. She walked to an older queen sitting in a rocking chair with a sleeping child on her lap. She picked up the little girl and cradled her in her arms.

"She just fell asleep," the older queen whispered.

Mayte kissed the child on the cheek and then lifted her head, her eyes glowing with fierce determination. "This is why I hid the geas from you. This is why my most powerful Blood guards the door. This is why I must be your sib. My daughter, Xochitl."

SHARA

A DAUGHTER. She had a daughter.

So much became clear now. Why Mayte was so desperate. Why she would go to such lengths to secure assistance from me, even if she must lie, cheat and steal to do it. The same as I would do to protect my Blood, and I didn't even have a child to worry about.

A queen. With a child. Gina's eyes were wide, her bond silent with shock, as were my Blood.

:When was the last time a child was born to a queen?:

:Keisha Skye's child, nearly a hundred years ago,: Rik replied, his bond grim. :And you. If she knew about this baby....:

My stomach pitched and I almost threw up the delightful oatmeal cake. Because if Skye was even half as vengeful and obsessed as I suspected her to be, she wouldn't take another queen with a baby well at all.

Tears rolled down Mayte's cheeks, but she kissed her daughter and handed her back carefully to her grandmother. "I'll be back later after she naps."

The older woman looked at me and the hair on my scalp tingled. Nerves zinged down my spine, as if a splash of cool water trickled over my head. "This is the one?"

"Yes," Mayte said. "She needed to see what we're fighting for."

She came toward me, and we walked quickly back toward her other Blood and then on up the tunnel and outside. I didn't say anything, but my mind whirled with questions. Keisha Skye had resorted to torture and, according to rumors, black magic, to conceive her child. Yet here Mayte, a relatively insignificant queen, had a two or three year old little girl hidden away. She wasn't strong enough to stand against Skye alone, yet she'd managed to conceive a child. A daughter.

A future queen.

Mayte took us back into the bright sunny breakfast room. Gina and I sat down once more and I nodded when she offered the coffee carafe again. Someone had whisked the other cup away. I didn't recall drinking any of it. Fresh plates had also been set at each place, though I wasn't hungry.

"Is it safe for us to talk openly here?"

Mayte nodded. "All my people know about Xochitl. She's usually out and about playing with Grandmama. We only hid her away while you were here, in case things didn't go well." She grimaced. "They haven't gone well, but I hope you understand a little better why I wasn't completely forthcoming."

"Does Skye know about her?" Gina asked.

Mayte paled and shook her head. "Goddess, no. If she did, I don't think there'd even be rubble left here at Valle de Zaniyah. We'd all be dead and I'm very certain she would take my daughter and raise her as her own."

To replace the daughter she'd lost. "Would it be rude to ask how you managed to conceive?"

"That's a story all of its own. Grandmama had been communicating with... with..." Mayte paused and took a deep breath. "I can't say her name. I hope that means something to you."

My mother. She'd been talking with Esetta Isador, her name not to be spoken by any living Aima. I nodded but didn't say anything to reveal my secret parentage. Not yet.

"She gave Grandmama the idea. After thousands of years, Aima magic wasn't strong enough to sustain a new generation. We needed to bring in new, powerful blood. New magic." Mayte poured herself another cup of tea and dropped in a single sugar cube. "If I wanted a child, I needed to find one of the old gods to conceive."

A dying god. The note Esetta had written about my father, Typhon, father of monsters.

"That's why you were in Dallas," Gina said. "But why there?"

"I've only ever called jaguars as Blood," Mayte said. "So I wanted the god of jaguars to father my child. When Tenochtitlan fell, many of the old gods and goddesses returned to Aztlan. However, after so many centuries, no one knows exactly where that ancient city is. I hoped that if I found the lost city, that I'd find at least one god there. All the references referred to an island in a lake, somewhere north of here. We searched for years with no luck, and I talked with every Mesoamerican researcher I could find. Then I realized I'd been searching with my eyes and my brain, when I needed to search with my blood and my heart. I used my power and asked my goddess to guide me, and with Her help, I found Tepeyollotl."

Her old and extremely powerful Blood who was so much more than alpha. "He's a living god?"

Mayte smiled at the incredulity ringing in my voice. "He's known by many names, including Tezcatlipoca, or 'Smoking Mirror.' When he felt my power and heard my plea, he roused from his long sleep and joined me. I don't know if it was me, honestly, or the jaguars with me. But he did come, and we did conceive my daughter. But then my worry increased a thousandfold."

Sobered, I could imagine all too well what would happen if Keisha Skye found out about the baby. Or her father.

"If she took me as sib, then she'd have access to Tepeyollotl too," Mayte said softly. "He's bound to me now. In many ways, he's vulnerable, because I'm mortal, even though I'm definitely harder to kill than a human and will live much longer. I'm under no illusions that she would allow me to keep such a powerful Blood who'd already proved that he was able to sire a queen. She would demand I surrender his bond."

"And take Xochitl," Eztli growled, his voice more jaguar than man. I met his fierce shining eyes and saw his beast prowling in his body. "We would die to protect our queen and her child, and without question, we would die first and hard, but we wouldn't be able to change the outcome. Skye would level this nest, and lay claim to our queen, her child, and her god. Zaniyah would be no more."

Mayte laid her trembling fingers over mine on the table. "This is why we need you so desperately. Why I didn't dare give you a reason not to try and enter the nest. Why I couldn't risk exposing Xochitl or her father, not until I knew for sure if I could trust you or not."

I sighed, my heart already tugged into this mess. I couldn't fault a mother for doing anything to protect her child, the same as Esetta had done for me, going so far as to use the last of her magic to place a geas on her entire people so she would be forgotten.

So I could be free.

And poor Eztli. In many ways, he was in the same position as Rik. Alpha, but put at risk because his queen took a powerful old Blood. In my case, it'd been my king, Mehen, and in Mayte's, her god. But it could have easily gone badly if our alphas didn't love us so much. If they weren't willing to compromise and risk their ego for the good of all.

I reached up to Rik over my shoulder, blindly lifting my hand. And he wrapped my fingers in his big powerful palm, as I knew he would.

:If you need to take a god, I will do all in my power to help you accomplish the task at hand.:

:I don't intend to take any god.: I squeezed his fingers and then put his hand on my shoulder and picked up my coffee cup once more. *:My alpha and our Blood are plenty for this queen.:*

His bond suddenly cut like hot steel through butter, melting around my heart. *:If you want a child and are not able to conceive with me, then I will find your god and you will have him and your child. So I say as your alpha.:*

Deciding it would be easier to ignore his promise rather than argue, I took a sip of coffee and met Mayte's intense eyes. Still shining, only now shining with fierce hope and determination. "What made you decide you could trust me?"

She cocked her head to the side, a smile playing on her lips. "Honestly? When you refused both me and my brothers last night."

My eyebrows rose with surprise. "Really?"

"Do you think if I'd offered to swear to Keisha Skye that she would have refused? Even keeping Xochitl out of the picture, she wants my power for herself. She wants my nest and everyone in it to serve her will and increase her power. Even more, she never would have refused to take such powerful Blood. My brothers have some secrets of their own."

I remembered the agonized longing in their eyes. I'd been fairly out of it after the geas knocked me on my ass, but I could feel their gazes following me all night. Taking them as Blood would be no hardship, that was for sure. I didn't want to add more to our number, but I had to admit I was intrigued. "Oh?"

"How old do you think Grandmama is?"

I grimaced. "I don't have any idea. I wasn't raised around

our people, so I have no idea how to judge age. You look like you're maybe thirty or thirty five years old."

Laughter bubbled up out of her throat, and I was struck again by her delicate beauty. Like a rose growing in the desert, seemingly tender and fragile. Until you remembered that the rose was growing in the fucking desert. "Oh dear, you are bad at guessing ages. I'm two hundred years older than your guess. Grandmama lived in Tenochtitlan at its height. Our goddess is Coatlicue."

I had no idea which goddess that was, or what Her significance was. "I'm sorry, my knowledge of the Aztec religion is sadly lacking."

"In some stories, she was the mother of Quetzalcoatl and Xolotl. Twin gods."

My eyes widened. I'm pretty sure everybody had heard of Quetzalcoatl, the great feathered serpent. "Are you saying your brothers are gods too?"

"No, not at all. But from the moment they were born, Grandmama said they were a throwback to the Twins. They have great power locked inside them, waiting for the right queen to make them Blood."

She must have called them to her. I felt Guillaume and Mehen both bristle as the twins approached, but they stayed outside the protective ring of my Blood. Though Mayte's older Blood gave them both looks that said he'd thump their skulls together if they didn't behave.

I looked out the bay window a moment, avoiding everyone's gaze, though they all stared at me. Waiting for me to make a decision. My Blood wanted to know how I felt about these twins. If I wanted them, period. Mayte wanted to know if I'd accept her as my sib. Even Gina wanted to know what my decision would be, so she could help me plan through our alternatives.

So what if I didn't take a sib. What would happen to us?

Keisha Skye had already attacked me twice. It was clear that she wanted to eliminate me before I could gain too much power, experience, and allies. She'd already missed out on killing me before I could establish a nest. She'd done everything she could to prevent Mayte from inviting any queen to help her. I'd broken that geas, but if Skye learned from her mistakes, she might lay an even nastier one on my nest. Who, then, could help me break it? Mayte, when she hadn't been able to protect her own people?

Unfortunately, Skye was only my most immediate concern. I still had to worry about the Triune. They had to know about me by now. They had to know about Guillaume and Mehen from the Christmas footage from Venezuela. From Skye, they'd know I had at least three other Blood that had originally been her sibs. Regardless of what I decided to do with Mayte, the Triune had to be plotting a way to either control me or eliminate me.

I didn't like either option. At all. Even more, neither did Isis or Morrigan. The necklace weighed heavily on my chest, the memory of the heart tree taking my blood and my life fresh on my mind. I hadn't grown the grove to watch Skye hack those glorious old trees down and raze my manor house to the ground. I hadn't traveled to Mexico to leave a fellow queen and her child defenseless.

But taking Mayte's side was another line in the sand. A battle cry to Keisha Skye. I'd already taken three of her sibs, survived her attacks, and broken her geas. If I also took the queen she'd been trying to take for herself for nearly fifty years...

Even if she never found out about Mayte's daughter, I would have made an enemy. A very powerful enemy, allied with one of the stronger European queens with an eye on the empty Triune seat.

Worse, I'd taken Guillaume from Marne Ceresa. She wouldn't be pleased at that, either. The Triune would give Skye free rein to do whatever she could to eliminate me. Probably even help her, to an extent. They certainly wouldn't help me if their most powerful and oldest living queen was pissed.

In a matter of a little over a week, I'd somehow managed to piss off two very powerful queens.

Great. Fabulous. *Fuck.*

Rik's fingers moved slightly on my shoulder. A reminder of all that I had gained in exchange. And I wouldn't change a single thing. Not as long as I had him and the rest of my Blood.

So the question came down to what I would do to keep them. How far would I be willing to go to keep my Blood safe? I'd already angered the oldest living queen and alienated the queen of New York City. We were at grave risk. At any moment, Skye could attack again. Or the Triune could demand I come to Rome or wherever they wanted. And I would have to go.

With seven Blood...

We would die. No matter how strong I was, I wasn't strong enough alone to protect the ones I loved. Not when Marne Ceresa had at least twice as many Blood.

:She had over ninety Blood the last I heard,: Guillaume said softly in my head.

:How many does Keisha Skye have?: I asked Rik.

:Twenty female Blood she calls her Furies, and a handful of male Blood, including whoever her alpha is at the moment. I've never felt her unleash her power, but in my heart, I know you're stronger.:

:But.:

He sighed in our bond. *:She has the numbers. Many sibs, plus an alliance with Rosalind. Eventually, she'll trap one of us. She'll get to Daire and use her old bonds to pull him home. Or she'll get to one of your human servants. Winston, say. Or Gina when she goes to town. They'll be vulnerable and easy pickings. If they get to Gina, she carries your blood. That gives them a foothold on your bonds.:*

And if I did nothing to protect Zaniyah, Keisha Skye would get to that sweet baby girl her mother had hidden with an Aztec jaguar god. Even he wouldn't be enough to protect them both if Skye managed to break through the nest.

I nodded and turned to meet Mayte's gaze. "I accept your offer."

Her eyes. Fuck. They gleamed with tears, shining with hope and relief, spilling over like a sparkling crystal waterfall. She threw her arms around my neck and pressed her forehead to mine. "Thank you. Thank you for helping us."

"And us, my queen?" One of the twins asked, his booming voice making me shiver.

I didn't turn to look at him or his brother, but I reached up and laid my hand on Rik's fingers, still on my shoulder. Closing my eyes, I brought up the tapestry in my mind.

Mayte's nest gleamed like her eyes, sparkling crystals and drops of liquid moonlight and soft, pink petals. Her jaguar Blood looked at me, their eyes flashing like predators hidden in the underbrush. But I saw them clearly. All five of them, even her god guarding her daughter.

Xochitl was like a colorful rainbow shining in the sky after a devastating tornado. I touched her shining dot in my mind and felt her power. She would be a queen to be reckoned with, ripe with power thanks to her father. I tasted sweet, pure rain in her gift and the sharp crack of lightning. Her eyes glowed golden and fierce, a jaguar, like her father.

Bracing myself, I let my mind drift to the twins. They blazed like the rest of *my* Blood. Bonfires in the darkness of my mind. One of them was a giant monstrous-looking dog, growling and slobbering at the mouth, snapping viciously in the air. The other was some kind of dragon-type creature, only instead of scales, he wore green, gold and red feathers.

:He's no fucking dragon,: Mehen retorted in my head. *:He's a cross between a chicken and a snake.:*

:A fucking dog,: Ezra muttered. *:Toss him a stick in the ocean. That'll get rid of him.:*

Oh joy I could only imagine the fighting and jostling to come. Though hopefully there would be jokes and laughter too. If nothing else, the twins had already put my two grumpiest Blood on the same side.

:A feat indeed,: Rik said.

He laughed, but I felt a heaviness in his bond. He expected problems. The twins had already made comments about challenging him or eliminating him entirely.

Gently dislodging Mayte's grip on my neck, I turned in my chair to look at them but didn't stand. *:Let them come closer,:* I told my Blood.

Guillaume dropped his hand and the two brothers strode to me, though they stopped a respectful few steps from my alpha and dropped to their knees.

"As I said before, I don't take Blood just to increase my numbers. I love my Blood. We've become friends and lovers in a very short time. I'm here because of them. I'm accepting your sister's offer so that I can keep us all alive, because I'm willing to do anything to protect them."

Rik squeezed my shoulder, pressing closer so that his thigh pressed to my side. "And we'll die for her. Gladly."

"I'm willing to die for you, my queen." The brother with the black sun tattooed on his face said. "We'll obey you. We'll swear to you. We'll do anything you ask for the honor to serve."

He said the right words, but I still wasn't sure. I didn't feel drawn to him or his brother. I couldn't imagine having sex with him, or asking him to join me and Rik in bed. For all I knew, he'd only want to come to my bed with his brother, and how weird would that be?

:Test him,: Rik whispered in his rock troll rumble. *:Give him an order. See if his ego will bend to your will.:*

"Rik's my alpha. Nothing's changing that. Ever."

The black sun brother's eyes flicked to Rik and back to me. "As you say, my queen, so it shall be."

"That's not enough for me."

He looked at his brother with a bit of panic spreading across his face. "What else can we do to convince you, my queen?"

I touched Guillaume's bond. *:Are you comfortable with a small demonstration?:*

:Absolutely, without question, my queen.:

"Surely you know of Guillaume de Payne's reputation."

Both brothers nodded, but their eyes tightened, and the brother with the red spiral on his cheek gripped his thighs firmly.

"When the last living Templar knight came to me, he did something very significant to show his willingness to submit to me and my alpha. Guillaume, would you please show them now?"

My knight strode into the room, inclined his head to me, and then lowered himself to the floor on his belly, hands flat against the floor, his eyes down. "I come in peace, my queen. I'm yours. Use me as you see fit."

The twins mirrored his movements without me saying a word, both going flat on their stomachs without hesitation.

Keeping my voice soft, I continued. "The great Templar knight who's famous for beheading alphas has gladly and willingly fucked me at the same time as my alpha. Even though Rik could have refused him access to me at all, he follows my alpha's orders to the letter."

"I obey my alpha without question because he guards my queen's heart," Guillaume said, his voice carrying through the room even though he was on his stomach.

"Leviathan, king of the depths." Mehen came closer and dropped to his knees before me. "Tell them how we welcomed you to my bed."

"Our alpha fucked me senseless while Guillaume fucked our queen on top of us," he replied without hesitation.

"Why did Rik need to fuck you into submission, my dragon?"

Mehen looked up at me, his eyes blazing with green fire. "Because I was... unruly," he said the last word with a rumble of sexual heat.

"And how did you entertain me last night?"

"I beat the shit out of Daire and then fucked him for you, though Daire enjoyed the hell out of it."

Daire let out a rumbling purr. "I sure as fuck did."

"And where was our alpha during this?"

"Beneath us. Fucking you, my queen," Mehen replied.

I looked back at the twins, judging their reactions. Their pupils were dilated, their nostrils flaring with each breath, their eyes locked on me. The one with the red spiral licked his lips, while the one with the black sun shifted his weight to the side. No doubt trying to make his erection more comfortable against the floor.

"I say these things to you crudely so you know what to expect if I take you into my Blood. I love my Blood. I fuck them all as often as I can, in as many ways as I can. Even if that means multiples at the same time. I like watching my Blood fuck each other. My favorite way to sleep is with as many bodies as possible crammed into my bed, and my nest is going to have the largest bed I can find so I can sleep with as many of you as possible next to me. I want to touch as many of you as possible, as often as possible, and everyone feeds from me, unless you've made a prior relationship with another Blood and want to continue feeding him. I don't play politics in my Blood. Rik's word is law. If he decides to punish you and ban you from my bed, so be it. You won't touch one hair on my head until he says otherwise."

I leaned forward, pinning them each, one after the other, with a hard look. "I won't take kindly to any thoughts of trying to dethrone my alpha. He's my alpha. Period. I *will* him to be my alpha with every fiber of my being and every ounce of my blood. I love him as my alpha. I won't accept anyone else as my alpha. If anyone tried to harm him with the mistaken idea that I'd be open to replacing him, I'd rip their skin and flesh off their bones and grind their skeletons into fertilizer to feed my trees. Is that understood?"

"Yes, my queen," the black sun brother said, while the other said, "Alrik Isador is my alpha."

I stood and stepped closer to them, but neither rose from the floor until I bent down and offered them each a hand. They took my hand and rose to their knees, their eyes locked on me. "When I take your sister as sib, I'll accept you as Blood, on one condition."

The black sun brother narrowed his gaze on me, pushed well past his normal limits for patience. "Yes?"

I laughed softly and tugged them to their feet. "You have to remind me of your names again so I can stop calling you black sun and red spiral in my head."

28

SHARA

I napped through midday and worked with Gina the rest of the afternoon to finalize the contractual side of a sib relationship with Mayte. I'd thought it was blood only, but evidently there was a whole other financial and legal side to consider. Taking Mayte as my sib meant she was entitled to my protection. To me, that meant she was part of my family and my court, and thus, my legacy. Though we had to define exactly what that entailed.

As far as I was concerned, it was an easy decision. She had a child. If I had no heir at the time of my death, I told Gina to give my legacy to Xochitl on the condition that she take care of my court as her own. If I did have heirs at the time of my death, Xochitl, and any other children Mayte conceived, would receive an equal portion of the legacy as my own children.

"Will you want an heir?" Gina asked hesitantly, looking up a moment from the stack of papers she was reviewing for signatures.

I shrugged uncomfortably. "I don't really know. I've never thought about it."

Gina turned her attention back to the contracts. "You have

plenty of time to decide. But it's a hell of a lot more paperwork once you have a child."

I huffed out a laugh. "That seals it then. No heirs, ever."

She knew I was kidding. Mostly.

Once the paperwork was organized, I had to select yet another dress. I groaned, rolling my eyes. "If I'd known I'd have to wear so many fancy outfits, I never would have come to Mexico."

"Nonsense. It's a wonderful opportunity to play dress up."

We finally settled on a sultry black gown that hugged my curves. Though it was floor length, the sides were see through except for bands that criss-crossed up my legs and hips. Daire picked it out, along with some incredible fuck-me red stilettos that didn't seem to go with the dress at all. But who was I to argue with the king of shopping and sandwiches?

"The order of presentation will be different this time," Gina told me as we headed downstairs to meet with Mayte and Bianca to sign the contracts. "You are going to be their queen, and so you will go first. Then your Blood. Then Mayte, alone. She'll present herself to you in front of her court."

I took a deep breath. "And I do the deed. At least she knows what to expect when I bite her."

Gina smirked. "But the rest of her court likely doesn't know."

Crap. I was going to make Mayte come in front of her entire court. She knew it, and she was still going to go through with it.

In her place, I wouldn't have minded, because my entire court was my Blood plus Gina, Frank and Winston. The latter two would be kind of embarrassing, I guessed, but nothing like the hundred or so people Mayte protected inside her nest.

"Then each of her Blood will come before you and you can choose whether to take them or not."

Ugh. "No way. I'm not taking any of her Blood from her."

"It's your right as her queen."

"Not happening."

Nodding, Gina paused outside a heavy set of doors where one of Mayte's Blood waited. "After that, the rest of her family will be presented to you. You can take her brothers at that time, or wait until later in private. That doesn't need to be done formally. Each sib will also be presented to you."

"I don't have to taste any of them though, right?"

"Not unless you want to."

"And none of them take my blood either."

"Again, not unless you feel moved to do so."

The Blood bowed low and pushed the doors open. "My queen, she's ready for you."

Having complete strangers refer to me as their queen was going to take some getting used to. "Thank you. I'm sorry, I'm terrible with names. Which of her Blood are you?"

"Luis, my queen."

I waited while Rik made his orders about how to position my Blood. Guillaume, Xin, and Ezra went before me. Nevarre, Mehen, and Daire took the rear. I gave my hand to Rik and he tucked me close to his side as we walked through the door.

This time, Mayte had set the meeting in the library. The walls were broken into panels by dark wood with murals painted in each section. Books lined the walls from floor to ceiling. A large round table sat before a fireplace with several heavy wood and leather chairs placed around it. Larger leather chairs were positioned in front of the fireplace and around the room. Mayte stood at the table with Bianca and her alpha, with her grand-mother, daughter, and the rest of her Blood behind her, including Tepeyollotl.

Her brothers stood on my left as I came in, but with a hard look, Guillaume kept them from approaching.

"Your Majesty, please let me formally introduce you to my grandmother, Tocih Zaniyah."

The older woman started to curtsy, but I quickly took her hand in both of mine. "I'm honored to meet you, Tocih, but please, let there be no formalities between us."

The older woman humphed beneath her breath. "The younger generation has no appreciation for formal courts or proprieties any longer."

I thought she was truly offended for a moment, but then I saw the twinkle in her eyes. "I'm afraid I couldn't care less for proprieties."

She laughed more openly and patted my hands with her free hand. "Me neither, truth be told. Thank you for helping us protect Valle de Zaniyah and all who live here."

"It's my pleasure."

I released her and Mayte stepped closer with Xochitl on her hip. Mayte was dressed in a formal pink princess gown with a huge sweeping train, and her daughter wore a matching dress in purple. With flowers in their hair, they looked like beautiful fairies dancing in a garden of flowers beneath a full moon.

"Is this the queen, Mama?" Xochitl asked.

"Yes, my precious. She's come to protect us from the bad queen."

Xochitl held out her arms to me.

Stunned, I glanced at Mayte to make sure she was fine with me holding her, and she nodded, smiling, and lifted her to me.

She touched the jet black and ruby necklace I wore and then gave a playful tug on a curled strand of my hair the hairdresser had pulled free of the braid she'd wound high on my head. "You're pretty."

"So are you."

"Are you going to kill the bad queen?"

I checked Mayte's face again to gauge how much she shielded her daughter and how open I should be. By the hard, fierce look on her face, I decided to tell her child the truth. "Yes, I'm afraid so. None of us will be safe until I do."

Xochitl wrapped her arms around my neck and pressed her cheek to mine, and I knew, beyond a shadow of a doubt, that I would kill anyone who threatened her.

"Good. She made Mama cry."

I handed her back to Mayte. "Well, we can't allow that to happen again, can we?"

"Please, sit, be comfortable." Mayte gestured to the chairs. Rik pulled mine out for me, and Gina passed a leather portfolio folder containing the contract we'd drawn up to Bianca.

The consiliarius read the summary page, looked up at me, eyes round, mouth hanging open. "This is unprecedented. Are you sure?"

Taken aback, I looked at Gina for help. She'd drawn it up for me. I trusted her guidance implicitly, and I had a very hard time thinking she'd made a mistake. "Isn't everything in order?"

"Well, yes, but... But..."

Mayte was looking a little pale around the mouth. Tepeyollotl pulled a chair out for her and helped her to sit. He looked at me with disgust, as if I'd called his queen a filthy name, and then turned a hard look on my alpha. His tattoos shimmered and moved on his skin, forming into spots. His jaguar. He bared his teeth at Rik and clenched his hands into fists.

I couldn't blame him for being upset that she was upset...

But what had we done that was so horrible?

Bianca passed the folder to Mayte. She scanned the page and then sat back in her chair. Hard. Even paler. When she started to cry, I felt worse than the lowest worm I could imagine.

"Mama, Mama." Xochitl squeezed her neck and puckered up too. "Don't cry. The pretty queen said you wouldn't cry again."

If the little girl started to cry, too, then I was walking out of here without looking back.

Mayte hugged her and kissed the top of her head. "This is a good cry, precious. I'm just... shocked. I can't..." She closed her eyes and squeezed her daughter tighter. "Everything's going to be all right now. Everything. I promise."

Rik squeezed my shoulder. :*I think she expected you to take everything.*:

A small sound of surprise escaped my throat, and Mayte looked up at me.

"You don't even realize what you've done, do you? No. I can tell by the look on your face. At most, I hoped that you would allow me to keep my nest and continue to provide for my court as Zaniyah has done for hundreds of years. But I never really thought it possible."

"Why would I take your home? I have a home. I have a nest. I don't want yours."

"It's your right to demand anything of me now. Anything at all. Do you think Keisha Skye would have allowed us to stay here as an independent court? A nest of power separate from her stronghold in New York City? Of course not."

I was starting to be offended myself. Her shock, her tears. Why had she asked for my help if she truly thought I'd take her home from her? "I thought we'd already established that I'm not Keisha Skye. So why is he glaring at me like he's going to eat me for lunch?"

Mayte took Tepeyollotl's hand and tugged him down beside her. "She's not only letting us keep everything, but she named Xochitl an Isador heir."

"What does that mean?"

Gina passed a heavy golden pen to Bianca. "It means that if my queen never has an heir of her own, your daughter will inherit the entire Isador legacy."

"I don't care about gold," the man grunted. "I only care that my family is safe and happy. For a moment, I thought we were going to have a chance to see how well Isador's alpha fought in hand to hand combat."

"And you're allowing this as the Isador consiliarius?" Bianca asked Gina.

My eyebrows arched but I bit my tongue. Gina laughed, shaking her head. "My queen does as she will, but yes, I do support her in this decision. My queen would never take

245

another queen's home or legacy. I knew better than to even suggest such a thing when we were writing up this agreement."

"I lived most of my life without access to the legacy. I could live without it now if I had to."

Rik squeezed my shoulder harder and his voice rumbled through me. "Not happening, my queen. You deserve every luxury and benefit the legacy will provide to you."

Bianca and Mayte signed the contract, then Gina, and then me. It was done. Mayte beamed as Tepeyollotl bounced their laughing daughter on his knee, but all I could think of was what would happen to her...

To them all...

If I failed.

29

SHARA

I took one look at the ornate throne they'd set up for me during the formal procession, and I balked. Hard. That was Zaniyah's throne with jaguars painstakingly carved into the burnished wood. Why on earth would I want to sit in *her* throne? Why would I want a throne at all?

After some arguing and insisting, they finally agreed to put one of the comfortable large leather chairs from the library beside the throne. It was big enough for Rik to sit with me and not be pretentious. This whole formal ceremony was already too pretentious for my taste, and if I had to sit for hours while Zaniyah's court was presented to me, then by goddess I was going to be comfortable.

Standing at the door while Bianca readied everyone in the plaza, I tried not to show how tired I was. How hungry. I hadn't fed yet today, and I hadn't fed my Blood either. They didn't need my blood every single day, but as much as they—we—enjoyed it, I preferred to give them all at least a taste. We needed to be strong at all times, in case Skye attacked, and now I had even more people to protect. I had more at risk than ever.

"You have more to gain now too," Rik whispered softly at my side.

I sighed and leaned my head against his shoulder. With Guillaume and Ezra standing in front of us, I felt hidden enough to drop my guard, just a little. "Right now it doesn't feel like it. It feels like Zaniyah has basically sold all their problems to me and I got screwed without a single drop of lube."

He rubbed his mouth softly against my forehead. "It seems like that now, because you haven't received the benefit of this arrangement yet."

A scuffle behind us alerted me to the approach of Mayte's brothers. Evidently they wanted to get closer... And, naturally, my Blood objected. Strenuously.

"Oh yes, here comes the benefit of that arrangement now." My tone sounded harsh even to my ears. "Let's see how many more fights and arguments we can have about who gets to do what first."

"They're not going to be a problem." Rik didn't say anything to them directly, but I felt him turn his head and look at the twins. His rock troll swelled in his bond, his muscles sliding toward granite. "I won't allow them to annoy you."

"Promise?"

"You know it."

Bianca opened the doors and curtsied to me. "Your Majesty, thank you for your patience. We're ready to begin the procession when you are."

"I'm ready." I bit back the impatient words I wanted to say. *"I've been ready for nearly half an hour now."*

She turned to the plaza and raised her voice. "Our queen, Shara Isador, and her alpha, Alrik Hyrrokkin Isador."

We stepped outside and everyone started clapping and cheering. The crowd was much happier this time around. Word must have spread about my deal with Mayte. These poor people. They must have thought I'd come to rip their homes out from beneath them. No wonder their reception had been so reserved that first night, even though I'd come at Mayte's invitation.

Rik held my arm as we walked down the aisle, and the cheers became deafening. I'd never heard so many people cheering so loudly before—let alone for me. Embarrassed, now, that I'd been so impatient, I stepped onto the dais and turned in front of the chair I'd asked for. I waited while Rik sat down behind me. Then his hands closed around my waist and he pulled me in between his thighs, cradling me against him.

The crowd fell silent a moment, and then the whispers started. Evidently they weren't used to such displays from their queen. It made me smile, because oh boy, were they in for a shock when I received Mayte's oath.

Bianca called out my Blood's names one by one, and they came to me, crowded close this time, because I didn't fucking care what the spectators thought now. Daire and Nevarre both dropped to the floor in front of the dais and leaned back to wrap an arm around each of my calves.

Finally, Bianca called out Mayte's name. Her people rose again, turning to face her and applauding as she approached me, alone, head high. She came to me with a smile on her face, her eyes shining with hope and relief and gratitude. I couldn't help but picture how things would have gone down if Keisha Skye had managed to gain entrance to her nest. There would be no smiles. No cheers. I didn't even want to try and imagine what would have happened to Xochitl. The thought of her sweet baby girl being harmed fucking wrecked me.

Pausing before me, Mayte turned to her people and held her hands up for them to quiet. "Today, Zaniyah and Isador came to a sibling agreement to the benefit of both of our houses. Tonight, you serve as my witnesses that I come to this agreement willing and gladly of my own free will. From this day forward, House Zaniyah is sworn to House Isador. My blood is given to our new queen to seal this deal. May Coatlicue strike me down if I ever think to betray my bond to Isador."

She turned to face me. With practiced elegance, she lifted the full sweeping skirt of her gown and dropped to her knees. A golden crown gleamed on her head. I'd have to get a closer look to be sure, but it looked like human hands and skulls entwined with snakes. "I, Mayte Zaniyah, daughter of Coatlicue, Teteoh Innan, Mother of the Gods, swear my blood and all my house to Shara Isador, daughter of Isis. I offer my blood to my queen to strengthen our alliance and increase her power. In exchange, I beg Isador's protection for my people."

I held out my hand out to her, and she rose and came closer, dropping back to her knees between Daire and Nevarre.

Holding my gaze, she tipped her head to the side, offering her throat to me.

My pulse thumped like a tympani drum in my skull. My fangs descended, more than eager to taste her. To claim her.

Her people watched breathlessly, waiting to see how I would handle their beloved queen. Images flickered through my mind. Mayte crying. Xochitl screaming. Tepeyollotl and Eztli bleeding, fighting, but unable to save their beloved queen.

I could save her. As long as I could protect myself too.

Leaning closer, I breathed in her scent, my lips brushing the soft line of her throat. She quivered against my knees, leaning harder into me. She wasn't scared or worried, even though I'd warned her about my bite.

Opening my mouth, I sank my fangs deeply into her throat. She cried out and her back arched, straining, her hands flailing to the side. I cradled her head, supporting her as she shook against me.

She tasted like sweet, delicate petals floating on a small pool of pure spring rain deep in the jungle. A hidden pool, secret and lush and warm. Her power rushed into me. She called jaguars, all big jungle cats. In fact, she could communicate with the animals. She'd sent the quetzal to warn me about the ants that would try and invade my nest. Yet there was a darker side to her power, a sense of destruction. She descended from the mother of gods, who represented both the womb and the grave. Mayte could stretch out her hand and will the crops to fail, plants withering and rotting with disease. People would starve. Famine and disease would spread in the wake of her power. Unleashing a deadly plague on New York City would have been her last line of defense in order to protect her daughter.

I sank into her mind, absorbing her bond. Her power. The feel of her Blood suddenly firmed in my mind. I felt their fur and smelled the feral musk of their scents. Prowling the night, mighty predators, sleek and deadly. Their eyes glowed in the darkness of my mind. Daire's warcat hissed a warning and Eztli's gigantic black jaguar made a coughing growl that sent goose bumps racing down my arms. The two cats crouched in my mind, tails lashing.

:*Be still. Leave him be.*:

Eztli's jaguar looked at me and lowered his sleek body to the ground. Surrendering to my will.

Through her bond, I could control them. I could feel them. I hadn't realized what that would mean. I could order them, as I ordered my own Blood. I'd never given orders to someone I didn't love. I'd never had to force someone to do my will. But I felt that certainty now. I could command them to do anything at all, no matter how opposite to their natural inclinations, and they would be forced to do so.

Such power. It terrified me.

I could only imagine what kinds of things Keisha Skye would order her Blood, or her sibs' Blood, to do. If she'd taken Mayte...

Rik's bond gleamed like a hot forge in my head. :*She could have made Eztli or even Tepeyollotl slaughter their own people and they wouldn't have been able to resist her command.*:

Mayte moaned, her arm sliding up to hook around my neck. *:Goddess, don't stop.:*

Her mental voice slid through our new bond like smooth, decadent chocolate. I tasted her pleasure in her blood. Her scent of flowers deepened, still sweet but now dusted with sultry spices. Hot cinnamon and chilies and dark chocolate.

Her skin beneath my lips was so soft, her smaller body so different from my big, powerful Blood. Soft curves instead of sheets of muscle. Sweet tender skin instead of hot velvet over iron. Both were wonderful temptations.

Desire pulsed through me. Through her.

I lifted my head and she blinked languorously, her incredibly long lashes fluttering like birds over her stunning crystal eyes.

Turning my head, I offered her my throat. Her arm tightened around my neck and she leaned up to lick my throat first, making me shiver. I expected her to bite delicately, sweetly, but her bite punched into my throat, making me groan. She wasn't shy about taking what she wanted.

Which made me groan again.

I could feel my blood flowing into her, lighting up her magic like a circuit board. My power fed hers, pushing her limits further and higher.

Gasping, she pulled back and drooped against me. "Too powerful. I can't take much or it'll burn me out."

Blood trickled down my throat, making me glad for the black material of the dress, though every person here could smell my blood, even if they couldn't see it. She settled against me with her head in my lap and I stroked my fingers over her hair and face, tracing her cheekbones and the curve of her forehead. She was so fucking beautiful. Her bone structure like fine hand-thrown china.

"Eztli Zaniyah," Bianca called out, and Mayte's alpha strode toward me.

Glowering, he went to one knee and bowed his head. I wasn't sure why he was mad at me, unless it was because his queen was draped in my lap. "My queen, I'm yours to command."

:You can access his thoughts through her bond now,: Rik reminded me. *:But I can tell you why he's upset without touching his bond. You have the right to claim him as your own. You could even order me or one of your Blood to fuck her, and we would. And she would allow you to make such an order, regardless of what her own Blood would prefer.:*

I squeezed my eyes shut, every cell in my body shuddering with revulsion. *:I would never order any of you to fuck anyone against your will.:*

:We know that. But he doesn't. Yet.:

I thought a moment, trying to find the best words to tell him politely I wasn't interested in taking him, without insulting him, and also making sure he understood how I was going to work in the future. "Eztli, you will best serve me by continuing to serve your queen."

Some of the tightness eased about his eyes. He saluted me, fist over his heart, and then stood. He hesitated a moment, looking among my Blood to find the best place to stand close to his queen without offending any of mine. I gave Mehen a mental nudge and he grudgingly moved down a bit so Eztli could stand by Nevarre and be within touching distance of his queen.

Her other Blood came to me as well, and I gave them the same order. A hush fell over the crowd when Tepeyollotl approached me.

I'd be a fool not to take such a powerful Blood. He was a god. If I ever wanted a child, he might be the only answer to me being able to conceive.

He smelled like ancient jungles lost in time, ruins of once powerful cities tumbled down and forgotten. Yet magic still hummed in his blood. I could taste his power, even without putting my mouth on him. Feeding on him even once would push my expanding power even higher.

But my heart did not stir in the slightest when I looked at

him. My blood didn't sing with excitement. My body didn't tighten with need. My fangs didn't even throb.

"Tepeyollotl, you will best serve me by continuing to serve your queen and Zaniyah's future queen."

His eyes flashed like black mirrors and he inclined his head, dropping down to one knee, fist to the floor. "I hear and obey, my queen."

Then her brothers approached, striding down the aisle toward me like an angry thunderstorm. Their energy hummed in the air, turbulent, violent, desperate. As one, they dropped to their knees before me. "My queen, we're yours."

I touched Mayte's bond flowing in my mind like a ribbon made of velvety petals. *:Are you up to moving aside so I can take your brothers?:*

She lifted her head, a smile curving her lush lips. She leaned up and rubbed her mouth softly against mine in a chaste kiss, and then accepted Tepeyollotl's hand to stand. She moved slowly, like her head was still stuffed with cotton. I hadn't drank that much from her. Had I?

I listened to her bond again, trying to sort through what she felt. She met my gaze and blinked, slowly, her tongue peeking out to wet her lips.

Oh. Goddess.

Her head was stuffed, but not with cotton. She gave me an image of silken sheets and soft down and her limbs entwined with mine.

I dragged my gaze away, my cheeks flushed.

The brother with the black sun tattooed on his face spoke first. "My name is Itztli Zaniyah, my queen. It means obsidian, and I always carry an obsidian blade." From a sheath on his hip, he pulled out a hand-hewn blade that sparkled like glass. Holding it in both hands, he bent low and laid the blade at my feet. "I would be honored if you would accept me as your blade."

I stared at him a moment, and I couldn't deny my response.

I'd looked at Mayte's Blood and seen attractive men and a powerful god, but they hadn't moved me at all. When I looked at her brother… I wanted to know what he tasted like. I wanted to know if I was right about what his power would be when he shifted. And yeah, I wanted to see how he'd fit in with the rest of my Blood. If he could be mine, wholly mine. Unlike Mayte's Blood.

I held out my hand out to him. Scooping up his blade, he stood to take my hand, coming closer between Daire and Nevarre, which was no easy feat. Daire hissed and rumbled a low warning, and even Nevarre, my normally very cheerful Blood, radiated a cold darkness that dimmed the bright lights of the party. It wasn't like Xin's fog of invisibility. This darkness had a weight to it that was suffocating. Dread prickled deep inside me, even though Nevarre was mine.

Itztli dropped to his knees once more and leaned against me, tipping his head so that I had access to his throat, though he kept one wary eye on my alpha behind me.

Rik made a low rumble that stilled the new man's advance. "Sheathe the weapon first, unless you wish her to use it on you and spare you the power of her bite."

Itztli flashed a broad grin that lightened the fierce lines of his face and he sheathed the blade. "Fuck, no, I'm eager for her bite. I'm all yours, my queen."

I sank my fangs into his throat and for all his eagerness, he still bellowed with surprise as he climaxed. His yell sounded strange, and it finally dawned on me why.

He sounded more like a giant dog than a man.

His blood burned down my throat and my nose suddenly seemed to be working overtime. Scent took on colors and textures and nuances that I'd never been aware of before. I could smell the grass he'd crushed beneath his feet as he walked outside earlier today. The soap he'd used. The healthy sweat and energy he'd burned off sparring with his brother, trying to take the edge off his desire before tonight's procession.

His bond formed in my mind. A gigantic black dog with a broad head and jaws that could engulf me in one bite. But his eyes were a deep, soulful brown and he whined, softly, creeping closer to lay his giant head on me.

I drank from him a long time. Long enough for his twin to make a low noise of dismay and impatience. I looked up at him, with my mouth still locked to his brother's throat, and offered him my hand.

He came closer, his eyes flashing gold. He dropped to his knees beside his brother, ignoring the growl Daire gave him, though my warcat did slide away enough for him to come close.

"Tlacel, my queen. I'm yours, however you wish to use me."

When I withdrew my fangs from Itztli, he made a low sound of disappointment. Until I offered him my throat. Eagerly, he lunged for me, as if he was afraid I'd change my mind and make him wait until after this formal presentation was over. I gasped as his fangs sank into me, my heart thudding heavily. Tlacel pressed closer, one arm around his brother, his other sliding up around me, daring my alpha to snap his arm off. As soon as he got close enough, I sank my fangs into him too.

He shuddered against me. His climax was quiet and controlled. In fact, the people watching may not have even realized that he'd climaxed. In his bond, though, I felt the depths of that release. I'd rocked him to his core. Green-gold feathers plummeted toward the earth, twirling, spiraling faster, harder. Much like when I'd taken Mehen and sucked his dragon into me along with the majority of his blood.

The feathers grew longer, Tlacel's wings bigger, more powerful. He shot into my mind with a rush of feathers that smelled like a jungle sky filled with a multitude of green, lush plants and thousands of wild creatures. He swept me up with him, higher into a bright blue sky, twirling toward the sun. So hot, so bright. For a moment, I feared that he was an agent of Ra, the god of light. But he enfolded me in those feathered wings and we coasted back down through the clouds.

I fed on one twin, while his brother fed from me. Both brothers pressed closer, pushing me up harder against Rik. My breath caught on a groan and my desire torched higher.

Itztli finally released me. He sprawled on the floor, his legs sliding off the platform. He would have slipped off completely except he hooked his hand in one of the criss-crossed bands that formed the side of my dress. Tlacel came up over me and locked his mouth to his brother's bite, and the sun we'd been flying toward exploded inside him. He shuddered, still quiet, but the taste of my blood made him come again.

Oh dear. This was going to be interesting.

Daire snickered. "I guess you're going to get him coming *and* going, my queen."

With the twins dealt with, I met Bianca's gaze across the plaza and gave her a nod to continue. Need pulsed inside me. With Rik's erection digging into my back and these two new Blood smelling of sex and desire and blood, the last thing I wanted to do was sit through hours of formal presentation.

But that's exactly what I was going to have to do.

One by one, court Zaniyah was introduced to me. My new sibs. My new family. They were all smiles and bows. Some wept. Some wanted to kiss my hand. A few gave lingering looks to my Blood, as if I'd allow them to take on a few new sibs. We'd talked about that before, and the idea still didn't thrill me. The twins probably had sibs in the court, since they'd been alive a very long time. If they wanted to keep those relationships...

Tlacel finally released my throat and leaned back enough to meet my gaze. His golden brown eyes were dazed and my blood trickled down his lip. "Why would we want to feed on sibs when we could have our queen's blood? You did say you feed your Blood regularly, yes?"

I nodded, letting my gaze slide down to his lips, then lower. His brother was bigger and broader, built more like Rik. Tlacel was leaner and slender. He moved with a delicate grace, like his bird, drifting through the air without effort. Tattoos scattered across his shoulders and chest, though on his face, he only had the red spiral. Some of them looked like tribal tats I was more familiar with, but many of them looked like glyphs of his people. They told a story that I couldn't understand.

And I wanted to understand that story. I wanted to read him like a book.

"How much longer is this fucking procession going to last?" Daire asked, nuzzling his head into my lap while his fingers inched up to my knee. I shifted my thighs apart as much as the tight dress would allow, and it was nowhere near enough for him to slide on up and stroke my heat. Much to my dismay.

"An hour at least," Mayte said, her words still slurred. "Though I can ask Bianca to speed things up."

"Fuck," Daire groaned, his fingers kneading my knee.

Which made me groan.

Which made Tlacel lean in harder against me, interfering with Daire's efforts to get his hand up my skirt. So he hissed a warning. Which made Eztli's jaguar make that coughing growl again.

Chuckling against my ear, Rik tightened his arms around me. "I think you should end this procession as quickly as possible, my queen."

Itztli straightened, shaking off the daze that had clouded his eyes after taking my blood. He leveled a hard look on Nevarre that said *move*. Naturally, Nevarre dug in tighter against my knee.

"Or they're going to start a fight?"

"Hmm. No. I wouldn't allow a fight." The rumble in his voice told me a fight was the last thing any of them were thinking about.

Mayte surprised the hell out of me when she dropped into my lap and looped her arms around my neck. She raised her voice so everyone in the plaza heard, though she looked only at me. "Thank you, all. We accept your continued oaths to

Zaniyah, now given willingly to Isador. But my queen is weary and needs to retire. Thank you for understanding."

Then she pressed her lips to mine and I decided that she was right. It was time to end this fucking event. Even if it pissed off some of her people.

Because I couldn't fucking wait any longer to take my queen.

30

RIK

My queen had accomplished much on this trip. She had taken her first sib, gained an ancient, proud court, and added two new Blood in the process. These men weren't lightweights, either. They weren't as old as Guillaume, nor as famous in Aima circles, but they brought new gifts to my queen that I knew without a doubt she'd need in this fight against Skye.

Though I might have to smash their heads together on occasion, which was far from a hardship. Or maybe I'd just pair them up with Mehen and Ezra. That would be hilarious.

Shara's power had already been so immense that adding Mayte and her court was like a drop in the ocean. But Zaniyah brought more than raw power to my queen. She brought a solid foundation and generations of experience, laid out like a feast for my queen to draw on at will.

Even more, Mayte brought a tenderness to my queen that we Blood could not give her, though we tried as often as possible. Many of us were predators. Aggressive males. While we could be tender on occasion, and I handled my queen as gently as possible, I could never compare to the soft, light touch of a woman.

My queen had grown up without many soft and pretty things. She'd grown up in a tower bedroom with no windows, because she feared the monsters outside. She'd never had a nest or a community of Aima to teach her our ways. Even the woman who'd raised her had struggled at times to balance her role in raising a powerful queen outside of any nest, with no protection, while under her sister's geas. Shara had said many times that her mother wasn't the same after her human lover died.

For my queen, that meant she had often felt alone. She hadn't had the warm, soft hug of her mother, or another family member.

So it was no wonder that she craved another queen's soft touch. She wanted laughter and tenderness and sweetness, and I would be no alpha if I didn't ensure my queen received exactly what she wanted. The only problem was my queen's potentially prickly pride. She wanted Mayte. But she didn't want Mayte's Blood, and she definitely didn't want any of us to touch the other woman. My queen was a jealous queen, which I loved. I didn't want to touch another, even though it would be more difficult to arrange her lovers to best meet her needs while remaining within her comfort zone.

Still on my queen's lap, Mayte nuzzled her ear playfully. "I have a place I'd like to show you."

Shara melted at the soft light shining in the other woman's eyes. "Then lead the way."

Mayte stood and offered her hand. My queen stood and winced, which put me on high alert. "These shoes weren't the best idea."

Mayte frowned. "We do need to walk a ways, but it's not far. Fifteen, maybe twenty minutes."

Worry nagged inside her. "Is this place you want to show me outside your nest?"

"Yes. Is that a problem?"

She turned to me as I stood. "Do you think it'll be safe?"

I cast my alpha senses out into the night, seeking anything amiss. Now that my queen had claimed Mayte as her own, the nest responded to her magic, and thus to me, with my queen's blood flowing in my bond. I sensed nothing out of place, but I wasn't familiar with this countryside. "Do you have many thralls in the area?"

Eztli snorted with disgust. "As if we'd allow any thralls to come within sniffing distance of our queen."

Shara leveled a hard look at him, which made him swallow and his eyes widen. "I trust my Blood's protection one-hundred percent, and we still have to deal with thralls. They follow me everywhere I go. They've hunted me my entire life and I almost died more times than I care to count."

He inclined his head slightly. "Forgive me, my queen, I had no idea. With your nine Blood and my queen's five, I highly doubt even a pack of thralls would dare come within a hundred miles of two powerful queens."

"What about Ra," she asked softly.

"The Egyptian god of the sun?" Mayte asked. "What does he have to do with you?"

"He attacked us in Kansas City before I established my nest. Does your religion have an equivalent aspect of the god?"

Mayte moved closer to Tepeyollotl, though she still held my queen's hand. "Of course. An entire pyramid was dedicated to Huitzilopochtil in Tenochtitlan, but he was never associated with Ra. Thousands of people were sacrificed to him before Tenochtitlan fell."

I felt her alpha searching the night now, too. He commanded three of her Blood to shift to their jaguar forms and they slipped into the night, silent hunters in search of anything out of place. "If there's anyone nearby, we'll know. I think it's safe enough to go to the grotto. Even Huitzilopochtil's power is weaker at night."

Shara gripped my arm and lifted her left foot, tugging on the strap of her shoe. Since Daire had picked them out for her to wear, he quickly stepped in and helped her remove them. She wriggled her toes against the tile and slipped her arm back through mine. "Should I change out of the dress too?"

Mayte glanced at her sideways through lowered lashes. "We can bathe at the grotto. I often take a dip and then walk back to the house naked. Unless nudity bothers you?"

"Not at all."

With her arm laced in mine and her other hand in Mayte's, we walked down a path lined with flat stones toward a line of trees. As we passed through the nest's boundary, Shara shivered and rubbed her arms. "That reminds me. Do I need to give your nest my blood too?"

"I don't know," Mayte admitted. "Bianca and Grandmama didn't know either."

Guillaume answered over his shoulder. "No, it's not necessary, unless you want to do it, my queen. Her blood is now your blood, so her boundary is now yours. If I may make a recommendation..."

"Of course, please."

"When we leave, you can add a small amount of blood to the boundary, which will reinforce and strengthen it. But there's no need for you to retrace the entire nest as we did in Eureka Springs."

"Good," Shara breathed out a deep sigh. "If I'm going to bleed that much, I'd rather give it to all of you rather than the ground. Though if I need to make that sacrifice, I'm willing."

I smelled water and sulfur before we reached the trees. The path steepened, cutting back and forth briefly to dip into a rocky canyon. The flagstones had been laid hundreds of years ago and had been ground smooth by time. Trees crowded in, giving the canyon a tight, dark feeling of safety and privacy from prying eyes. I sent all her Blood, including the two new ones, to guard positions in a ring around the grotto. Eztli did the same, though he did not command the father of his queen's child to leave her side.

:*Since she has two with her, do you want to choose another to join us?*: I asked in her bond. :*Or do you want to invite both twins?*:

:*I think inviting her brothers would be icky. I'm not even sure I want to invite them both at the same time. Which would you prefer?*:

I lifted her hand to my mouth and kissed her knuckles. :*Whatever you wish, my queen.*:

:*Then I want only you with me tonight.*:

Love surged through me so powerfully that I could only nod, not trusting even my mental voice in the bond.

"The water smells of minerals, but it's nature's hot tub." Mayte turned to smile at my queen. "There's a spring a bit further up in the cave, but the water's so hot that it's not really comfortable. I usually use this pool. It's still warm, but it's deeper and the submerged rocks give plenty of places to sit."

Shara looked around at the deep pool, easily ten feet across, and grinned. "This is fantastic. Too bad we don't have a hot spring at home. I've asked Gina to find me the biggest tub she can, but a natural spring would be even better."

Deep inside me, I felt a whisper of magic, as if my queen's words whisked off into the night, her intention spoken aloud made manifest in her magic. It wouldn't surprise me in the slightest if we returned to her nest and found her very own grotto among the trees she'd grown with her blood.

Mayte turned, giving her back to her alpha. He immediately unzipped her gown. She let the material flutter to the rocks, and the same as my queen, she wore nothing underneath.

Staring at her body, I could admit that she was attractive. Shorter than my queen and curvy, her breasts full and heavy, her stomach gently rounded from having a child. But she did not move me. I could look at her like she was a priceless statue and admire the craftsmanship, but not covet her body as a man.

How could I, when I loved my very own goddess?

I turned my gaze to Shara, and my dick swelled even more,

pushing against the fabric of my pants. Her eyes glowed as she looked at the other woman. Her lips parted on a soft sigh. Her nipples hardened and I could smell her desire. To me, that was everything beautiful and priceless in the world. My queen wanted. My queen needed. And she would receive exactly what she needed.

I unzipped her dress and helped her work the tighter-fitting gown down her body. She had to shimmy her hips to get the dress to slip down her thighs. Watching as my queen undressed, Mayte unbraided her hair so it fell in loose waves about her shoulders. Mirroring her, Shara took the pins out of hair and handed them to me one by one, letting her hair cascade down her back. Her hair was much longer than Mayte's and darker, heavier.

Holding out her hand to Shara, Mayte stepped closer to the pool. Two gorgeous Aima queens slowly stepped into the water and time seemed to stop and roll backwards, thousands and thousands of years, so that it was two young goddesses laughing and playing in the water. Isis and Coatlicue, two goddesses who never would have interacted in this world. Now here, splashing each other, laughing, and then shyly reaching out to touch the other. Mayte pressed a soft kiss to my queen's lips, and Shara sighed, her hand gliding down the other woman's back. Then she turned to me, her eyes glowing like jewels. "Join us."

I stripped off my clothes, unwilling to look away from her for a single moment. I assumed Mayte's Blood did the same, but I didn't wait for them. Surprisingly hot water inched up my calves, knees, and thighs as I went to my queen. A splash told me Eztli and Tepeyollotl weren't far behind.

Shara turned partially toward me, slipping her arm around my waist and lifting her mouth to mine. I kissed her, opening my mouth to her tongue. She touched my fangs and made an eager sound deep in her throat. "You hunger, my alpha. Please. Feed."

"I'm fine, my queen. I can feed later."

She pushed against me hard enough that I sat back on one

of the boulders that ringed the pool as a natural boundary. Moving between my thighs, she slung her hair back over her shoulder and curved her throat in offering to me. I should have waited. I should have ensured her pleasure first. But I had waited while she fed others tonight, and now that she offered, I couldn't find it in myself to wait another second. I slid one hand beneath her heavy hair to cradle her nape and wrapped my other arm around her, supporting her back as I sank my fangs into her throat. Her blood surged into me, shooting straight to my head like a massive shot of whiskey. I groaned, my senses flooded with power. Her blood sparked a supernova inside me. My rock troll swelled, drumming fists against my ribcage, making me groan. Yes, it hurt. My own power threatened to tear through my control. But it was a good hurt. I loved that she could move me so easily. With a simple caress, she could make me crazy. Drive me wild with need. Set my soul on fire with lust.

I lifted her astride my hips and she took my cock inside her. I felt a moment of regret. This wasn't how I envisioned her night with her queen going. Not with her alpha immediately fucking her, too hard, too fast, out of control. I tried to pull back some semblance of control but she tightened her thighs around me. *:Don't even think about it. I want you wild and out of control tonight. Please. I don't want to be in charge right now. I want you to take me hard and fast. Without thought. Without holding anything back. Exactly as you want.:*

I fisted my hand in her hair and tugged her head back, straining her throat beneath my mouth. *:Is this too much?:*

She ground her hips against me, desire rising in our bonds like a rising tide. *:Never.:*

Something broke inside me. My control snapped, freed by her words. I had made love to my queen many times. I'd fucked her in a multitude of ways with all of her Blood.

But since our very first night together, I'd never fucked her by myself.

Even that night, Daire had stood guard. He'd had the first taste of her desire. He'd given her pleasure first.

Tonight, I would give her pleasure first. Alone. I would hoard her pleasure and her sighs and yes, especially, her screams. They were all mine. She was mine. My queen.

She cried out, her pleasure ringing like sweet music in the night. I pulled her harder against me, not thrusting but giving her every inch I could push into her. Filling her as deeply as I could go. Shuddering, she sagged against me. I licked my puncture marks and then lifted her up off me, high in my arms, and buried my face between her thighs.

I sank my tongue deep between her folds and drank her cream as eagerly as I'd taken her blood. Nothing compared to my queen's desire mixed with her blood. Absolutely nothing. I could feast between her thighs for hours and never drink my fill. She clutched my shoulders, her head falling back, giving herself over to me. Trusting me to hold her and keep her from falling. My queen. My goddess. Letting me do as I would with her body, simply because she loved me.

Fuck, it was the most powerful and wondrous gift she'd ever given me. That she'd trust me enough to let me take control, when she had enough power to destroy not only me but this entire ranch for miles in all directions.

I'd forgotten about the rest of our party, until Mayte's hands slid over my queen's body while I licked her. Mayte stood behind her, giving Shara something to lean against. I lifted her thighs up around my shoulders, my hands supporting her buttocks. I pressed tiny bites along her pussy, making sure she felt my fangs but not penetrating her skin, while Mayte stroked her. Slowly, her hands smoothing Shara's throat and shoulders, her fingers gliding over Shara's breasts. Stroking down her sides and stomach, kneading her thighs while she kissed Shara's neck.

"Please," Shara whispered. "Bite me again."

"Are you sure? I don't want to take too much, my queen."

Shara half groaned, half laughed. "You barely took any

earlier. You won't weaken me. But I want to feel your pleasure flooding our bonds at the same time."

Mayte sank her fangs into my queen and Shara quivered against me, a fresh surge of cream flooding my mouth. I drank her down eagerly, just as the other queen took her blood. I suddenly envisioned her Blood coming to feed from her, one after another, while I fed from her pussy like this.

:Yes. But not tonight. This night is for you alone:

I wasn't sure which of Mayte's Blood took her, but her moans filled the night. She squeezed Shara's breasts, rolling her nipples in her fingers. Gasping, she lifted her mouth, my queen's blood on her lips. She rocked against Shara, which rocked her hips against my face. In moments, I felt her desire cresting again, her need humming through her body. A need my mouth alone would not be able to satisfy.

Mayte cried out her pleasure, her Blood's deep grunt of satisfaction pushing her higher. Which only increased Shara's need. She twisted in Mayte's arms, trying to get off my shoulders and get my dick back inside her.

Letting Shara's thighs slide off my shoulders, I turned her around so she faced the other woman. My queen pressed her lips to Mayte's as I stood. I lifted Shara enough to push into her from behind. She hugged her thighs around Mayte's waist and locked her hand behind Mayte's head, her fingers tangled in her hair. When her other Blood moved behind her, she moaned against Shara's mouth.

Tepeyollotl stood with me, eye to eye, toe to toe, our two queens pressed between us. We were nearly the same height. Nearly the same build. And yes, fuck him, he was slightly taller and bigger than me, but he was a god, after all. An unspoken dare hovered between us. Who would break first? Who would come first? I had an unfair advantage and I knew it. My queen's bite would seal the winner of this challenge.

In our arms, our queens clung to each other, stroking and kissing as we moved inside them.

We fucked our queens in a hot mineral spring in a secret grotto, but they held the power. They commanded our hearts to beat. They gave us their blood and magic to sustain us. They drove us, their desire a burning urge that seared my skin and demanded every ounce of strength and control I could give her.

Shara sank her fangs into Mayte's throat and she screamed, a sweet, high sound that rang like a bell in the night. Her Blood's face tightened, muscles standing out in stark detail beneath his skin. He tried to fight back his climax, but his queen's pleasure rolled over him and pushed him over the edge while my queen fed.

Shara drank Mayte's pleasure from her blood, wallowing in rose petals and silk, a luxurious combination that went straight to her head. Tightening on me, Shara groaned, her mouth locked to the other woman's throat.

I squeezed her hips, pulling her hard against me as I thrust, harder, losing my careful rhythm. I tried to slow down, tried to hold back. I'd tasted my queen's desire, so when I came, I'd likely be done for the night. I didn't want to end her pleasure. Not so quickly.

:Please.:

My determination to last cracked and splintered. My lust broke free and tore through me, casting aside my usual chains of steady control. I sank my fangs into her throat and spewed like a volcano. I roared with release, spurt after spurt tearing through me. I emptied myself into her so thoroughly that my knees quivered and I sat down hard on the boulder. At least it caught me so my head didn't go under the water.

Shara turned in my arms and nestled beneath my chin. Tepeyollotl dropped beside me, his breathing still a deep wheeze as he tried to recover. On his lap, Mayte draped an arm around my queen's shoulders.

Eztli had recovered enough to laugh, though breathlessly. "That was... incredible."

"Agreed," Tepeyollotl said, even though his chest still heaved for air. "We may have to ask Maxtla to bring a car down and pick us up."

Mayte laughed softly. "Your pride would never allow such a thing and you know it."

"I don't know, my heart. Watching you with our queen took our lovemaking to all new heights."

I agreed, though my lungs burned too much to try and talk yet.

"Perhaps you could stay with us well past the new year," Mayte suggested, twirling a lock of Shara's hair around her fingers.

She slid her palm up and down my back, her fingers strumming my spine. And yes, miracle of miracles, my dick stirred again. "I would love to, but I have a great deal to do at home. We just established my nest and we're renovating the house. Plus I need to make some plans."

"For Skye?" Mayte asked softly.

"Yes."

Sudden fear tore through our bonds so viciously that I almost shifted to the rock troll. Shara's other Blood surged toward us, tearing through the underbrush. Daire's warcat leaped down from the top of the canyon to land beside us. Nevarre cawed from a tree. Ezra roared, Guillaume reared and screamed a challenge into the night, Leviathan exploded into the air, his breath pluming smoke into the night sky. Xin's silver wolf appeared at the edge of the pool, wavering like a ghost for a moment, and then he disappeared once more.

But that fear wasn't our queen's.

It was Mayte's, though we felt it through our queen's bond.

"I'm sorry," she whispered, blinking back tears. "I've worsened your situation, haven't I? Now Skye will come gunning for you with everything she's got."

Shara shrugged, a smile tugging at her lips. "She was already gunning for me. Now I know you'll be safe."

"But what about you? Who'll protect you?"

"Me." That single word crashed out of my throat like a thousand-pound boulder.

Shara's other Blood all declared the same in her bonds. *:And me.:*

Her eyes burned with tears, but her heart soared as high as Mehen flew above us. "And I'll protect us all."

Mayte threaded her fingers with Shara's, her voice hesitant. "Why are you willing to risk yourself to protect us? To protect me, and Xochitl? You barely even know us."

Shara lifted their clasped hands to her mouth and kissed each of Mayte's fingertips. "What this queen takes, she loves, and she keeps safe for all time."

SHARA'S STORY continues with the next book, QUEEN TAKES ROOK. An excerpt isn't ready to share yet, but if you'd like to chat about these books and get sneak peeks as soon as they're available, join Joely's Triune on Facebook, or sign up for Joely's newsletter to receive the latest updates.

ABOUT THE AUTHOR

Joely Sue Burkhart has always loved heroes who hide behind a mask, the darker and more dangerous the better. Whether cool, sophisticated billionaire, brutal bloodthirsty assassin, or simply a man tortured by his own needs, they all wear masks to protect themselves. Once they finally give you a peek into the passionate, twisted secrets they're hiding, they always fall hard and fast. Dare to look beneath the mask with delicious BDSM in a wide variety of genres with Joely on her website, www.joelysue-burkhart.com.

If you have Kindle Unlimited, you can read all her indie books for free!

Wondering what's next? Sign up for her newsletter and receive exclusive free content.

Mythomorphoses, Paranormal/SF Romance

Free in Kindle Unlimited

<u>BEAUTIFUL DEATH</u>

The Connaghers, contemporary erotic romance

Free in Kindle Unlimited

<u>LETTERS TO AN ENGLISH PROFESSOR</u>

<u>DEAR SIR, I'M YOURS</u>

<u>HURT ME SO GOOD</u>

<u>YOURS TO TAKE</u>

<u>NEVER LET YOU DOWN</u>

<u>MINE TO BREAK</u>

<u>THE COMPLETE CONNAGHERS BOXED SET</u>

Billionaires in Bondage, contemporary erotic romance

(re-releasing in 2017 from Entangled Publishing)

<u>THE BILLIONAIRE SUBMISSIVE</u>

<u>THE BILLIONAIRE'S INK MISTRESS</u>

<u>THE BILLIONAIRE'S CHRISTMAS BARGAIN</u>

The Wellspring Chronicles, erotic fantasy

Free in Kindle Unlimited

<u>NIGHTGAZER</u>

A Killer Need, Erotic Romantic Suspense

<u>ONE CUT DEEPER</u>

<u>TWO CUTS DARKER</u>

<u>THREE CUTS DEADER</u>